Dedication

For those still on this journey with me.
Thank you.

THE DEVIL'S CARTEL HIERARCHY

PRESIDENT
DAMON JUDGE
"JUDGE"

—

VICE PRESIDENT
JAMES CREED
"CREED"

—

ROAD CAPTAIN
SOREN REYES
"HAWK"

—

SERGEANT AT ARMS
KYLE WILLIAMS
"ARMI"

—

SECRETARY
JASON ROTH
"STOIC"

—

TREASURER
MATTHEW ROYAL
"CASINO"

—

PROSPECT 1:
KACE RYAN

Burning
Daylight

A Devil's Cartel MC novel

Book Two

BY
SKYLA MADI

Burning Daylight

Limitless Publishing, LLC
Kailua, HI 96734
www.limitlesspublishing.com

Formatting: Book Pages By Design
Cover Design: Deranged Doctor Design

ISBN-13: 978-1-64034-907-0

PROSPECT 2:
IRIS SAITO

—

NOTABLE PATCH MEMBERS
CYRYS "*CY*" AHMADI, SORA "*RAH*" KIMURA, AARON "*AYR*" ST. CROSS, MODO, AMANI LEWIS, HARLEI HART, PEARL HART

—

OLD LADIES
ISABELLE LAURENT ♥ JAMES CREED

TERMINOLOGY

1%ER (ONE PERCENTER): The term was coined when the AMA (American Motorcycle Association) was said to make a statement in response to the 1947 Hollister Riot that 99% of motorcycle riders are law-abiding citizens. The remaining one percent belonged to outlaw clubs/gangs who took the term and wore it proudly on their cuts, usually encompassed by a diamond shape.

43: The numerals that coincide with the alphabet letter "D" for Devil's and "C" for Cartel.

BITCH: Another word for "girlfriend," a term of endearment.

BRAIN BUCKET: A small beanie-like helmet not usually approved by the Department of Transport.

CAGE: A vehicle that isn't a motorcycle. For example, a car, truck, van etc.

CABBAGE: Idiot.

COLORS: The club emblem/numbers/insignias.

CUT: Leather vest with club colors. Usually has no sleeves.

DCMC: Devil's Cartel Motorcycle Club.

DRAG BARS: Low, flat, and straight motorcycle handlebars.

FENDER FLUFF: A female passenger invited for a ride on the back of a motorcycle. Not an old lady.

FLYING LOW: Speeding.

MAMA: A woman who is willing to have sex with all members of the gang, usually at the same time (see "Pull a Train"). The term is only used for women who regularly associate with the club and entertain multiple members on a very regular basis.

NOMAD: An individual who isn't a member of a motorcycle group and isn't locked to a certain territory.

NORMIES: Civilians/towns people.

OLD LADY: A wife or long-time girlfriend. It has nothing to do with age and is *not* a derogatory term.

PATCHWHORE: A female who has sex with members of a motorcycle club, solely members who have been patched into the club. No one has ownership over these women, and they can have sex with whoever they like. Other variations include: Patchrider, clubslut, and clubwhore.

PIG: A derogatory term for a police officer.

PULL A TRAIN: The act of having sex with multiple (if not ALL) of the members.

RUNNING 66: Riding without wearing club colors.

SMOKE: Cigarette

SNOW: Cocaine. Other variations include: Blow.

"She conquered her demons and wore her scars like wings."

— *Atticus*

ONE

Damon Judge. I heard the roar of his lonesome motorcycle before I saw him speed down the main strip heading out of town. The thundering of his bike sent goosebumps skittering over the surface of my skin and stirred warning deep in my belly. I knew better than to pull my white Ford Fiesta away from the curb and follow such a dangerous man, but I was desperate. I'd chased every lead and exhausted every option, and if the police wouldn't help me get my son back, I was going to ask the one person who could.

I didn't know Damon Judge, but I knew *of* him. He was a criminal, a murderer, president of Exeter's Devil's Cartel Motorcycle Club, and I was certain he was the one responsible for the disappearance of Jonathan Laurent, our previous mayor. But despite

1

everything Judge was involved in, and everything he'd done, I suspected he wasn't an unreasonable man. It was obvious with the line-up of men and women he allowed into Exeter's DCMC chapter. Across the states, The Devil's Cartel MC were notorious for the ways they regarded women, the LGBTQ community, and people of color. They were treated worse than dirt under their boots, but the Devil's Cartel Exeter chapter was the only place you'd find female, gay, and colored members, and that was all thanks to Judge. He was a businessman too, that I knew, but I had no money and no power to offer him. My only plan was to appeal to Judge's paternal instincts since it's public knowledge he lost his daughter to domestic violence.

I swallowed the lump in my throat and continued to follow Judge's taillight out of town. Nervous, sharp-winged butterflies nibbled my stomach lining at the thought of asking him for help to get my son, Nicolás, back.

At the age of five, Nicolás was as tough as nails, but his father knew how to break him. I knew Nicolás could heal any physical wounds his father inflicted. It was the emotional torture he stood no chance against. My ex-husband knew how to climb inside Nicolás's sweet, beautiful soul and tear him apart. He knew how to make him feel like there was something wrong with him, even though I spent every day of the last five years telling him how perfect he was. I swiped at a hot tear that dripped onto my cheek. I hadn't felt this useless in a long time. This fight had cost me everything—my job, my house, and the only family I had left. I'd experienced the worst of life, so chasing a biker down a dark highway in the middle of the night didn't seem so scary.

Judge rode for ages, into the thick of nothing. I followed at a safe distance, my speedometer indicating I was still going well above the limit. Nerves ate at my veins and my heart leapt into my throat every time he turned his head. He had to know I was following him. I hadn't turned off my headlights and the only things out this way were trees, a river, and an abandoned fireworks shack. Sure enough, Judge pulled into the drive of the abandoned shack and got off his bike to walk into the thicket, heading toward the river. I knew I wouldn't be able to follow him any further in my car, so I pulled up, turned it off, and trekked the rest of the way. As twigs and leaves crunched under my worn sneakers, I stretched the sleeves of my navy sweater over my knuckles and wrapped my arms around my torso. I was more nervous than cold since I was intruding on something private, something Judge couldn't do in town, or with any of his men. There was every chance he'd shoot me and throw my body in the river. I'd be found within days, of course, but no one would investigate.

Thanks to my ex-husband, I was the town's resident nutcase and everyone avoided me like the plague. He painted me as an anxious, suicidal wreck who had PTSD issues and paid sexual favors to a long list of bad, *bad* men. Everything he said was a lie, but he was an expert with his brush, and he stained my reputation with every stroke.

The thicket thinned out and I strode cautiously toward the dry riverbank, glancing left and right. It was quiet, too quiet for a peaceful night like this. I straightened my posture and blew air between my lips. Judge was here, somewhere. Nature told me so. The frogs were quiet, and the crickets didn't dare sing, so *where'd he go?* Then I heard it, the snap of a twig nearby. Gasping, I whirled on my heel and reached for my hip, as if I were carrying a gun. I wasn't. I hadn't carried a gun in a long time.

I saw the moonlight shine on the damp end of his gigantic boot first and watched his dark jeans absorb it as he stepped out of the undergrowth and onto the riverbank. The notorious DCMC skull on the chest of his shirt pulled my attention and I fought a shiver. Seeing the Devil's Cartel insignia on paper was one thing…seeing it in real life, on the towering frame of the infamous Damon Judge, was another thing entirely. It was as if…as if it were alive, demanding I hand over my body and soul right here by the water's edge.

"Lost, sweetheart?" he asked, his gravelly,

demanding voice rumbling over the surface of my skin, eliciting goosebumps.

I swallowed hard and lifted my stare to his shadowed face. He was taller than I expected. I wasn't a tiny woman. I was slightly above average in height and carried my fair share of excess fat around my belly, thighs, ass, and hips, but standing in front of Judge, I felt small.

Too small.

And worse, from his shadow, he'd stolen my courage and my voice. All I could do was stare at him like a mute, equal amounts of surprise and fear tangoing in my belly.

"Do you speak?" he demanded, impatience clipping his tone.

"I…"

The words I wanted to speak, the favors I wanted to ask, were on the tip of my tongue. I'd practiced it before bed more times than I prayed these last few months. Still, Judge rendered me speechless and I hadn't even seen his face in the full light yet. I moistened my lips and swallowed again, then I straightened my shoulders and steeled my spine. "Yes, I speak."

He stepped into the harsh moonlight, perfectly silent. His leather didn't rub and the dry leaves under his boots didn't crunch. Strangely, it scared me that a man his size could be so stealthy. What scared me more was the way his dark, ocean eyes, pursed lips, and chiseled jawline made my entire body clench. Even before tonight, I knew he was terrifying in the most beautiful way...but I wasn't expecting his arresting appearance to freeze me on the spot. A heavy, dark curl of dread twisted down the length of my spine. When I first met my ex-husband, Elias Vergara, on a yacht in the Bahamas, I couldn't take my eyes off him. He consumed my entire being with an angry glance, a glance much like Judge's. My ex was tall and athletic, had luscious locks the color of midnight rain, and at the age of thirty with a ticking biological clock, I was no match for his smooth, tanned skin, and eyes that glittered like black diamonds. Men who looked like Elias—men who looked like Judge—were bad news, and I had more bad news than I could swallow.

The click of a hammer being pulled on a handgun tugged me from my thoughts, and I flicked my attention to his large hand. I wasn't afraid of guns. I'd lost count of how many I've stared down the barrel of.

"I need your help," I said, my voice holding a fraction of the confidence it did in my head.

A gentle breeze blew by, moving thin strands of my burgundy hair out of my face. With it wafted his cologne, a rich, woodsy smell that kissed my nose and warmed my chest. I expected him to smell of blood, cigarettes, gunpowder, and B.O., but he didn't. He didn't smell like a criminal and, for some reason, that further cemented the fact he could help me.

"My help?" His full lips quirked and his eyes warmed, as if I said something amusing. Exhaling, he released the hammer of his gun and lowered it. "I don't help people."

He stuffed his gun into his waistband, then turned his back on me. I frowned. That's it? He didn't want to know what I needed his help for?

"I can pay you," I shouted at his broad back, loud enough for him to hear, but not loud enough to stir the demonic skull on his back. I glanced nervously at it, at the upside-down crucifixes that flanked each side of it. *God. It's creepy.* "I can pay you a lot of money."

It was a lie. I had no money to my name.

"Don't want your money. Don't need it."

Sticks cracked and crunched under his big boots as he walked away, and that made him seem more human, less godly, so I followed him. In a few strides, we were drowned by the shadows of the undergrowth and Damon Judge wasn't so scary as he stomped alongside trees that towered over him.

"If you just listen to me—ouch!" A rogue stick slipped between my sneaker and my skinny jeans and dug into my ankle, breaking the skin. I stumbled forward and, out of reflex, I reached out and grabbed his cut to stable myself. "Please,

Damon—"

A vicious growl ripped through the forest and I gasped, my entire body tightening. I glanced over my shoulder, expecting a ferocious black bear to be right on my tail, when Damon's cut was wrenched from my hand. I barely managed to straighten before he grabbed me by the shoulders and slammed me against the trunk of a thick tree. I hissed as the back of my skull connected with the solid wood and pain seared over my scalp, embedding in my eyes. Stars exploded then dissolved as quickly as they appeared, leaving me staring into the cold eyes of my last hope. How did my life dissipate to this? Me, Yasmine Garcia, begging the president of an outlaw motorcycle gang for help. *I wish I never went to the Bahamas all those years ago. I wish I never met my ex-husband. I wish I never had my son, so I could spare his pure, beautiful soul this horrible life.*

"Please," I whispered, hating how many times I'd said that six-letter word to him tonight. "I'll do anything."

Judge pressed his hips to mine and dug the barrel of his gun into my jaw. It smelled like it'd been fired a hundred times in its lifetime. Would it take my life tonight?

He was everything the stories made him out to be. No. He was taller, wider, more handsome than I ever imagined. He smelled of bad things, of leather, smoke, and burned rubber. Judge hit me with a glare so frightening, but in their depths, curiosity and concern swirled.

"You'll do *anything*?"

I regretted saying it already. "Within reason."

"Reason," he repeated, his upper lip twitching at the corner. Judge looked down at my covered breasts, then back to my face. "I'm not a reasonable man."

My stomach knotted. Men like him were rarely reasonable, but I knew Judge could be. There were too many stories for it to be a myth. I stared at Judge, kept my eyes on his, not daring to glance at his lips. He didn't need encouraging and, if I was wrong about him, who was around to hear me shout for help? Then he grinned and I slipped and watched his lips as they curled, exposing his white, and surprisingly perfect, teeth. My heart thundered.

"Mm," he hummed, craning his neck to ghost his lips over mine. "Listen to that shallow breath. You want me to kiss you…"

I swallowed and shook my head. We were on a slippery slope and it confused me. I was a natural negotiator, born confident and steadfast, but in Judge's presence, it was hard to communicate what I wanted. Perhaps it was because of all the things I knew he'd done—the things that weren't so noble or lawful—that kept me from pushing him. Regardless, I was above exchanging sex for favors.

I'd go back to my ex-husband long before I became the woman he told everyone I was.

"I think you do," Judge whispered, and he softly flicked the tip of his tongue against my lower lip.

I gasped as my heart stuttered and my blood pressure went through the roof. *Who the hell does he think he is?*

"Get away from me," I growled.

I thrust off the tree and slammed my hands against Judge's wide chest. I gritted my teeth, clenched my jaw, and shoved him with everything I had. I didn't thrust him off balance, hell, he didn't even stumble, *but* he did step back, giving me the space I physically demanded. We stared at each other in silence and a nervous sweat formed in my palms

He simpered, wide and ridiculous, then turned away from me. *Oh.* I lifted my eyebrows. *He's leaving?* I balled my fists and steeled my spine.

"Is that how Isabelle Laurent paid for your help?" I barked at him and he stopped, turning his head. "What kind of sick shit did you make her do?"

Judge slowly turned around and faced me again. I remained unfaltering, unshrinking under his irritated gaze. I liked it better this way—with this much space between us.

"I didn't make her do anything since it wasn't my help she wanted."

He was talking about James Creed, the club's Vice President. I didn't know much about Isabelle's relationship with him, but I saw them around town enough to know he claimed her as his. It even said it on the back of the tiny leather cut she wore. There wasn't much I could say about Isabelle Laurent. She looked out of place with the Devil's Cartel men, since she still dressed like her father was in office, but she appeared happy, at least.

"You helped her," I said. "Now I need you to help me."

"I didn't help her," he replied. "If it was up to me, I'd have left her for dead."

"I don't believe you."

Judge turned his back on me one more time. "Believe what you want. I don't give a shit."

He stormed off and I marched behind him, following him back toward the road. By the time we made it out of the shrubs, I was sweaty and irritated beyond belief and Judge continued to ignore me, like I wasn't on his heels begging for help. I insulted him, his club, his mother, and he didn't react. Not even once. I stopped in my tracks as Judge approached his monstrous motorcycle and threw his leg over its black and silver body.

"Please," I sighed, exasperated, my voice turbulent with the emotion wreaking havoc in my chest. I was done being strong. Judge was the only person left who could help me and if he left...I didn't know what I was going to do. "It's my son. He's only five and...and..." My voice cracked, painfully, and I swallowed hard, choking down the pain the way I'd been doing for a long time. "He needs help, and I can't save him, Damon. Not on my own."

Judge paused atop his bike, his large hands resting on his thighs. I waited, letting the apprehension his silence created eat me up.

"I told you," he replied, not bothering to look at me over his shoulder, and I let out a small rush of frightened air. "I don't help people."

He sat forward and grabbed his handlebars, sending my soul into a panic, then he started the engine, bringing it roaring to life.

"You couldn't save your daughter," I shouted over the rumbling, using the last of my ammo. "But you can save my son, *please*."

Judge's shoulders tightened, and he clenched his handlebars in his hands. I held my breath for the umpteenth time tonight and waited as he hung his head. Hope ignited in my chest...until he shook his head, lifted his foot off the ground, and zoomed off, sending dirt and stones in my direction. I shielded my face until the dust settled and, when I lowered my hands, Judge was but a single, distant taillight that disappeared a heartbeat later. *No.* I slumped into myself and sniffled as warm tears dripped onto my cheeks. I couldn't stop my body from hunching

12

forward as familiar and painful tendrils of failure burrowed deep in my heart, making my whole chest ache.

"God damn it," I whispered.

And then the uncontrollable sobbing started.

TWO

JUDGE

We arrived at the clubhouse just as the sun set below the horizon. We parked our bikes out the front and lined them up along the entrance, the way we always did on the nights we partied.

"They couldn't wait?" Creed huffed as we sauntered toward the doors of the establishment.

"Impatient assholes," Hawk added, kicking a stone across the drive. "Better not've drank all the good beer."

"Quit your bitching," I said. "More beer in the cellar to last us a lifetime."

"Or until ten p.m., if Modo's drinking," Armi added, fixing his stupid hair into its usual stupid bun.

"Modo's always drinking," Creed said, and I laughed.

"If you want to take his drink away from him, be

my guest," I chimed in. "Don't come crying to me when he chops you into little pieces and feeds you to his alligator."

"Wait. Modo's scared of snakes but he owns a goddamn alligator?" Hawk shouted. "What the fuck, Judge?"

I shrugged. I didn't pretend to understand that crazy bastard. As long as you stayed on his good side, you were A-Okay. If not...well, I pitied anyone on the receiving end of his wrath.

We drew close to the clubhouse entrance and I smirked as Metallica seeped from the walls and blasted from the windows. The smell of cigarettes and beer hung in the cool evening air, comforting every anxious cell in my body. *Home.*

Finally.

I couldn't get inside fast enough. I bounded up the steps and shoved the doors open. Members cheered and I inhaled. Leather danced with oil, metal, and sweat in my nostrils and I couldn't breathe it deep enough. Nothing was better than noisy, reckless nights spent at the clubhouse I helped build with people who'd die to protect it. I loved it. I lived for it.

We'd been gone two days—Creed, Armi, Stoic, Hawk, and I. Rah caught wind of some nomad Twisted Sons camping between Exeter and Venton Vale. After the fuckery they pulled with Blondie eight months ago, we voted the Twisted Sons were to be killed on sight, no exceptions.

And we did just that.

I peered sideways at Creed who stood beside me, combing the crowd with his gaze, looking for Blondie. I made a mistake bringing him on the kill run. His thirst for revenge on the Twisted Sons made him sloppy and unhinged. I counted on him to be my word of reason. As my right-hand man, he always had to have his head screwed on straight and never let his emotions get the best of him. He lost it in Venton Vale. What he did was so fucking demonic that Stoic had to stop eight times on the way home so he could puke. If I hadn't encouraged him to burn everything, he'd have brought their spines home as a trophy for his woman.

Rolling my shoulders, I pushed off the last two days and left it at the door where it belonged. The clubhouse was my sanctuary and I did my best to keep it that way.

Hawk, Stoic, and Armi pushed past Creed and me and sank into the crowd. I began to do the same when Creed caught me by my bicep. I turned my head and looked at him.

"I lost my head," he finally admitted after fighting me on it the past twenty-four hours. "Don't tell Izzy."

I frowned. Did I look like a goddamn snitch? Did I look like the type that would go running to someone's woman, looking for a pat on the back? I shrugged out of his grip.

"Why would I tell her?" I asked, and he pinned me with a look.

He'd been increasingly suspicious of me and I couldn't deny it wasn't warranted. I bumped into Blondie often…sometimes not by mistake and I didn't know fucking why. I flirted with her, played with her, and it drove him mad. Maybe that was what was piquing my interest…the fact it made Creed mad. If I wanted to end their relationship, I could. I was president and my higher rank meant I could take Creed's woman and there wouldn't be a thing he could do about it. Lucky for him, I needed him more than I needed Blondie.

"Relax," I told him. "I won't tell her shit."

I moved away from Creed and headed toward the private quarters, toward my room, where I showered and put on fresh clothes. When I came out, the party was raging harder than before and I didn't know where to start my fun. Topless women strolled by me, touching and stroking me, encouraging me to follow, but a flash of pink out of the corner of my eye stole my attention. There was only one person who wore pink around here.

Blondie leaned over the bar in a pink bralette—I hated I knew exactly what it was called—and tight denim jeans that reached just under her newly pierced belly button. Her blonde hair, tied back in a high ponytail, cascaded over her shoulder and pooled on the bar surface. She beamed at Kace with a white, perfect smile, and he happily poured her a drink. Based on the contents of the cup, the drink was for Creed. I knew better than to approach her but fuck it. I needed a drink anyway.

I leaned on the bar beside her and she turned to smile at me. She was sickeningly sweet, a breath of fresh air through the dusty tunnel of club life. I knew the clubwhores hated her guts and convinced some of the lesser members to hate her too, but they should be thankful she was Creed's and only his. If she weren't, all the men would be eating her up.

"Welcome home," she said, tilting her head. "I'd ask you about the trip, but something tells me you're only going to say it was—"

"Fine," we said at the same time and she laughed.

"That's what Creed said too."

She shook her head, grabbed her drinks, and sauntered off, heading in the direction of the sitting room, and I turned my attention to Kace, who finished pouring a beer for me. He slid it over the lacquered bar, and I caught it in my hand.

I was still resting against the bar, talking to whoever showed up for a drink, when Blondie returned for another round. Unfortunately for me, I was four beers deep and my filter had long since left the building. She rested her taut stomach against the bar's edge and drummed her fingernails against the surface, their pearl hue glistening under the harsh light.

"You started craving me yet?" I teased.

Izzy whipped her head in my direction, surprised, and a gentle blush flared in her cheeks. "What?"

I moved closer to her. "You heard me."

She flicked her stare down to my shoes, then back up. When our gazes met, she was no longer coy and innocent. She was serious, the flash in her eyes resolute. I hated it. I also loved it.

"Honestly?" she said in a low tone so only I could hear, then she leaned in until her lip grazed my ear. Her light, floral perfume wafted over me, making me feel—I don't know—stupid. I licked my lower lip and spared a glance at Kace, who watched on, his boyish face twisted uncomfortably.

"I haven't thought about you at all," she whispered in a sexy, husky tone.

Oh, fuck off. I pulled a face as she retreated from me with a smug smirk. "Bullshit."

"I haven't."

I didn't believe her for a second. She was the one who begged Creed to let me fuck her when we had our three-way. I tapped my finger against the bar surface once, unable to bite my tongue.

"You're mine too, you know."

Blondie cut her eyes at me, but it wasn't out of anger, more so disappointment. I regretted the words the second they flew out of my mouth. I had no claim on her and I knew better than to suggest otherwise. The thing was, I didn't want Blondie. Besides sexual attraction, I had no connection to her. I didn't want her heart, not even a slice of it. I wanted what she represented: *a future.* I had a future and I let it slip through my fingers…maybe I was jealous Creed would eventually get what was taken from me. Maybe I wanted to sabotage it.

Isabelle levelled me with her stare and leaned closer. "Don't do that to him, Damon."

I couldn't bear the look she gave me. It sent shockwaves of guilt through my chest. "Do what?"

"Be so disrespectful. He trusted you and so did I." She protected my wrongdoing by talking quietly and I admired that. She lowered her voice even further when Kace placed her drinks in front of her. "You're the president of the Devil's Cartel, Judge. You don't need to take someone else's woman. Go get your own."

I brushed her off and reached for my glass. "Just testing your loyalty," I said, before I swallowed a large mouthful of my cold beer.

"Don't concern yourself with my loyalty. I love Creed and he knows it," she said, grabbing the drinks. "There are plenty of women here tonight. Why don't you go bother one of them?"

I didn't glance over my shoulder, not at any of the whores in the club, definitely not at my usual lay, Liv, whose glare I was certain burned holes in the back of my cut. "Nah."

I didn't know why I wasn't in the mood. Perhaps the last two nights sleeping outside on the hard ground had taken it out of me. Or maybe, with my thirty-sixth birthday looming, I realized I wasn't twenty anymore and the thought of fucking for hours left me exhausted. It was odd. I used to love the way women threw themselves at my feet. Now, they bored me. They bent over backwards for me, did everything I said, because I was president. They'd fight each other to the death to be my old lady if I asked. It drove me up the wall that Izzy wasn't attracted to me. I'd surrounded myself with women who wet their panties at my every movement, like I was a God, but Izzy didn't give two shits about me or what I did. I turned on the spot and watched her go.

"You look good, Blondie," I called after her and she grinned over her shoulder at me, a fucking beautiful beam.

"I know. Creed told me already."

I simpered and laughed under my breath. He was gone two days…she was going to fuck him later and good too. *Lucky bastard.*

"Creed will kill you." Kace's voice ripped me from my train of thought.

I twisted in his direction and looked at him, just looked at him. Regret etched its way over his features every second I held him in my silent gaze.

"Mind your own fucking business, prospect," I said finally, then finished my beer. "Where's Iris?"

"At the range."

I frowned. "At this time of night?"

That girl was obsessed with guns—more than Armi—which was messed up. I thought back to the night Kace brought her tiny ass in here and we laughed her right back out the door. My finger twitched. I could still feel the heat and vibration in my hand as her bullet tore through my beer can, demanding my attention. I happily gave it and now, well, now she was like a daughter to all of us.

"She likes it there."

"Hey!" Armi's boom drew my attention and my concern for Iris fell to the wayside.

I straightened and turned toward the front door. I couldn't fucking believe what I was seeing. I expected a brawl. What I didn't expect was a short, petite woman shoving her way through the crowd, her dark eyes trained on me, her white teeth bared.

"You can't just walk in here!" Armi snapped at her, his dark glare zeroed in on the back of her head. He reached out to grab her, but she was always a few steps ahead, evading his grasp. "Damn it!"

"You!" she growled as he broke through the crowd and entered the clearing to my left, pointing her slender little finger in my direction. "You stole my driver's license."

"Me?" I rested my elbow on the bar and crossed my feet at the ankles. "I don't know who the hell you are."

She seethed and planted her hands on her curvaceous hips. "I think you do."

I flicked my stare from her pretty face to her impressive bust that warped whatever was written on the front of her white tank top. Then I dragged my stare down the rest of her gentle, pear-shaped body. Her tight, black jeans fit her like a dream, her legs filling every inch of them, and her slender feet held firm inside a white pair of heels. Inhaling, I lifted my stare to her face and surveyed her angry pout. Something about her rang familiar, but I couldn't put my finger on it.

Armi muttered an apology to me, then grabbed the woman's bicep and pulled her toward him. She yanked free with a growl and took another step forward, entering my personal space like she had every right to. Armi reached for her again, but I lifted my hand and he backed off. Those who stood around us stared, waiting to see what I'd do. I clenched my jaw, squared my shoulders, left my beer, and towered over the small woman. No one entered my personal space unless I allowed it—not Creed, not Isabelle, not fucking anyone.

"We met at the river four days ago," she said. "I asked for your help, but you turned me down and stole my driver's license."

Ah. A cold chill swept down my spine. The bitch with the kid. I remembered now. I went through all her pockets when I had her pinned against the tree. The five-foot-four woman in front of me was the brown-eyed, brown-haired *Yasmine Lolita Garcia*, the woman who followed me out of town in the middle of the night and asked for help, talking like I owed it to her. I'd forgotten I took her license. It must still be in the pocket of a pair of my jeans somewhere.

The corner of my lip threatened to curl and bare my teeth. I made myself clear that night by the river and I wasn't in the business of repeating myself. I cut my eyes at Armi. "Get her out of my sight."

Armi grabbed her by the bicep and tugged her toward him, sending strands of her long, dark hair into her face. I turned away.

"If you're gonna have me thrown out on my ass, at least be a man and do it yourself."

I froze on the spot. My ears burned hot. Did she just fucking challenge me? Members surrounding us sucked air between their teeth. They wolf whistled, cheered for her to give me hell, and for me to throw her out on the street where she belonged. I slowly turned to face her again and she swallowed hard as regret etched its way across her features. Armi stopped tugging and let her go. Yasmine was mine to deal with now.

All mine.

She was at my mercy and, unless you were naked and hogtied, that was never a good place to be. I stepped forward until my boots kissed her white heels. Yasmine didn't shrink into herself. If anything, she squared her shoulders and straightened her spine more, craning her neck to look up at me.

"If I have to leave this building, I'm gonna make you regret going toe to toe with me, little woman."

Yasmine's glance flickered between each of my eyes, her big, toffee irises holding back so much pain. "I'm not scared." Her left eye welled but didn't dare drip over the edge. "I'm already facing my greatest fear, Judge, and it isn't you."

I blew impatient air out of my nose and grabbed her around the waist. She squeaked as I lifted her into my arms and put her over my shoulder. Hooting and hollering filled my ears and drowned out one of my favorite Lynyrd Skynyrd tracks. No one followed me outside. It was just me, her, and the wind. Yasmine shouted and drummed her fists into my back, she kicked her legs and called me every name under the sun—a colorful variation of insults in English and Spanish.

I walked her as far as I wanted to, then I dropped her ass on the gravel drive in front of our motorcycles.

"Don't come back," I warned, and she lifted

herself to her feet.

This time she didn't stand so tall and the defeat in her bones aged her pretty face. I didn't notice it inside the clubhouse, but in this light, she looked gaunt and exhausted. I didn't understand it. I didn't understand her. Why did she want my help? Me, of all people? Even if I wanted to help—which I didn't—I was already neck deep in shit with enemies all over the goddamn place. Yasmine was a sexy woman, anyone with eyes could see that. The problem with sexy women was that psychotic and possessive men usually followed.

I'd bet our entire club fund that her villain was a bad, *bad* man.

"I'll come back again and again," she promised, and I rolled my eyes and turned from her. Rocks crunched under my boots as I walked away. "You're the only one who can help me. Please, as a parent, I'm begging you to help me save my boy—"

"My daughter wasn't saved!" I boomed as something snapped inside me. I faced her and just looking at her scared expression made my chest grow hot. "What makes you think your son should be? What makes you think I give a shit what happens to your kid? It's not mine."

Even at a distance, I saw the tremble in her chin. "I'm sorry for what happened to your daughter, truly—"

Emotion broke her voice and she swallowed the

rest of her sentence, then exhaled. Without thought, she dropped back to slump against a motorcycle and it toppled, knocking over the one beside it, which knocked over the next one.

And the next one.

Altogether, eight bikes toppled like dominos, filling the night air with sounds of scraping, scratching, and crunching.

"Oh, my God," she whispered loud enough for me to hear.

I started toward her and she whipped her head in my direction, her perky ass still on the fallen first bike. Her mouth was the perfect 'o' shape and I smiled wickedly as she exposed her palms to me.

"On second thought," I said, dark amusement lighting my tone. "You're not going anywhere."

THREE

YASMINE

The music.

The moaning.

The banging.

It's doing my head in. I lift my head from my knees and drop it against the wall, dinging the back of my skull. I've been in this small room for hours. It's dark. The light above doesn't work properly, casting an eerie, yellow glow around the room. It's not a cell, more of a sparse guest room. It smells clean, like citrus air freshener and washed linen. The bed I'm cuffed to is queen sized and the pillows I perch on are surprisingly plump.

I don't know what's going to happen to me. When the bikes fell, Judge simply smiled a terrifying and calculating smile, then he dragged me back inside the clubhouse. He whistled, *loudly*, and all eyes fell on us. He told them what I did, and they descended on me like bloodthirsty psychopaths. I thought Judge was going to feed me to them and let them pull me apart. I didn't cling to Judge's massive body as he stood beside me, watching the side of my face as I refused to yield to the verbal onslaught of his men. I simply stood there and took it all. When, and only when, a single tear dripped over the rim of my eye and onto my cheek did he stop them from shouting, swearing, and spitting at me. Then he dragged me down a hall and tossed me in this room. In smug silence, he handcuffed me to the slim railing of this queen bed and left. I don't know what his plans are. I have no money to pay for damages and every second wasted here is a second longer my son suffers at the hands of his nasty sperm donor.

A gentle knock patters on the door and I straighten as if a steel rod has been jammed in my spine. I purse my lips, not granting anyone access, but it doesn't matter. The handle is tugged down and a high-pitched squeak rings around the room as the door opens. A low grumble, a male's disapproving voice, vibrates into the room followed by a feminine whisper, and a thin layer of hair lifts on the back of my neck. My uneasiness doesn't let up, even when a solo Isabelle Laurent enters the room with a red cup in her hand and closes the door behind her.

"Hello," she greets me, smiling softly. She flexes

her slender fingers at her side and lifts the cup. "Brought you some water. Are you thirsty?"

I flick my stare down the length of her slim body. I don't think I've seen the mayor's daughter dressed so casually…or have so much skin exposed. If I hadn't seen her with my own eyes willingly kissing James Creed, I would've denied she'd ever be interested in a man like him. Sure, he's hot as sin, but girls like her marry politicians and celebrities. They marry filthy rich men thirty years their senior, not bikers.

Isabelle clears her throat and slowly moves toward the bedside table closest to her. "I asked Judge to let you go, but he's a hard man to negotiate with."

I scoff as she sits the cup down. "He can't keep me here forever."

"He will if you give him reasons to," she shoots back, planting her hands on her hips. "Don't challenge him. It won't end well for you."

I lift an eyebrow. "Is that a threat?"

"Take it however you want."

I avert my gaze to the bed and watch my red painted toenails as I nervously wriggle them against the black comforter. Maybe she's right. Maybe I should play nice so I can get the hell out of here. It's clear I'm not going to get any help from Judge and I'm burning too much daylight trying to get it.

"Your son…" Isabelle says, shifting her weight.

"Judge said something happened to him?"

I tighten my jaw and swallow hard. "He was taken."

"By who?"

"His father." I peer at her and she pinches her pretty face in confusion, the way everyone's does when I tell them Nicolás is with his father, but Elias has hated our son from the moment he was born. "He's a bad man."

"He'd hurt him?"

Pressure fills my chest and builds behind my eyes. I nod as tears well. No child should ever have to worry about their dad hurting them, but Nicolás has lived with that fear every day of his life. Why? Because he's different. Because he needs extra love, attention, and support, and that makes him weak. The one thing my ex-husband hates more than the law is weakness.

Isabelle shuffles toward the bed. Her brow is furrowed with concern, her arms folded tightly across her chest. "Why Judge? Can't you go to the police?"

I snort, then swipe the back of my free hand across my nose. "The police won't help me."

"Why?"

"They're in my ex-husband's pocket, just like they were in your father's." I drop my head back in exasperation and glance at the ceiling. There's too much to explain and I'm tired of reiterating it. "I'm on my own…and I need help."

The bedroom door is thrown open as the last word leaves me my mouth and I jump, nearly falling off the edge of the bed. In strolls a young man, no older than nineteen, donning a brown leather cut. His head is shaved, a buzzcut close enough to his scalp to show the scary swirls of ink that paint his skin. He finds Isabelle with his bright irises and offers her a small shrug.

"Sorry, Iz." He looks to me and flicks his long fingered, tattooed hand in my direction. "Judge wants to see her."

"I don't want to see him." The words shoot from my mouth with a clench of my stomach.

"It don't matter what you want." He crosses the room and rounds the foot of the bed, spinning keys on a ring around his long index finger. "You'll do as you're told."

I remain still as the young guy releases my wrist from the tight metal handcuff and requests I get off the bed. He demands I listen to him over and over, threatening to drag me out by my hair if I ignore him one more time. Reluctantly, I follow his orders, letting him escort me out of the room, barefoot, and right past James Creed, who leans against the hall wall, his knee bent, his giant boot planted on the wall's surface. I lift my eyebrows at the sight of him. He's tall and broad, like Judge, and just as intimidating. I swallow. I've heard my fair share of violent stories about Creed, Judge's VP, too. Maybe he'll help me if I ask? If I convince Isabelle to ask? James flicks his attention down the length of my body, then back up to meet my stare.

"Where're you taking this one, Kace?" he asks the man behind me.

"Judge. He wants to see her."

"She's his type, all right." A wicked smile pulls at Creed's lips as Kace ushers me past. "Good luck, Minnie."

Minnie? I balk, digging my heels in. "My name is Yasm—"

I try to turn around and face Creed, but Kace shoves me forward. A strange squeak leaves my lips as I stumble into the main room. It's busier than before—*louder*. Heavy metal music batters the walls and vibrates the floor. Its rough, messy, and consuming beat devours the voices of the wild and wayward men in front of me.

"Other side of the room," Kace shouts in my ear, poking me in the back. "Move it."

I shuffle forward and enter the throng of sweaty men and women. I wrinkle my nose. It smells of beer, sweat, and sex in here. How can they stand it? As I walk, I'm purposely shoved and tripped, but I keep my head high. This isn't about them. I'm not here to make friends.

When the thicket of leather and denim becomes too strong for me to push through, Kace takes the lead and I hold onto his brown cut. They don't move out of the way for him either and they shove and trip him as much as they did me. Every inch he moves, they make him work for it, until he's irritated and dripping with sweat of his own. When we break through to the other side, Kace snatches my bicep in his big hand and yanks me through a sheer set of black curtains and into a dark, moody room. Strange hints of grapefruit linger in the air. I straighten my spine in the darkness and open my eyes wider, desperate for them to adjust. All of three seconds pass before Kace releases my arm and the blaring music behind me dissolves into a low hum as it's closed behind heavy doors. When the lights kick in, I hold my breath. Faint, thin LED strips around the edge of the room glow and the space begins to take shape. Armchairs. Loveseats. Stages. A long bar in the corner of the room. The LEDs grow brighter, morphing from red to purple and I spot him, Damon Judge, sitting in a large, dark armchair directly in front of me. A woman perches on his lap, topless, her breasts in his face. She moves seductively, her hips rolling at a gentle pace, and she touches his chest, her hands bunching the black fabric of his t-shirt. The lights change from purple to white, lighting the room further, and his dark blue eyes find me. I exhale. When he looks at me, mischievous fire ignites in his expression, and it turns my stomach. *He thinks I'm a shiny new toy*. He's going to drag this out and waste more of my goddamn time.

I keep my stare on him as he eases forward and speaks in the woman's ear. Without hesitating, she slides off his lap and walks away, her firm breasts swaying as she fades into a dark corner by the long, skinny bar. He flicks his chin at me, summoning me closer. I clench my teeth and saunter forward, stopping a foot away from him. Tilting his head, Damon stares up at me.

"Sit."

Heat flares in my cheeks. I haven't sat on a man's lap in five years, I haven't let a man touch me in five years, and the thought sends unease hurtling through my veins.

"On you?"

He doesn't answer, only watches, his eyes sharp with impatience. I let out a slow exhale and move forward. I grip the armrests of his chair and lift myself onto his lap, placing my thighs either side of his. Behind me, whispers swirl, and it's unsettling. Our pelvises touch and our torsos are close—too close for comfort. To avoid touching him with my hands, I place them against my stomach. Scents of whiskey, cologne, and feminine perfumes tickle my nose, and the warmth emanating from his large body kisses my skin, making me hot around the collar. I guess I forgot how nice men feel...

I glance over my shoulder as the lights fade to

red, darkening the edges of the room.

"This is humiliating," I murmur, licking my dry lower lip.

Judge scoffs and I look at him. "Humiliating? You got the best seat in the house." He flicks his chin in the direction of the other side of the room. "Some would kill to sit where you're sitting."

I peer over my shoulder again and wait for the room's LEDs to change to a brighter color. When the blue comes, it allows me to see just how many people are in the room. There's more than I can count. A handful of men. But mostly women— young women, older women—and the way they glower at me...I believe him.

Some women are dressed, most are naked. As the blue hue reaches its peak, I'm sure I spot three people having sex on a love seat on the far side, but the color changes to a dark purple before I can register what I'm looking at.

"I spoke with my men and we came to an agreement," Judge says, pulling my attention back to him. I hold my breath. "You're free to go...once you've helped Wrench repair the bikes."

I lift my eyebrows. Is he serious? "I don't know the first thing about—"

"Alternatively." He pinches my tank top between his thick fingers and lifts the fabric, exposing my stomach. Self-deprecating thoughts about extra skin and pregnancy stretchmarks snake their way to the forefront of my mind, but Judge doesn't take his eyes from mine as he hangs the fabric over my breasts, exposing my white bra. "You can work off your debt another way."

I scowl. "A clubwhore?"

He rakes his stare down my chest to my stomach, then back up. "Your choice."

"I'd rather die than let any of you touch me." I say it with venom, with as much malice as I can muster, but it dies quick when Judge grabs my biceps and yanks me forward, my body slamming against his. My fast, shallow breath dances over his face and the corner of his lips twitch as if he's fighting the beginnings of a smirk.

"Afraid you might enjoy it?"

"I'm afraid I..." I swallow as tears sting my eyes. *Shit.* Crying at the drop of a hat is a new superpower of mine, thanks to my ex-husband. I've spent so long bottling my emotions up they now seep from the cracks.

And being here isn't helping my anxiety. I inhale slowly through my nose as my chest tightens and my gut churns painfully. *Get through it,* I tell myself. *You need to get through this.* I clear my throat and sit back, lifting my chest off Judge's.

To answer his smug comment, the men here scare me. They all scare me.

"I'm just afraid."

Judge flexes his fingers against the armrests and

turns his head to peer across the room. In the dim green lighting, shadows flicker on his jaw as he clenches and unclenches it.

"Your son is with his father," he says eventually, still avoiding eye contact. "There are worse places he could be."

"His father is a bad man."

Judge whips his head in my direction and his dark, aggressive gaze kicks my heart rate up. "I'm a bad man."

"But you're not evil."

"Is there a difference?"

"There's a world of difference." I inch closer, feeling as though I've got him on my hook. I just need to reel him in. He turns his head and I lean close to his ear. "I need you, Damon. Help me and I'll be forever in your debt. I'll do anything, be anything."

It's not a lie. I'll happily suffer the rest of my life as a piece of meat for the Devil's Cartel if it means Nicolás is safe, healthy, and happy.

"I don't believe you."

I cup Judge's face in my hands and guide his head back to mine, until our noses graze. Nervousness and excitement twirl recklessly in the pit of my stomach. The desire to kiss the most powerful man in the building has no business creeping through my veins, but I can't stop it. The need spreads like wildfire and he does nothing to discourage it. Judge moistens his full lower lip and tilts his chin, encouraging me to close the distance.

"Go on," he demands. "Fucking kiss me."

"I don't want to."

"Liar." He snatches my hair in his hand and yanks my head back, exposing my throat. "I'll give you what you want, and you can say I took it if it'll ease your guilt."

He presses his nose to my collar bone and my breath hitches as he touches his tongue to my throat and licks me all the way up to plant a kiss on my jaw. Electricity dances across my flesh and the skin behind my ears pulls tight. Judge eases my head forward until our eyes lock. The shade of the room changes from green to red and his eyes darken like the sky before a deadly storm. My heart beats fast— at a speed I haven't felt in a long, long time.

I tighten my grip on his face and crush my mouth to his. His lips twitch smugly against mine before he opens his mouth. When I open mine, he takes control of the kiss, shoving his tongue inside my mouth and squeezing me to him, forcing my hips to move against him. Judge moves his large, strong hands all over me, pinching and squeezing, appraising every inch of me. I've never felt so thoroughly appreciated as a woman and it leaves a thick swirl of confusion deep in my soul.

Judge breaks the kiss with an abrupt, disapproving growl. I pull back, blinking, letting my equilibrium sort itself out. When it does, I focus on the little baggie he holds in front of my face and the white, powdery substance nestled in its clear depths. My heart sinks.

"Cocaine." He cuts his eyes at me. "You're a druggie, bitch?"

The audacity of him to judge me given his line of work. It's public knowledge, the amount of drugs distributed by the hands of the Devil's Cartel, so he can shove his righteousness where it hurts. I shrug. "Sue me."

He swears and stands up. I fall to the ground with a thud, only to be picked right back up and lifted onto his shoulder. I grip the edge of his leather cut and lift my torso. "Put me down!"

Judge ignores me as he storms from the dark room. I wince at the harsh light and pounding music—Slipknot—as he carries me into the main room again.

"Again, Judge?" someone shouts, and Judge tightens his grip on me.

"Shut up."

"There she is." A sharp slap on my ass sends pain searing over my left cheek and I yelp, gritting my teeth. "Bit off more than you can chew, Prez?"

"Fuck off, Modo."

I spot Modo as we pass him. He grins at me, his blue eyes dancing mischievously. Lifting his large hand beside his face, he wiggles his fingers at me, a childish wave. I glare and flip him the bird, making him toss his head back and howl with laughter.

Judge marches down the hall to the very end and throws a door open. I gulp and hold on for dear life until I'm dropped from his shoulder and tossed away. My heart shoots up my throat as I freefall, and I bite my lower lip when I'm caught by a soft mattress. I hiss and lick my lip, lifting myself on my elbows. I scowl as Judge surges through the room toward an open far door. He flicks on the light and opens the lid to a toilet. I watch, silently, as he drops the bag of cocaine in and flushes it. He pins me with his glare, daring me to do something.

I cut my eyes at him. "You're awfully triggered by some blow for being a drug dealer yourself."

"I don't use it." He tramps back into the room, slamming the bathroom door behind him, drowning us in darkness. "Any of it."

I laugh once. "Bullshit."

"Believe whatever the fuck you want." Judge crosses the space, rips open the door, and storms out.

I lift my shoulders and brace against the loud slam that shakes every wall in the room. In the silence, the sound of metal locks clicking into place is all I hear. Then, the rapid pounding of my heart takes over, followed by a throbbing pain at the base of my neck. I sit up and shuffle back on the bed and rest against the pillows as thick, painful tendrils of dread burrow through my chest.

What the hell do I do now?

***

By the time Judge comes back, it's lighter outside—not quite morning, but getting close. He doesn't come alone, either. I lie on my side and stare at the wall as the sounds of kissing and sugary giggles grate on my nerves. A body hits the mattress and I bounce and grit my teeth. Then, I assume, Judge's weight also compresses the right side of the bed. I pull a face. These people are disgusting. I shift closer to the edge, not wanting either of them to touch me, but it doesn't matter. Judge grabs my thigh and pulls on it, forcing me onto my back.

"Don't touch me," I shout, swatting at his hand and kicking my leg.

Judge lifts himself from between the woman's legs and rears back on his knees. I glance at the woman, who wears nothing but lacy black panties and a matching bra, then back to Judge, who shrugs out of his cut and drops it on the mattress. He cuts his eyes at me as he grabs his shirt by the hem and pulls it off over his head. I don't look at his bare chest, or the ink that covers almost every inch.

"You make me sick," I tell him, and in the dim light, he smirks at me.

He keeps his attention on me as he reaches into

the pocket of his jeans and pulls out a small, black vial. I frown, confused, as he opens it up and leans over the woman. He taps the vial with his thick index finger and white powder falls onto her skin, like snow. My frown deepens. Happy with the thin, white line, Judge sits back and flicks his chin.

"Go on," he demands, and I notice the swell in his lips from passionate kissing. "I poured you a line. Let's have some fun."

Fun? He doesn't get it, does he? I don't use cocaine for fun. Even if I did, I'm not here to have *fun*. I'm here to get my fucking son back. I clench my teeth so hard my jaw aches and the pain radiates into my ears.

"That's what you're here for, right? Drugs?" Judge narrows his dark, dark eyes. "Did your husband even kidnap your son, or was he taken from you because of your bad habits?"

I flinch and my eyes begin to burn. I blink slowly, careful not to let tears form. Inhaling through my nose, I steel my spine and sit up. Judge's lips tug at the corner, the beginnings of a smug, disgusted smirk. I shift closer to the petite woman, who remains silent, and lower my face to her breasts, to the thin white line between them. I feel Judge's stare burning holes in the side of my face and it makes me uncomfortable. I pucker my lips and blow the cocaine off the woman, sending powder everywhere, making her cough.

I sit back on my heels, square my shoulders, and pin Judge with a glare. "You have me all wrong."

Something wicked flashes across his features. "Is that right?"

"That's right." My left nostril twitches as emotion builds in my chest, eating away my courage. "I don't use it for fun," I tell him, hating the way my throat trembles. "I use it to buy myself more time in a day. I can't save him while I'm sleeping."

Judge scans my face, looking for my lie. He doesn't find it. His throat bobs with a hard swallow, but his tense expression doesn't crack. "Can't save him jacked on coke, either."

I lift my shoulder with a half-hearted shrug. I suppose he's right...but what am I to do? I turn away and lie back down on the bed. Silence fills the room and weighs down my eyelids. I don't want to sleep. Sleep brings my son back to my arms and fills every crack in my aching soul. When I wake from my sweet sleep, I'm cracked in half all over again.

"Get out," Judge demands, and I'm swinging my legs over the edge of the bed before the last syllable falls from his lips.

"Gladly." I lift myself an inch off the bed when I'm grabbed by the bicep and tugged back on.

"Not you."

I whip my head in his direction as the woman

leaves the bed with a huff and exits the room, slamming the door behind her. Judge keeps his hold on my bicep and his stare on my face. I stare back, confused, hating the way warmth from his touch creeps through my veins and soothes my bones. He looks like he wants to say something, but he's holding back. Inhaling through his nose, he gives his head a gentle shake, then expels the breath through his lips.

"You need a good night's sleep," he says, his voice gruff and tired.

"I can't remember what a good night's sleep feels like."

He releases my bicep. "Get comfortable. I'll be back."

I shuffle up and rest my head on his fluffy pillows while Judge walks about his room, doing god knows what. He enters the bathroom, turns on the tap, then turns it off again. When he returns to the bed, he extends a pill and a glass of water to me. I eye it suspiciously.

"It'll help you sleep."

Unease pins my stomach, but I sit up and take the pill and water from him anyway. "What if I don't want to sleep?"

"If you wanna stay up, I've got some ideas."

I flick my stare over his naked torso. In this light, his tattoos look like oil poured over his muscular body. The bleeding heart in the middle of his chest catches my attention and holds it. I wonder what it's about. His daughter, maybe. I open my mouth and place the tiny, tasteless pill on my tongue. Then I bring the cup to my lips and pour the cool water into my mouth. I swallow it all with a single gulp, then finish the rest. Judge holds out his hand and I place my empty cup in his palm.

"More water?" he asks, and I shake my head.

Judge sits the cup on the empty bedside table, and I settle further into the pillows, preparing for sleep. Soon after, the bed dips with his weight and he lies on his back. I stare at the side of his face, at the gentle slopes of his facial structure. In all seriousness, he could be a model.

"I'll put you out with the dogs if you keep staring at me."

"Where am I supposed to look?"

"At the back of your eyelids," he grumbles. "Go to sleep."

I close my eyes only to open them again a heartbeat later. "How long until the sleeping pill kicks in?"

He shrugs, then turns his back to me. I frown at it, at his muscular back, until I slip into a dreamless slumber. When I wake, the sun is higher in the sky, its bright rays lighting up the room through his skylight. I stare at the blue sky from where I lie on my back, blinking only when a murder of crows fly overhead. I think of my son and my lips twitch at the corner. Most people prefer to lie under the moon and watch the stars, but not my Nicolás. He likes doing it during the day. Planes, shapely clouds, and flying birds move him more than sparkly stars.

I roll onto my side and Judge still has his back to me. In the light, I try to make sense of his tattoos. There's a forest, intricately inked into his skin, and at the center of it, the leaves of the trees give way to the shape of a tormented skull. At the base of the trees, the ground dissolves into what can only be described as *Hell*. Skulls and wilting flowers, a destroyed teddy bear, ripped flesh, and more screaming skulls. Across the center of Hell, written in small breathtaking cursive, *what doesn't kill you makes you wish you were dead. What doesn't destroy you, leaves you broken instead.* My heart stutters in its beat and my fingers twitch with the urge to reach out and touch the two musical notes that adorn each side of the lyric.

...*what doesn't kill you makes you wish you were dead.* I press my tongue to the roof of my mouth. I can't imagine living in a world without Nicolás. Guilt swallows me up inside. My son may be gone, but he's not dead. Judge lost his daughter. The reports say she was pronounced dead at the scene and Judge, despite the paramedics' protest, carried her lifeless body for miles to the hospital for further investigation. I shudder, recalling the man who committed manslaughter against Judge's daughter went missing hours later. No one has seen him since and I don't think he's in the Bahamas living his best life.

"Judge?" I murmur, his name flying out my mouth before I can stop it.

"Mm."

"Why put the lyrics on your back where you can't see them?"

Silence. I rub my lips together, cringing. I shouldn't have said anything. I shouldn't—

"Don't need to see it," he says, interrupting my train of thought. "I feel it every day."

I nod. I understand the feeling, in my own personal way.

"I've always wanted a tattoo," I say.

"Of?"

I shrug and roll onto my back. Not knowing what I want is the reason I don't have one.

"I want something meaningful. Maybe my son's name, a lyric from a song, or a quote from a book. I want something that stirs my soul every time I look at it."

He rolls onto his back and looks up at the ceiling. I flick my gaze over his torso and bicep tattoos. They're a lot different than the ones on his back. They're more...superficial. Naked women, thorny roses, and flaming skulls. Do they stir his soul, like the deeply personal tattoos on his back?

"Your son's father," Judge grumbles, taking me

by surprise. "Who is he?"

I catch my lower lip between my teeth. It has to come out sooner or later, especially if Judge and his club are going to help me. "Elias Vergara."

Judge lifts his eyebrows and turns his head, pinning me with a surprised look. "Spanish drug-lord Elias Vergara? What the fuck, Yasmine?"

"I know—"

"How the hell did you get tangled up with one of the world's most wanted?"

My stomach churns. If I go into too much detail about how I ended up on Elias Vergara's superyacht in the Bahamas all those years ago, I'm as good as dead. It's not an easy story to tell and if I tell it, it won't be the most honest story either. I'd have to lie to Judge and the rest of the MC. For my own sake, I need to limit the amount of lies and bended truths.

"It's a long, *awful* story. I'd rather not relive it." I scratch my cheek. "Now you know why I can't get my son back on my own."

"We can't take on Elias Vergara," he states and turns on his side.

I frown at his back as he sits up and swings his legs over the edge of the thick mattress.

"Why not?"

"Because it's suicide."

I sit up and cross my legs. I follow him with my eyes as he saunters about the room. His ropey bicep and forearm muscles tighten as he bends low and picks up his t-shirt from last night.

"You have the men. You have the weapons—"

"Do you have any idea how many men I could lose? *Good* men." He pulls the shirt on over his head. "Men who don't deserve to be caught up in the shitstorm you call your life."

"Good men?" I scoff. "None of you are good. If anything, I'm giving you an opportunity to actually do some good for once in your miserable, corrupt lives."

Judge cuts his eyes at me, pinning me with a glare so cold I feel it right down to the bone. The muscles in his jaw flex and relax over and over as he bends down and scoops up his cut. He takes his time brushing it off and pulling it on. When it's on, he squares his shoulders and my steeled spine wavers at the sight of him towering over the bed.

"You fix the bikes, you leave," he says, resolute. "Set foot on my property again and I'll have Armi shoot you on sight, *entendre?*"

I scowl at him.

Culero.

FOUR

J U D G E

From the side porch of the clubhouse, I watched her work. I dragged my stare over the flat of her stomach that was exposed every time she leaned over to see what Wrench, our mechanic, was doing. I followed the bend of her back to the curve of her ass as she bent over and searched through the small, red toolbox. The soles of her feet were as black as night, her white shirt now a dusty gray. I didn't want to admit it, but she looked sexy as hell with her wild hair haphazardly tied into a high ponytail and a swipe of dirt across her cheek. I liked a clean woman, a proper woman, like Blondie, but I coveted women who weren't afraid to get dirty. Our clubwhores weren't afraid to get dirty...but they weren't afraid to do anything for a member. If it got them attention, drugs, and money, they didn't bat an eyelid. I wasn't interested in the kind of loyalty that could be bought. I was interested in unshakeable loyalty, like Blondie had for Creed, like my men had for me.

Yasmine grew more frustrated the longer she searched through the toolbox. Eventually, Wrench got up off the floor of the garage and sauntered toward her. He placed his dirty hand low on her back. I thinned my eyes, unfamiliar with the gross tendril of jealousy that burrowed through my chest. Yasmine straightened, clenching a screwdriver in her hand. Her lips moved quickly, aggressively, as she stepped away from his touch and shoved the screwdriver at him. Wrench tilted his head and grinned.

"How's she doing?"

Creed startled me with his low voice, but I absorbed my surprise well. I cast a side glance across the wooden table to Modo, who continued to watch Yasmine and Wrench in uncharacteristic silence, his eyes covered by his black Ray-Ban sunglasses.

"Don't know." I turned my head and peered out over the green land that stretched for miles. "Don't care."

Smiling, Creed moved in front of me and leaned against the black porch beam. He bent his leg at the knee and folded his arms over his chest. "You've been watching her for an hour."

"So has Modo." I looked at him again. His lips

parted, but he didn't utter a word. "Modo."

I angled my hips and stretched my leg under the table. I shouted his name and kicked his plastic chair. Gasping, he choked on a snore and jumped a few inches out of his seat, his sunglasses falling from his face. "What?"

Creed laughed. "Were you sleeping?"

"Nah. Nah." He rubbed at his tired face, stroked his beard, then adjusted his cut. "Just resting my eyes."

He propped his elbow on the armrest and rested his cheek on his tattooed fist. Creed and I watched him. Three silent seconds passed before a soft snore vibrated the table. *Useless.*

"I'm supervising." I propped my legs up on the chair across from me, crossing them at the ankle, and I slouched. "Making sure she's doing what she's told."

"I think Wrench can handle her."

I blew air between my lips. Wrench couldn't handle shit, especially Minnie. He hadn't left the property in seven years. He spent his days and nights in the garage, talking to himself. He was a recluse, a fucking weirdo, but he'd taken a liking to Yasmine.

And she didn't like it.

I didn't like it either.

"What do you want, Creed?" I demanded, hating the way he stood there, smug, like he knew everything I was thinking.

"The weekend off."

"The weekend off," I repeated, pulling a face. I couldn't hide the bitterness in my tone. "Didn't you just take a weekend off? You went to Sacramento."

"I've got no runs scheduled this weekend, Judge. Got no meetings, and no duties. I want to take Blondie away for a couple days."

Away? They lived in their own big-ass house, not at the clubhouse anymore, for God's sake. Besides, sometimes things weren't scheduled. Sometimes shit happened and he needed to be here when it did. The rules had never changed. The club came first. It always has and always will. Blondie was fun, but fuck her. She didn't need to stay at a five-star resort every month, but there she was, dragging my VP out to day spas and nail salons. Creed happily went with her whenever he could. He did everything for her—fucking spoiled her—and I couldn't help but wonder if he did it because he was trying to keep up with her old, lavish lifestyle. Maybe he was afraid she was gonna get bored of him and leave. God knew she had the money to go wherever she wanted.

"Where're you two headed this time?" I asked.

I wasn't going to argue with him. He deserved the time off. He'd been my right-hand man since we were teenagers, and he did everything I asked without question. I owed him the private moments he wanted with Blondie during this rare peacetime. It wouldn't last. Once the heat died off and the FBI permanently left the town, we had a lot of money to recoup, and a lot of ground to recover—years of it. Isabelle better stay the hell out of my way when the time came.

"Vegas."

I lifted an eyebrow. "Ventilli territory? Ballsy."

"I won't wear my colors. We'll be fine."

I knew they'd be okay. Ventilli wasn't stupid, even our small Exeter chapter could wipe them off the map, but if Creed gave them one, shitty reason to kill him, they would without hesitation.

"Don't recall you asking me if I wanted to go to Vegas…"

"One of us needs to be here." He flicked his head toward the garage where Wrench stood close behind Yasmine, his covered cock inches from pressing against her ass. My cheek twitched. "Anyway, you've got your hands full with that one."

"I want nothing to do with her."

"Maybe you should have a little fun with her," he said, and I looked at him. "Who knows, maybe you'll like her enough to keep her and leave Izzy the fuck alone."

I laughed. Shit. She really did tell him everything. I wondered how long he was gonna wait before bringing last night up with me. It was a marvel, really. Since dating Blondie, he'd developed some restraint. Old Creed would've murdered me where I stood.

"She doesn't want you, Damon."

I smiled. "Is that what she told you?"

"Yeah, that's what she told me." He pushed off the porch railing and sauntered closer. "Then she showed me how much she doesn't want you. All night, all morning, and well into lunch."

I tipped my head. Riling him up was too much fun. "She must be a good liar."

He gripped my chair's armrest and leaned in. His dark, whiskey eyes weren't glistening and there wasn't a drop of humor to be seen. He wanted to beat the living shit out of me.

"When you get a woman, I'll be right there," he warned. "Breathing down her neck."

Creed's threat fell on deaf ears. I didn't want my own woman. I'd already been there and done that, and it ruined my goddamn life. "I'm shaking."

"I'm going to Vegas and I'm gonna enjoy my weekend, fucking Isabelle all over the city, while you sit here, all by yourself, playing with your limp dick."

I simpered. *Lucky bastard.*

"Damon!" Yasmine snapped, pulling our attention. She stormed toward us, her thin arms swinging at her sides and Wrench hot on her tail. "I'm *done*!"

"What now?" I shouted as Creed released my

seat and straightened.

Modo choked on another snore and pushed his sunglasses to the top of his head. "What the— what's happening?"

Yasmine stopped in front of the porch as I lifted myself out of my chair and walked over to the railing. I leaned on the wood and peered down at her.

"You're not done. You've still got four bikes, mine included. You're not leaving here until every one of them is scratch free."

She stood on an awkward angle and pointed back at Wrench, the fucking idiot. "I can't do it with him. He keeps touching me and breathing all over me—"

"So?" Creed says dryly, as he came to stand beside me. "He's helping you. Give him some."

My cheek twitched again, and Yasmine pinned him with her dark, sexy eyes. "I'm not talking to you, *asshole*."

"Oop." Modo roared with laughter behind us and my lips kicked up at the corners as amusement swirled through me.

Creed arched an eyebrow and cut his eyes at me. Most women turned to jelly in Creed's presence. He could make a female do whatever he wanted without uttering a word. I'd seen it with my own eyes. Maybe he was losing his charm. In his defense, Yasmine wasn't an ordinary woman. She had fire in her eyes and fuel in her soul and I was certain there wasn't a feeble bone in her body. Even if she gave Creed a shot, he couldn't handle her. He loved being a woman's knight in shining armor, the hero who opened jars and reached items too high in the kitchen. I'd never been attracted to women like that. I liked women who'd break the jar long before they'd ask for my help. Yasmine was that kind of woman and I wanted her to prove it to me. I wanted her to prove she already tried her hardest to get her son back and I really was her last resort.

"You don't need me to fight your battles for you." I straightened and she pouted her lips, reminding me of the way she kissed me last night. She wanted it. She was hungry for it. If I hadn't found that little baggie of cocaine, would it have gone further? Would we have done more in my bed than argue and sleep? "You've got four more bikes to do. You can leave when they're done, and only when they're done."

Yasmine clenched her fists at her sides and seethed. I recalled the night I first met her, by the lake. I was the one she wanted. She was awed by me. Her eyes held all the hope in the world, as if she believed her son was finally within arm's reach. Now, she detested me. As she glared up at me, there was no awe in her features. No respect. Not even fear.

"You're pathetic, you know that?" She spat it in Spanish, and I translated without fault. My ex spoke

Spanish and I spent the first few years of Nila's life taking nighttime Spanish communication classes. "I hope you rot in hell."

Minnie whirled on her heel and stormed back to the garage. I turned my attention to Wrench and stared at him. I expected an apology, a vow to leave her the fuck alone, since she verbally detested even the feel of his breath on her gently tanned skin. Instead, he shrugged his fat shoulders and turned away, trudging all the way back to Yasmine where he stood way too close. She looked at me, and if looks could kill…

"I like her," Modo said, leaning back in his chair. "She's fun."

Creed, Modo, and I continued to watch Wrench and Yasmine. He violated her personal space more times than I could count, and she took it all with a dipped head and gritted teeth until she couldn't take another unsolicited touch. Wrench brushed his palm by her breast, smirking like the pervert he was, and Yasmine snapped. She chopped him in the throat and punched him in his bulbous stomach with enough force to make him hunch and clench his torso.

"Jesus," Creed uttered, folding his arms across his chest.

But Minnie wasn't done. She bent and grabbed the bucket of dirty, soapy water by her feet. She lifted it, spilling it down her white shirt as she went, then slammed it over his head, dousing him completely. *Holy shit.* I fought a wicked smile as something ignited in my veins. An excitement I hadn't felt in the longest time coiled through my body and burrowed through my bones. *Modo's right. She's fun.*

Trouble too. I didn't have time for trouble.

Yasmine adjusted her ponytail as she stormed from the garage and barreled up the drive.

"Hey!" Creed shouted.

He shot forward and hooked his leg over the porch, ready to jump it. I hit the back of my hand against his chest as she flipped him off and kept on going.

"Let her go."

"Let her go?" Creed frowned at me. "Why the hell are we letting her go?"

I turned and strolled across the porch. Irritation and disappointment danced around my ribcage as I bounded down the stairs and closed the distance between me and the garage. My men weren't the best. They'd all done things in their lives that put them on God's naughty list, but none of them had touched a child, purposely murdered an innocent, or raped a woman. When I took over, those sick fuckers were the first to go. I had no tolerance for it. We didn't traffic human beings, we didn't play with blood diamonds, we didn't sell drugs to kids. With my bare hands, I lifted this chapter out of the dirt, out of the dregs, and I gave my men something to be proud of.

Wrench ripped the bucket from his head and tossed it away as the soles of my heavy boots hit the concrete garage floor.

"Fucking whore," he grumbled, pushing his knuckle-less fingers through his long, soaking hair.

He froze as he righted his head and saw Creed, Modo, and I standing there, staring.

"What'd you do, Wrench?" Creed asked, stuffing his hands into the pockets of his cut.

"Nothing."

"Nothing?" Modo stepped forward. "We saw you do a whole lot more than nothing."

I screwed up my face. "You didn't see shit. You were sleeping."

He shrugged his shoulders. "Still…"

"Oh, big-fucking-deal," Wrench spat. He shrugged out of his cut and dropped it to the floor. Then he wiped his hands down the front of his shirt. "Bitch was up her own ass anyway."

I sauntered forward and circled Wrench while Creed went out onto the drive. I dragged my gaze all over him, then all over the garage. He'd been in here with her for hours. The scratches weren't deep, and he was repairing whole panels on some bikes instead of buffing them out. There was no reason to do that unless he was trying to keep her in here longer than she needed to be.

I use it to buy myself more time in a day. I can't save him while I'm sleeping, her words echoed in my mind and guilt wormed its way through my organs. I stopped in front of Wrench and watched him. He wrinkled his nose and blew air from his lips, apparently nervous. Yasmine was trying to get her son back and here this asshole was, burning up all her daylight, and for no good reason.

"She's gone," Creed sighed, planting his hands on his hips. "What about the bikes, Judge?"

I clenched my jaw and jolted forward. I slammed my fist into Wrench's stomach, right where Yasmine got him, and forced the air from his lungs. He gasped and wheezed, this time collapsing to the floor.

"Wrench'll fix them." I crouched by his head and brushed hair out of his reddening face with my index finger. He squeezed his green eyes shut and focused on getting his lungs to work the way they should. "Won't you, Wrench?"

"Yeah, Prez," he gasped, curling into the fetal position. "I'll fix 'em."

FIVE

YASMINE

I turn my key in the keyhole of my motel room door, a room generously—and unknowingly—paid for by a Charlotte Waller. Guilt twists through me and tightens around my ribcage. This is what my life has been reduced to. Cheap motel rooms, credit card fraud, and associating with criminal bikers. When will it end? I've become the thing I hate most in the world. Lawless.

I jimmy the key in the lock and push down on the handle. With a satisfying click the door unlocks, and I tilt my head back, lifting my chin in thanks to a God I don't believe in. I step inside the tiny, self-contained room and close the door behind me. In the quiet, my mind turns toward thoughts of a hot shower, so I can wash away the dirt and sweat I accumulated on my three-hour trek from the Devil's Cartel clubhouse.

Then it hits me…

…the smell of old eggs.

I sniff and wrinkle my nose as I inhale the sulphur scent deep in my lungs and hold it. My eyes go wide. *He's found me.* I whirl on my heel and grab the door handle. As my fingers connect with the metal, a hand clamps around the back of my neck and I shriek as I'm yanked backward. In my stumble, I drop my keys and trip over my own feet.

"Elias isn't happy with you, *Camilla*."

I gasp at the use of my fake name. *Jorge*. I know that husky smoker's voice from anywhere. He was my babysitter for the duration of my miserable time living with my ex-husband. Jorge moves his gigantic hand from my neck to my hair and grips it tight. I hiss and clench his wrist as he drags me back, my ass inches from the dirty floor, toward the kitchenette.

"Let me go!" I shout, and I'm lifted by my hair, my sore feet no longer sliding along the floor, and I grit my teeth against the unbearable pain of my scalp holding my bodyweight. "Shit."

I'm slammed into a wooden chair hard enough to knock the wind out of me. I grip the flimsy armrests and hang my head, taking shallow breaths to give my lungs time to recover. Jorge crouches in front of me and pushes my hair out of my face, forcing my head up. Our eyes lock—brown to ice blue—and he smirks. His lips pull at the corner, stretching the deep scar that runs vertically through them. I swallow hard. I doubt he's forgotten I gave him that scar... I attacked him with a playdough knife the night he and Elias came for Nicolás. It's healed atrociously, but at least it matches the one running down the middle of his bald scalp.

"What do you want?" I ask, sniffling as tears well in my eyes. "What more could he possibly want?"

Jorge leaned in close and surveyed my tears.

"You're crying?" He thins his eyes. "You disappoint me."

I straighten my spine and my fake tears dissolve. "*You* disappoint *me*. How can you still work for him, Jorge? After everything he's done to Nicolás?"

Jorge was Elias's right hand man—a brute that could fell impossibly large groups of men in no time at all. At one point in time, Jorge was my only friend. He became my brother, always looking out for me when Elias was gone, always playing with Nicolás, and keeping him busy while Elias and I fought like cats and dogs. I thought I could trust him. I thought he'd help us escape...but he was only loyal to Elias. And he betrayed me.

"I owe my life to Elias."

I sneered. "Then you'll die with him too."

Jorge grinned and stood. I watched as he rolled the sleeves of his black button up shirt to his elbows.

"I've missed you," he says, then cracks his knuckles.

"You haven't missed me."

I lift myself out of my seat and roll my shoulders. I don't have it in me to fight him, but what choice do I have? My heart pounds and I peer at the front door.

"He only sent one of you?"

"One today." He squares up. "If I don't get it done, he'll send two tomorrow."

Nausea rolls through me, a result of breathing in the gas Jorge filled my room with.

"Something to look forward to, then." I grit my teeth and launch forward. I slam my fists into Jorge's fat stomach, then swing for his head. Grunting, he catches my wrist and punches me in the side. I shout as my organs ripple and my legs give out from under me. I drop to my knees, clenching my side. Jorge extends his hand and I stare at his gigantic palm.

"I'm exhausted," I tell him. "I can't fight you."

"Yes, you can. You will."

I close my eyes. "I won't."

"You're not a victim, Yasmine." He bends and takes my hand. I hiss as he forces me to my feet. "I once saw you jump a dining table and drive a steak knife through Elias's chest. You want to see your son again? Fucking prove it...or die trying."

I blow air from my lips. He's right. I didn't end

66

up on Elias's yacht by accident. I chose to be there—worked my ass off to be there. It went further than I ever expected it to go, but I made my own choices.

Jorge swings his fist and I duck it, planting three swift punches to his ribs. He grunts and hunches, tucking his elbows in to protect his torso. I shift my assault to his head and connect with his jaw. Pain flares in my wrist, but I ignore it and hit him again. The force of my punch throws his head to the side. Growling, Jorge barrels forward and grabs me around the waist. His gigantic, wide-set body hits mine like a freight train and I'm lifted off my feet. I grab onto him and brace for impact as he dives into the kitchen and slams me into the cupboard. I hit it hard and the cheap plywood cracks and splinters. Pain slices across my scalp and zips down my spine. My brain rolls in my skull as space dances in front of my eyes, pretty stars obscuring my view. Jorge rears back, keeping his hands on my hips, and drives forward, thrusting his shoulder into my torso repeatedly. Each hit feels like it fractures my spine, each hit drops me lower and lower until I'm sitting on the floor, my palms exposed. Jorge towers above me, his fists clenched at his side, his nostrils flaring. I'm no match for him. I never have been, even when he was teaching me how to fight in secret at Elias's villa in Greece.

"I can't..." I pant, wincing when the muscles

around my spine spasm. "I can't fight you."

He licks his bloody lower lip and steps forward. "Get up."

I shake my head. "Promise me you'll look after him. Promise—"

He snatches my hair and punches me in the mouth. Reality falters, blood fills my mouth, and I swallow it, tasting my life. My shitty life.

"Promise me, Jorge," I gurgle, unable to see his expression through the blur.

"Elias is going to kill him." Jorge rears back and hits me again. I think I lose a tooth and swallow it, like a pill, with a mouthful of blood. "There's nothing I can do."

He releases my hair with a shove, and I tip over, my cheek hitting the dirty linoleum floor. I close my eyes. When they flutter open, all I hear is the sound of my heart beating in my ears. It plays like an anthem, demanding I get up and fight for my son.

Jorge paces back and forth right outside the kitchen, slow, calculating steps, as he draws his cellphone to his ear and speaks into it. I roll onto my front and crawl toward the bottom kitchen drawer, barely able to pull my weight along on my shaking arms. Every inch I move feels like the drawer moves further away, a trick composed by my shattered equilibrium. Blood rolls freely from my lips and I choke on a sob, then collapse, squeezing my eyes closed.

"Are you sure this is what you want?" Jorge asks, glancing over his shoulder at me. "Yes. She is."

Jorge's shoes tap the floor and the linoleum dips by my face. I hear Elias's deep, smooth voice before I register the feel of a warm phone screen on my face.

"I told you, Sweetheart, didn't I? I told you what would happen."

Hot tears burn out the corner of my eye. "I hate you."

"You hate me?" I hear his smile in his tone. "It was you who infiltrated my life and fucked everything up." He pauses to drag on a cigarette and it's like I can smell it through the phone, the rich, European tobacco. "I gave you everything you wanted. I laid the world at your feet, made you a queen, and what'd I get in return?"

I don't answer.

"I got lies, betrayal, and a monster child only you could love."

My lower lip trembles. Just when I think my heart is as broken as it can possibly be, he shatters it a little more.

"You may hate me, *Camilla*, but you ruined my life." He takes another drag. "I was content knowing you were alive and suffering without Nicolás, but then I hear you're conspiring with the Devil's Cartel—"

"They won't help me," I rasp. "They refused."

He laughs. "Lies fall from your lips so easily, don't they?"

"I'm not—"

"This will be the last time we speak. I'd tell you to rest in peace but that's the last thing I want for you. I hope you rot in hell, you cunt!"

I wince and flinch away from the phone, dropping my head to the floor. Jorge turns away, returning to his phone call with Elias. He begins to wrap it up, agreeing to whatever Elias wants just to get off the phone. Thick pumps of adrenaline and stubbornness fills me. This isn't how I die. I lift my head and continue army crawling to the bottom drawer where I stashed a handgun months ago. Hope ignites in my veins when I make it across the small kitchen and quietly open the drawer. Like I expected, my little black handgun sits amongst washed take-out containers. I reach inside and grab it without disturbing the stacking order and alerting Jorge.

Shaking, I lift my torso and pull my legs underneath me, wincing at the fire that rips through my tired bones. Jorge exhales and lowers his phone. Without a glance over his shoulder, he stuffs it into his pocket.

"I really wish things were different, Yasmine," he says, looking up at the ceiling. I force myself to stand up and I straighten my arms, holding the gun outstretched and pointed directly at the back of his skull. "If you had—"

I pull back the hammer and it clicks loudly into place. Jorge freezes.

"Don't be stupid. You shoot that gun and this whole building goes up."

I shuffle forward, then shuffle backward off to the left where the front door remains unlocked. Jorge slowly turns to face me and pins me with a softened stare.

"Eight people are currently staying at this motel. One a family—mom, dad, and three little babies."

My eyelids flutter at his lies. They've always manipulated my good morals and used my humanity against me. They've always abused my big heart. Not this time. I know for a fact eight of the twelve rooms are being refurbished due to asbestos. At this very moment, the only people in this building are me, Jorge, and the motel owner, but I'm not sparing a thought for that child-sex offending pig. Getting rid of him would be doing the town a favor.

I back up, keeping a firm hold on my handgun and I reach behind me to open the front door. Cool air rushes in as I back out onto the ripped welcome mat. Jorge steps forward, his eyes darting to either side of where I stand as he tries to decide what he's going to do. Nausea turns my stomach and scratches at my throat. I aim my gun off to the side, pointed at a dirty pan I used to make soup the night I went to the clubhouse. I stride backward, giving myself as much space as possible.

"Yasmine!" Jorge runs at me, his heavy stomps causing the room to tremble. "Don't!"

I part my lips with an exhale as the urge to vomit rises and I shoot the pot. I don't have time to turn or run. The flames eat up the room quicker than I can blink, and they explode out the door and the windows, blowing me off my feet. The ground falls away from me and glass whips through my skin like tiny diamond bullets. Where I hit the ground, I don't know, but it's hot and sharp and the shrapnel that rains down on me burns like lava.

That's enough. I've done enough.

I let out one last exhale, then succumb to the darkness pulling me under by my ankles.

SIX

JUDGE

"I need you, Damon. Help me and I'll be forever in your debt," Yasmine pleaded, her sweet breath blowing over my ear. "I'll do anything, be anything."

It'd been a long time since I believed words spoken by a pretty female tongue. I wanted to believe her, but I'd been burned in the worst possible way too many times before. She couldn't use her God-given beauty to manipulate me. The only reason she was here was because she wanted something from me.

"I don't believe you."

Yasmine cupped my jaw in her soft hands and guided my head back to hers. I flicked my gaze over her face as our noses gently grazed. My eyebrows draw closer. It felt genuine, the way she touched me. Yasmine blinked, enrapturing me with her long lashes and pretty, dark irises, and something changes in her posture. She leans harder against me and holds me tighter with her thighs. Hot blood begins to travel south and pool between my legs, stirring my cock. I wanted to kiss her, to crush my mouth to hers and rip her clothes from her body. I wanted her naked—no—needed her naked, and on me. I licked my lower lip and eased my mouth closer, encouraging her to give me what I want.

"Go on," I demanded when I really wanted to beg. Please, *please* kiss me with those gorgeous lips. "Fucking kiss me."

"I don't want to."

"Liar." I snatched her long, thick hair in my hand and yanked her head back, exposing her throat. It was one of my favorite parts of a woman's body. It was an easy part to please, an easy part to punish. "I'll give you what you want, and you can say I took it, if it'll ease your guilt."

I lowered my head and pressed my nose to her collar bone, deciding if I wanted to kiss and lick her, or nip and suck. She did barrel in here uninvited, then called me out in front of my men...so I should punish her. Show her who's boss.

But...

I pushed my tongue out and touched it to her throat. Her breath hitched, sending shockwaves of pleasure down my spine. The girl on my lap was too pretty to punish. I licked her along the column of her throat and planted a soft kiss on her jaw. Then I eased her head forward until our eyes locked. Yasmine's chest rose and fell with shallow breaths and her wide eyes were now hooded and lusty. She tightened her grip on my face and crushed her mouth to mine. It caught me off guard. I was never caught off guard and never let a woman take a kiss from me like she deserved it. I gave them if I wanted to give them. No bitch in this club had the balls to steal one from me and the gasps from clubwhores hiding in the shadows of the room confirmed my thoughts.

But…in the moment, I was powerless against Yasmine. I pushed my tongue inside her sweet mouth. I devoured her. I gripped her bare hips and ground her against me. I hadn't dry humped since I was twelve, but here I was, wanting to get a girl off with my jeans. And she was sexy in a way none of the women at the club were. I couldn't explain it. I moved my hands low to cup her ass. I grabbed her bare cheeks in my hands and forced her harder against me. I groaned as I felt the warmth from her pussy through my jeans and on the tips of my fingers. Then, I broke the kiss and pushed Yasmine back enough to take her in. The LED lights in the room brightened to a blue and…my attention fell to her exposed breasts and flat, naked stomach. She was naked.

She wasn't naked before…

I touched the space under her ribs, where her body curved in, and I slid my hands north until my thumbs touched the underside of her breasts. Minnie was perfect—untouched by the club, by this way of life. She had no tattoos, no scars, no silicone trapped under her smooth, soft skin. She let her long, dark hair down and it tumbled over her breasts, covering the nipple and tickling my forearms.

"Damon, please," she whispered, placing her hands on top of mine. "Please."

"Please, what?" I asked as she peeled my hands from her and placed them on the chair's thick armrests. "What do you want?"

"You. I need you."

Yasmine cupped her breasts and I watched excess, pliable flesh spill from her slender fingers. They needed bigger hands. I tried to lift mine to show her, but all I got was a twitch from my middle finger. *What the hell?*

"I need you," she repeated, moving her hips against me. "I need you so bad."

I tried to grab, to squeeze her soft flesh, but I couldn't move my damn hands. She turned me on so bad and I wanted to touch her more than I've wanted to touch any woman, but I couldn't. Releasing one breast, Yasmine slid her pretty hand south over her taut stomach to the mound of her pussy, covering the thin, maintained strip of hair that teased me.

"Touch me," she sighed, pressing her fingers inside her creases.

"I can't touch you." I flexed my hips again, wanting to be closer, needing to be closer. "I can't touch you."

Her eyelids flutter as a shiver rippled over her body. She continued to move, to grind, to moan, as she brought herself closer to her orgasm. I didn't know which part of her deserved my attention more, so I flickered it everywhere. Her eyes, her mouth, her throat. Her breasts, her stomach, her thighs. *Fuck.*

Yasmine grabbed my face again and her quick breath skittered across my cheeks. I stilled as she grazed her index finger along my lower lip.

"You look like you want to taste me," she murmured, pleasure flashing in her eyes. "Do you?"

I kept my stare on hers as I flicked my tongue out and touched it to the tip of her finger. Her full lips parted, and she slipped her finger into my mouth. I salivated the second her taste hit my tongue. I groaned and closed my mouth around her finger. She tasted good—better than good. She tasted like everything I was missing.

Yasmine replaced her finger with her tongue and kissed me deeply, hungrily. I got lost in it, lost in the way it felt, in the way it made my heart beat into my ribs, and the way it turned my blood to lava. I fell deep into her, into her passion, that I didn't notice her moving my hand between her legs until I felt her slick arousal coat my fingers. *Oh, god, she's wet.*

"Yes," I groaned, breaking the kiss. "Fucking hell."

I never allowed a woman to be in control of me, not ever, but since I *literally* had no control over my own body, I allowed her to do whatever she wanted with me. She sat on my hand and flexed her hips, smiling wickedly.

"Your fingers are so much thicker than mine," she said, positioning my finger at her tight entrance. I pushed up as she sank down on it with a shuddering moan and it caught her by surprise. She fell forward and pressed her chest to mine. "Jesus, Damon."

All I could do was hold my finger inside her and desperately wish it were my cock instead. Yasmine tilted her head back, giving me access to her slender throat and I ran with it. I kissed, sucked, and bit her flesh until she was a quivering mess, until she was begging me to make her come. A loud moan seeped out between her lips and turned my blood to hellfire.

"Judge," she bit out, then buried her head in the space between my shoulder and my neck as her body went rigid and her muscles trembled.

I dropped my head back against the headrest and focused hard on not ruining my jeans as the feel of her contracting around my finger propelled me to the edge of ecstasy, to the edge of madness. Her body shook, her thighs clenched me sporadically, until she couldn't bear to move against me anymore. I shut my eyes, willing my body to calm with hers even though I was still worked up beyond belief. Yasmine's panting breath warmed my shoulder and dampened my shirt, but I didn't mind…

…until the panting turned to sobbing and the fabric of my shirt became thoroughly soaked.

I frowned. "Minnie?"

She spoke, but her words were muffled by my shoulder.

"What?"

She pulled back and I shouted at the sight of her, at the blood seeping from her scalp and rolling down her face. Her gently tanned skin was red, and black, and gushing. I tried to recoil. I couldn't.

"He's dead" she cried, baring her white teeth. "Because of you!"

"Me?" I pulled my hand free and gawked at the blood that spread down my forearm and dripped onto my jeans. I tried to stand up, tried to push away, but my limbs were useless. She was an anchor on my lap and I had no way of getting her off. "What the fuck?"

A banging thundered in the distance, the sound of a heavy fist colliding with wood, and my world wavered, pulling me out of my chair, away from Yasmine the psycho, and into nothingness. My eyelids fluttered, and I felt my bed mattress beneath me. Recollection of where I was floated into my consciousness. I was in my room, alone.

A nightmare? Thank God for that.

When my heartrate settled, I let myself drift off again.

"Prez!" Casino shouted though my door and rapped his knuckles on the wood. "Prez, wake up! There's something you need to see."

I groaned and rolled onto my back. I blinked into the dark, my room lit only by the light that seeped under the door since I kept the skylight closed. My naked chest was clammy with sweat, my cock still hard and tenting my sweatpants.

Bang. Bang. Bang. "Prez?"

"All right," I shouted, running a hand over my face to pinch the bridge of my nose. With my other hand, I adjust the waistband of my pants, easing the pressure on my length. "Better be good."

I peered at the alarm clock on my bedside table. **2:00 A.M.** Nothing good happened around here at this time of the morning. A few scenarios ran through my head and none of them were pleasant.

I switched on my bedside lamp and squinted into the lit room. Yawning, I sat up and threw my legs over the edge of the bed, planting them on the carpet. I let my eyes fall shut as I bent to pick up my t-shirt from its crumpled heap on the floor. I pull it on, slip into my boots, and leave the room. In the hall, Casino waited for me, dressed in full colors, which meant he was about to ride out.

I frowned at him. "What's the problem?"

"I'll show you."

I followed him through the clubhouse. The place was quiet tonight. A few alcoholic members lingered in the main hall, whining and spending time with the clubwhores. They shouted their hellos to me, but I walked right on past. Casino didn't need to say anything as we stepped out the front door. I saw it on the horizon, the smoke and flames as they billowed high in the sky. It was coming from town and we were miles away, our clubhouse situated at the very end of Burning Road.

I peered at the men who waited just outside the doors of the clubhouse. Seven of them in total— Creed, Amani, Hawk, Ayr, Casino, Modo, and Cyrus. There had to be a reason they were standing here, waiting for me to give the orders.

"Am I missing something?" I asked, un-fucking-impressed. "You woke me up because there's a fire in town? Are we the goddamn fire brigade?"

Creed stepped forward. "Judge—"

"Is it one of our warehouses?"

He shook his head.

"One of our rackets?"

He shook his head again. Why was he here anyway? He spent most nights in his home, snuggled up to Blondie. Getting him out here after nine p.m. for a job was like pulling teeth. Unless they were fighting.

"No?" I glanced between them once more, making sure they knew how pissed they made me. I turned away. "I'm going back to bed. Anyone wakes me for something this stupid again, there'll be consequences."

"Could be Twisted Sons, Prez," Amani called after me, and I paused, turning my head.

"We chased the last ones out of the area," I said.

"They're like cockroaches, you know that. They always come back."

She had a point. I rubbed my tongue along the roof of my mouth, in thought. It was better to be safe than sorry. If another club was messing around on our territory, without our permission, then we needed to act on it before word got out that we weren't protecting what was ours.

Exhaling, I turned around. "Creed, Hawk, Amani. Go for a ride." I looked at the others. "You four stay here. No need to wake the neighborhood over something that might not concern us."

Creed, Hawk, and Amani marched toward the drive, where their bikes lined the curb. That was when I saw it, a small figure making its way down the drive.

"Who's on sentry?" I asked Armi, squinting to work out who the hell it was.

"Stoic."

A whistle sounded in the distance, Stoic's whistle, but he was slack on his timing. We should've known the second the intruder crossed the gate's threshold. I'd be on his ass about that later. I whistled back, acknowledging I heard him, and Armi strolled up beside me, lifting his sniper rifle. He cursed as he peered down the scope.

"It's a woman," he said. "It's—"

"Better not be," I grumbled, knowing exactly whose name was going to fall from his lips.

I held out my hand and Armi placed his rifle in my palm. I lifted the heavy gun to my face and peered down the scope. It was blurry, so I adjusted the sharpness, twisting until the picture was clear. Under the drive spotlights, I looked at the intruder's bare, slender feet. They were black and bloodied. I dragged my sights up a pair of dirty, ripped jeans. Her tank top fared no better. My pulse increased as Yasmine stumbled down the drive, her long, brunette hair no longer in a ponytail but frayed and frizzy around her filthy face. It was clear where she'd come from. The explanation for why she looked so beaten down billowed high on my left. I continued to watch through Armi's scope. Creed and Hawk approached her, and she collapsed to her hands and knees on the gravelly ground at their feet.

"What the fuck…" Casino swore as I handed my rifle back to Armi. "What's this bitch's deal?"

Creed and Hawk made no move to help Yasmine. They simply stood there, looking down at her as she barely held her weight on her shaking arms. Creed glanced over his shoulder at me and flicked his head. I started forward and stormed up the drive.

"Want me to drop her back in town?" Hawk asked and Creed cut his eyes at me.

He didn't think that was a good idea, but what was I supposed to do? This was a clubhouse, not a shelter or a hospital. I clenched my teeth together. If I helped her, I was involved. If I left her for dead, her ex-husband might even send chocolates. She said herself that none of us were good men, so why start now?

I peered down at Yasmine, who sobbed and lowered her head to rest on her forearm. Blood seeped from her skin and stained her scorched clothes. She reached out and touched my boot with her small hand, sending a pang of guilt through my chest. I crouched and caught her chin with my finger. She winced as I lifted her head and made her look at me. Her full lips were busted at the corner, her cheek swollen, her eye bruised. Anger spilled through my veins at the sight of her. What kind of animal would do this to a woman?

"I give up," she whispered, her breathing turned labored and painful. "Kill me. Just kill me."

That should be the end of it. I should have one of the men take her body and dump it somewhere else…but *fuck*.

"Wake Harlei," I ordered, not caring who was the one who did it. "Help her prep the surgery."

Amani and Hawk left, leaving Creed and I alone with Yasmine. I released her chin and her head fell like a stone.

"We'll help her with her injuries, not with her problem," I told him, glancing over at the smoke that continued to plume. "When she's better, she's on her own."

Creed frowned. "You think she's come from the explosion? That it's got something to do with her?"

I looked at the ash that clung to the fabric of her clothes and dirtied her skin. Creed shifted his weight and pinned me with an accusatory look. He was good at doing that.

"What aren't you telling me?"

"Nothing."

I stepped over Minnie and rolled her onto her back. Her eyelids fluttered as she sucked in a hard breath and I scooped her fragile body into my arms. I was careful not to bend and jostle her too much since I didn't know the extent of her injuries. As I carried her toward the clubhouse, and Creed spewed bullshit about me being secretive, I kept looking at her face. She was going through hell for her son…and I admired that. It was my first time seeing a mother's love in action. My ex didn't love our daughter the way Minnie loved her son.

I bounded up the stairs, Creed hot on my tail, and marched toward the front door where Casino stood.

"Jesus Christ," he said, leaning against the door frame. "I guess she's got some enemies."

"One," I told him. Fuck it. It was gonna come out sooner or later. "Elias Vergara."

Everyone behind me swore as Casino pushed off the frame and blocked the door.

"Elias Vergara? As in the—"

"Drug lord," Creed answered for me and I felt his glare burning holes in the side of my face.

"That's the one." I flicked my chin at Yasmine. "She's his wife."

Everyone lost their shit, like I expected, but I'd deal with it later. Yasmine needed to see Harlei and quick. I stepped forward, but Casino didn't budge. Was he challenging me? I narrowed my stare, a silent warning for him not to be stupid. I ran the fucking show and I had no qualms proving who was in charge of this chapter.

Casino bared his teeth at me. "And you want to bring her inside the clubhouse? Are you fucking insane?"

"Get out of my way."

Armi put his hand on my shoulder. "He has a

point, Prez."

I shrugged him off and turned to push Yasmine into Creed's arms. He took her without hesitation and he held her close, protecting her while I stepped up to Casino.

"I told you to get the fuck out of my way."

Casino squared his shoulders and flexed his jaw. He wanted to contest me. No doubt he wanted to punch me in the face since I was risking everyone's lives by bringing Yasmine in, but what was he gonna do about it? He was the fucking treasurer. He should be in a back room counting pennies, not sticking his nose in my business. Swallowing hard, he shook his head and stepped aside. I took Yasmine from Creed and carried her into the clubhouse.

"This is insane!" Casino shouted after Creed and me. "She's gonna get us all killed!"

In the surgery, Harlei was washing her hands and Hawk was wrapping the bed in a blue sheet. I placed Yasmine on the bed, turned around, and left the room. I surged back through the clubhouse and found Casino leaning against the wall, talking quickly to Modo and Ayr, who stood there with their hands stuffed into the pockets of their jeans. Casino saw me coming and pushed off the wall as I shoved Ayr out of the way. I grabbed him by the collar of his gray shirt and yanked him forward before slamming my fist into his jaw. He grunted and his jaw made a sick crack when I connected.

"After everything I've done for you?" I snapped, hitting him twice. Creed and Ayr wrapped their arms around mine and dragged me back. "Show me some respect."

I hit him hard, not enough to knock any teeth out, but enough to remind him who the fuck I was and the horror this chapter faced when we saved his ass from the Ventillis and brought him into the club.

He spat blood on the hardwood floor and clenched his jaw. "I'm sorry."

"What?" I shrugged Creed and Ayr off and stepped forward, making Casino flinch. "I didn't hear you."

"I said I was sorry." He swiped his mouth and cut his eyes at me. "All right?"

I stared at him, and he stared right back. "You're gonna help Rah find out everything you can about Yasmine Garcia, Elias Vergara, and the boy they share."

He opened his mouth to protest.

"And then you're going to help Harlei tend to Yasmine until she's feeling better. Got it?"

Casino pursed his lips, then blew out a defeated exhale. "Yes, Prez. I got it."

"Good."

I held out my hand. Casino took it and I helped him to his feet.

"What's the boy's name?" he asked, touching his

lip then looking at the blood on his fingers.

"Nathan, or Nathaniel, or some shit." I waved him off as I turned away. "Start with Elias and you'll find the kid."

***

A couple hours later, as the sun was sliding over the horizon, Casino and Sora approached me while I was setting my bike up for my monthly ride to the cabin.

"Well?" I asked, slipping two handguns into my saddlebag, not sparing them a glance. It took them longer than I expected. "What'd you find out?"

"She's crazy, Judge," Rah started, scratching his head. "She's been in and out of various mental hospitals, in and out of prison, has multiple restraining orders against her—"

I shrugged, trying to get the clasp on my bag closed. "Who doesn't?"

"There's no record of a kid," Casino chimed in and that got my damn attention. I lifted my head and pinned him with my stare. "No record she was even married to Elias Vergara."

My gut sank and I straightened. "What'd you say?"

He smirked at me, like he knew that piece of information made him right and me wrong.

"There's no record of her being pregnant, no

record of her giving birth. She's full of shit."

Something inside me snapped. Whatever it was, I'd only felt it a handful of times before. It was like rage, but stronger. I tore away from my bike and shoved past Rah and Casino. I surged into the clubhouse, right past Modo, who slept on the stairs with his sunglasses on, and right past Creed, who was cleaning rifles on the tables inside. He called my name, but I ignored him. There was only one person I wanted to speak to. I was sick of this woman. From the moment I met her, she drove me up the wall with her demands and wasted my time. Enough was enough. I wanted her out of my life for good.

I kicked in the door of the surgery and Harlei jumped out of her skin, dropping a bag of sterile gauze on the floor.

"Christ, Judge. You scared me."

She went back to doing whatever she was doing as I stalked toward the bed Yasmine laid on. She blinked up at me, shrinking at my aggressive approach. Her hair was washed, her skin clear of any ash and dirt. Only her cuts and bruises remained. I stood beside her, seeing red the longer I looked at her. She looked awful, she looked like she was in pain, and it tugged at my heartstrings, but I knew better. This was her game. She was crazy, a con-artist, and I'd fallen for her act.

"I've advised her not to speak," Harlei informed.

"Burned lungs from smoke and all that. It's not comfortable for her. It should get better as the hours go on—"

"Is Elias Vergara really your ex-husband? Do you even have a kid?" I demanded and she winced. "You better speak through the pain or I'm throwing you out on your ass."

Her eyelids flickered and a tear dripped from her eye. She tried to speak, all I got out of her was a rasp, a painful sounding rasp.

"I had you checked out, Yasmine, and all my sources tell me you're a crazy bitch." I leaned in close, so close our noses almost touched. "Give me one good reason to believe you are who you say you are…or God help you."

Disappointment flared in her pretty, watery irises and she winced before she rolled onto her side and turned her back on me.

SEVEN

YASMINE

The Bahamas 2011

I breathe the salty ocean air as deep into my lungs as I can. Under my bare feet, the smooth, wooden deck of Elias Vergara's superyacht feels like victory. I lift my crystal flute of expensive champagne and smile into the golden liquid. I deserve this. I worked myself to death to get here, to be on this boat. Warm sea breeze blows my long, brunette locks over my shoulder and into my face, and I revel in it. All those years spent in my office, or in my car. I'm finally out doing what I've wanted to do since I started. I'm finally doing the work that counts.

"Look at her." The smoothest voice I've ever heard floats into my ears and kicks every nerve ending in my body, sending tingles spiraling over

my skin. I turn my head in time to see him approach. "The most beautiful view I've ever seen from the top deck."

I flick my gaze down the length of the notorious Elias Vergara. He's everything his bio said he would be. Going off the grainy black and white photo alone I knew his beauty would be dangerous, but in person, it was lethal. I move my attention to his toned, sculpted stomach, then back to his black diamond eyes. Warmth spreads up my neck and swells in my cheeks. I clear my throat and peer out at the ocean. He's right. I can't imagine a view as perfect as this. I was born and raised in Exeter, California. I've never seen an ocean as blue, or a boat as big.

"It is beautiful," I say.

"I wasn't talking about the ocean."

Oh. I look at Elias as he takes my hand.

"What's your name?"

"Camilla," I lie, fixated on his sparkling, onyx irises. "Camilla Degas."

He lifts my hand to his lips and kisses my knuckles. "Do you speak Spanish?"

I shake my head, more lies. "I'm afraid I don't."

"Es una pena..."

I'm ashamed to admit that Elias and I slept together the same evening we met. I didn't mean for it to happen, but Elias knew what he wanted. He wasn't an easy man to turn down. He wielded his power, money, and sex appeal like a sword, and I fell for it. I was mentally ready to weather Hurricane Elias, but I wasn't emotionally or physically ready. Despite being way in over my head, I was determined to do what I floated into his life to do...

...and that was to fuck it up.

It wasn't until I was standing at an altar with Elias opposite me that I realized I was in too deep. All along I thought he was playing into my hands, but I was playing into his. By then, my superiors couldn't pull me out. By then, I was three months pregnant with our son and no longer a queen in the game, but a pawn. Unknowingly, I became tangled in the web of lies I created, and I was suffocating. All along he knew it, he knew what I wanted, what I was after, and he strung me along.

And I let him...

...because somewhere, somehow, I fell in love with him and I remained in love with him until our son was born. Being who he is, Elias refused important pre-natal scanning and testing. It bruised his ego to be told there's a chance there might be something wrong with his precious heir.

Our son, Nicolás, was born seven weeks early and was labelled as Down's Syndrome at birth. The label didn't matter to me, so I didn't pay much attention. When the midwife handed Nicolás to me,

I'd never seen a baby so perfect. Elias, however, made it vocally clear he'd never seen a baby so...*not*. He used the most magical moment of my life to expose me, to shatter my world and rip me to shreds. From that moment, we became his prisoners. We weren't allowed to leave his villa and, as far as anyone knew, Nicolás died during childbirth.

***

I blink up at the ceiling of the clubhouse medical room, ignoring Harlei as she loads a sterilizer. I still remember Nicolás's shrill screams as Elias tore him from my breast and violently shook him. Sickness spreads through me, thick like oil. All I've suffered through...for him to wipe it all away. Our history. Our life together. Our son. Judge wants me to prove I am who I say I am, but how can I? Elias left nothing behind for me to use and the Devil's Cartel MC has been reduced to no more than names I can add to the long list of people who think I'm crazy. I draw my knees as close as I can to my chest without hurting my back or opening any of Harlei's dressings. At least I still have my life. Elias came close to taking that away too. If it weren't for the taxi driver who pulled up right after the motel exploded, I'd be dead. He wanted to take me to the hospital, but I convinced him to take me to the clubhouse. He dropped me off a couple yards before the clubhouse drive and I stumbled the rest of the way, fighting unconsciousness with every step. If I'm lucky, Elias will believe I died in the explosion and I'll have time to heal and figure out my next move. Judge has given me seventy-two hours to be gone, so my plan is to get as much healing done as possible, then make my way to Venton Vale. I hear there's an all-female MC club there. On the plus side of having my life wiped clean, I'm safe from Judge learning my biggest secret of all—a secret I fear even thinking about under his roof.

"You've rattled him, you know," Harlei says, pulling me from my depressing thoughts.

"Who?" I rasp, my throat burning.

"Judge."

Oh. She writes on a clipboard, then closes it and sits it on top of the stainless-steel counter.

"He hates me."

"You're here, alive, and getting medical treatment at his expense." She turns her slender body to snatch a pair of gloves out of their tightly packed white and red box. They snap against her fingers. "Trust me, he doesn't hate you."

I watch in silence as she moves around the room, confident, and in her element. I wish she wouldn't do that—make me believe that, maybe, Judge will help me. I've pushed and I've pushed for his help, but he's made himself clear. There's no help here, only chaos.

"All the girls were talking about you two—"

I shift my hips to turn away and wince as pain sears over every inch of my flesh. It takes me a while, but I eventually turn my back on Harlei, the clubhouse doctor. I don't want to hear what she has to say. I just need to heal and leave. I close my eyes and the raspy, panicked scream of a newborn baby—*my* newborn baby—is all I hear. I shake my head against the pillow and try to turn my thoughts in another direction, but the morphine keeps dragging me right back into my deep pit of despair.

"Elias!" I shriek, my arms outstretched as Jorge holds me away from the monster shaking my baby. "Elias! Stop it! Please! Stop it!"

I can't see. My eyes are flooding, my nose running. I feel blood, lots of it, pouring down my legs from the recent birth. I slip in it multiple times, but I manage to keep my hold on Jorge's expensive Armani suit.

I grimace and open my eyes. Maybe, if I don't close them, my mind can't take me back to the past. I stare at a blank, white wall. Seconds tick by and the torturous noise in my head goes unaccompanied by the images…until my mind projects them onto the white surface and I'm watching that day play out in front of my eyes.

Elias stills and Nicolás goes quiet in his tight grip. He makes cute gurgling noises, blinks his tired eyes, and curls his skinny fingers into the smallest, sweetest fists I've ever seen. Elias flicks his head at Jorge and Jorge steps away, leaving me unbalanced in my own mess. I shudder, my breath loudly trembling along with it. I hold out my arms, silently begging for Elias to put my son in them.

"Let me hold him," I whisper, unable to take my eyes off Nicolás, my lips wet with the water leaking from my nose. "Please let me have my baby."

Elias screws up his face in disgust and peers at Nicolás. He turns our baby in his hands, appraising him as if he were a new iPhone, then he turns toward me, grimacing when he sees the blood and gore I stand in.

"Take your thing." He shoves Nicolás into my arms and I gratefully take him and hold him close. Elias looks to Jorge. "Get the midwife. One who can speak English."

While Jorge fetches the midwife, I climb back onto my big bed and put Nicolás on my breast. He attaches like a good baby and I don't care that it hurts, that it feels like my nipples are being pulled in half. I just want him close. Where he's safe. Elias watches from the left side of the room, indifferent, but I don't care. We don't need him.

We don't.

I'll give Nicolás a good life away from Elias,

where'll he be surrounded by only people who love him for who he is. As Nicolás falls asleep, Jorge returns with the midwife. She gasps at the sight of the blood on the floor and my footprints in it and rushes to my bed. She says something in Greek I can't decipher. I look to Elias as he pulls a set of keys from the pocket of his pressed, black slacks.

"English?" he asks her.

She nods. "Yes."

"It's unfortunate," Elias begins, pinning her with his soulless glare. "that my son died during a traumatic childbirth and could not be resuscitated."

The midwife's eyes go wide. Mine do too. He...he wants her to forge papers to say Nicolás died? My heart bleeds.

"Elias—"

He points a slender, tanned finger at me. "You shut your mouth, or I'll have this pretty little midwife write that you suffered the same fate."

The midwife, who wasn't the one in the room when Nicolás was born, starts to shake her head. She looks at me.

"Don't look over there," Elias demands. "I don't know what that thing is, but it is not my son."

My heart splinters and every memory I hold of Elias singing to, and caressing, my swollen belly shatters. I glance down at Nicolás and can't help the tears that drop all over his perfect, pink skin and wet the remains of his birth still left on his fragile, little body.

Elias does his usual thing to the midwife. He threatens her, her family, and her children. He threatens to blow up the entire maternity ward if she doesn't forge the paperwork to say our son died. She brings up the hospital board and, of course, Elias is already making the calls to pay them off. Within twenty-two minutes, as far as the world is concerned, Nicolás is dead.

And what do I do? Well, I purse my lips into bloodless lines and I don't say anything. I don't say anything as I verbally confirm the death of my son, nor as I sign off on it with an official pen on official papers.

My tears soak into the pillow I rest my beaten head on. I didn't fight for Nicolás then, but this time I won't go quietly. This time I will fight for his life, even if it gets me killed.

I owe it to him.

I owe him everything.

EIGHT

J U D G E

In the darkened room, Liv moved against me. I kept my hands on the armrests of my deep, velvet chair, and tried hard to focus on the task at hand, but I couldn't. I saw Liv, semi-naked, her firm, fit body draped in black leather and lace, but I didn't *see* her. She was there, a gentle flurry of sensual movement, I just couldn't keep my attention on her. Music played, one of my favorite tracks by Santana, the lighting was just right, and there was no one else in the room...still, I found my mind drifting to Yasmine Garcia—if that was her real fucking name. I dreamed of her frequently. Sometimes, they were awful dreams. I had my hands around her throat, and I squeezed the life out of her for betraying me. And sometimes, the dreams were sexy and sensual—romantic even. I didn't know what to make of it, but what I did know was that I was abetting a goddamn liar—a con-woman—and as president, I knew better. When I confronted her, she gave me no explanation, but I'd get it out of her as soon as she could speak without pain.

Liv's weight on my lap dragged me from my thoughts and I peered into her volcanic glass eyes. She used to be a brunette. Once Blondie started hanging around more often, she dyed her hair platinum blonde. It didn't suit her, but it was a fun change since I'd never have Blondie again. It bored me now. *She* bored me.

"Where's your head tonight?" Liv asked me, rolling her torso against mine, pushing our hips together.

Her pleasant, minty breath blew across my face and her warmth grew in my lap. Any other night, I'd be well aroused and ready to go. Tonight, burying myself deep inside Liv was yet to cross my mind. If I was being honest, I didn't want it.

"All over the place," I said to her. "I don't know what to do."

"About the random Latina woman?" She dipped her head to my neck and kissed me. "You get rid of her."

Get rid of her. If only it was that easy. Liv slid her hands underneath my shirt and rubbed my torso up and down, massaging me, coaxing me into accepting what she was trying to give. I closed my eyes and thought about her small, slender hands and how she touched me with them. Liv was eager—desperate, almost. Tonight was the first night in weeks I was giving her any attention—if you could call this that.

"Did she sleep in your bed?"

I opened my eyes. There it was—the motive behind her telling me to get rid of Yasmine. She was jealous, but that wasn't news to me. Liv was always jealous. She was jealous of Blondie and that I was her benefactor in the event of Creed's death. She was jealous when I spent too much time with the men, and jealous when I spoke to other women. Liv was jealous of every part of my life that didn't involve her, and I hated that Minnie was on her radar. Liv could be cruel and cunning. She knew better than to fuck with Blondie since she was Creed's property, but Yasmine was fair game.

"Did she?" she pressed.

To be honest, the night I put Yasmine in my bed, I forgot I put her there. It was the first time I shared a bed in years, and I had a shit sleep. Yasmine didn't, though. She slept soundly, softly snoring, until the sun was up.

"Yes."

Liv tensed. My answer bothered her. She'd barely been in my room and had never spent the night. In a way, she was exclusive to me and she felt it gave her leverage over the other women. It also boosted her ego, made her feel like I owed her

103

something. She wasn't better than any other woman we employed. I didn't prefer her over anyone, I just wasn't in the habit of sharing with every patch member in the club.

Sighing, Liv moved her cheek against mine and searched in the dark for my lips. She got close, but I turned my head, not giving her what she wanted. Tonight, her lips weren't warranted north of my belt.

Her body tightened against mine and she pulled back, no longer moving to the music. "You don't kiss me anymore?"

"Not in the mood."

In my defense, I barely kissed her. I could count on one hand the amount of times I'd willingly pressed my lips to hers in the last four years. I was certain the only times I did kiss her, I was drunk off my ass. If I was being honest with myself, kissing Liv drained me. It didn't fill me with adrenaline or excitement. It was a fucking chore, something I did to keep her from bitching at me.

"I guess I'll have to get you in the mood, huh?" Liv sat back and peeled off her little black bralette. Her fake breasts sat high and proud and I looked at them. My dick barely twitched. Liv took my hands in hers and placed them on her breasts. I palmed them, squeezed them in my hands until Liv was moving against me once more, acting like my touch was better than crack, as if it breathed life into her.

"You don't love me anymore?"

I stilled and frowned. Liv and I weren't friends. I never thought about her. Never wondered where she was or who she was with. I didn't even care if she didn't show up to club parties.

The problem with Liv was, although I'd been careful when setting the boundaries of our casual-sex relationship, she allowed herself to fall in love with me. I knew it years ago, but she never said the "L" word aloud until now. Over the years I was careful never to confuse her, never to make her feel that I felt the same way. I didn't. There was no chance she'd ever be my old lady.

"I never loved you," I told her, and in the distance, there was a knock on the door. "Not even a little bit."

Hurt cracked her pretty, mature features and she pulled away from me, crossing her arms over her chest, hiding her breasts from view.

"Never?"

I looked her dead in the eyes so there was no confusion. "Never."

"Well…" She scratched her cheek as the door to the room opened, letting in a sliver of light. "That fucking hurts, Judge."

With exceptional timing, Casino approached from the left and cleared his throat. "Prez?"

I flicked my chin at Liv, and she slid off my lap. With her head hung low, and her tail between her legs, she sauntered off. I exhaled in relief. Thank God I didn't have to talk my way out of that.

"I found her kid."

My heart stopped and I stared at the small, white paper he held in his hand. *She wasn't lying?*

"Turn the lights up," I demanded, correcting my posture in my armchair.

Casino did as he was told, and I squinted as the bright lights lit up the seedy room.

"I couldn't find anything on Yasmine, as you know, but I did find something on a Camilla Degas."

I frowned. "Am I supposed to know who that is?"

"No, of course not. It took Rah ages, but he found out Yasmine went under a different name while married to Elias."

"Why?"

He shrugged. "Fuck knows. Camilla's records say her son, Nicolás Vergara, died at birth," he said, crossing the room toward me. "I'd bet my life savings Elias faked the papers. Her son goes by Nicolás Garcia officially."

I flicked my head toward the paper he held in his hand. "That a photo?"

Casino nodded, then scratched at his forehead. "Did she mention anything about Nicolás? Any medical conditions or—"

"No. Why?"

"The kid is, well, he's…" He frowned. "He's *different*."

I held out my hand and he gave me the photograph. I stared at the white back of it for a beat, then flipped it over. My lips parted at the sight of her son. Casino spoke, but it went in one ear and out the other. I flickered my stare over Nicolás's tuft of dark hair, his upward slanting eyelids and the shiniest irises I'd ever seen. I couldn't help the adoring curl in my lips as I surveyed his short, flat, and wide nose, and his cheeky tongue poking out of his irregularly shaped mouth. He wasn't what I was expecting at all. *He was Down Syndrome.*

"I want to know why she had another name. See what you can find out," I said to Casino and he left me alone with the photograph.

As I sat there looking at the photo, it all fell into place. Minnie was his protector, his *only* protector, like I was for Nila. The things she said about Elias…he couldn't stomach Nicolás because he wasn't what he was expecting. No doubt he wanted a strong heir, someone he could pass the family business off to. I guess he felt he felt he couldn't do that with Nicolás.

Nausea inducing guilt wormed its way through my chest, spreading its anxious roots through my limbs. I lifted myself out of the chair and left the room. It was quiet in the main bar. A member I didn't know the name of was sleeping against the far wall, his dirty boots propped on a chair. I made a mental note to have Kace hose him off if he was still here when the sun came up.

I moved over to the bar and placed the photograph face down on the oak surface, then I grabbed a glass, put some ice in it, and poured myself a drink. Minnie was telling the truth.

And I treated her like shit.

I took a swig and gritted my teeth.

"I thought you were too important to pour your own drinks?"

I smirked and turned my head to watch Iris as she approached from the right. She stuffed her small hands into the front pocket of her over-sized Devil's Cartel hoodie. It looked like she stole it. It didn't suit her. Her features were gentle, and she was so young and pure, but I knew better than to file her in the *"little girl"* drawer. She could outshoot all the men here and she could kick the fuck out of a heavy bag. I'd seen it with my own eyes. I felt sorry for those who had to go up against her when her initiation came around. *If* her initiation came around. It was likely her dad would come for us once he found her here. Yakuza—just to add to the list of dangerous men that were gonna descend on the clubhouse in the future.

Iris slipped onto a stool across from me and flicked her chin toward my bottle of whiskey. Her straight, black hair swung around her shoulders and she drummed her finger against the bar. I pondered it. At the tender age of twenty, she was too young for alcohol, but fuck it. I could use her company. I grabbed ice from the ice drawer and put it in a new glass. Then I poured a little whiskey into it and slid it across the bar to her. She caught it in her hand and lifted it to her lips. She sipped it and hissed as she swallowed, making me laugh. Iris had a long way to go before she was a certified biker bitch.

Iris lifted the picture of Nicolás and flipped it over. Her dark eyes lit up the second she saw his smiley face. "Cute kid. Is it hers?"

I nodded.

She lowered the photo and tilted her head. "Why don't you help her, Judge?"

I downed another mouthful of whiskey and swallow hard. "Because it's none of my business."

"I was none of your business." She glanced around. "I'm pretty sure most of us are here because you made us your business. Because you helped us."

I leaned on the bar. Iris didn't know what she was talking about. I turned my back on more people than I helped. If it was too much of a risk, *bye*. I could count on two hands the members I went out of my way for.

"Yasmine's ex-husband is a dangerous man," I told her.

"My father is worse, and you took the risk for

me." Iris pushed Nicolás's little black and white photograph closer to me. "If you didn't think you could beat Elias Vergara, you wouldn't have let her step foot in the clubhouse."

I stared at the photo. Poor kid was probably scared shitless without his mom...but this was a conversation I needed to have with my main men, not a twenty-year-old prospect. If Creed knew I was consulting with Iris instead of him, I'd never hear the end of it.

"It's past curfew for you," I said, taking her glass. "Go to bed."

Smiling, she slipped from the stool and sauntered back toward the hall where her quarters were.

"Iris," I called after her and she stopped and glanced over her shoulder. "Put the rifle back in the armory before Armi notices it's missing. You know it drives him up the wall when they're not where they're supposed to be."

Her lips quirked. "Yes, Prez."

Iris disappeared down the hall and I was left alone with the photo again. It called out to me, to my soul. There was a sparkle in Nicolás's eyes that begged for help. If the roles were reversed and it was my daughter...what would I do? I knew the answer.

"Fuck," I swore, lifting my glass to my mouth.

I had to help Yasmine get her son back.

NINE

YASMINE

Harlei was in the room applying new dressings to my burns when Judge entered the infirmary two days later. I don't look directly at him, but I listen to his heavy boots as he walks, and I see his large, intimidating body as he moves closer to where I'm sitting. I fear what he wants to say and what he's going to do. Perhaps today's the day he tosses me out—or worse, he's found out my darkest secrets. I turn my head and his eyes crinkle at the corners when our gazes meet, as if fighting a wince. I must look awful, but he doesn't. He looks amazing, as always. Smooth, tan skin with a stubbly jaw of dark hair. I notice he's not wearing his cut, or his chains, so whatever he wants can't be club business. Harlei gave me some tips on club life while I've been laying here and if a brother isn't wearing his cut, then it isn't official club business.

111

Judge stops a few feet in front of me. "You didn't tell me your son was D—"

"Judge." I cut him off, not wanting to hear those words fall from his lips. "Don't."

How deep did he have to dig to find out about Nicolás? Not too deep, I assume since he hasn't shot me dead.

"Why didn't you say anything?"

I swallow hard. He's referring to Nicolás's condition and it bothers me that putting a label on my son had the power to change Judge's mind.

"What difference does it make?" I snap. "Girl, boy, black, white, Down syndrome, or not. A child is a child and you still refused to help me."

Judge turns his dark, ocean blue eyes on Harlei and she nods. With her slender, subtly tattooed fingers, she finishes dressing the burn on my forearm and leaves the room. With her gone, the tense barrier between Judge and I dissolves. There's no hiding, no holding back, now there's no one else in the room. It's me and him.

"If you're here to tell me you've changed your mind because you found out Nicolás is Down syndrome, save your breath." I lick my lower lip, hating my voice for getting so thick and raspy. I clear my throat. "I'd rather face my ex-husband alone than bring a bunch of people who only want to help because they pity my son."

"Pity," Judge utters, slipping his hands into the

pockets of his dark jeans. "I don't pity Nicolás."

My heart stutters at his name said aloud. I feel like I haven't heard it in so long in a voice other than my own. Elias didn't call him by his first name. He opted for horrible nicknames and insults instead. I love the name Nicolás. It's been at the top of my baby name list since I was nineteen.

"And I did change my mind," he continues, pulling something out of his pocket—a small, rectangular piece of paper. He looks at it, focusing on whatever is on the other side. "Because I saw him…and I saw my daughter in his face. It reminded me that, although my girl is gone, I'm still a parent. I'm still a dad."

My lungs tremble with every breath and my sore throat vibrates. I squeeze my teeth together and take deeper breaths through my nose as I stare at him. Judge steps closer and I straighten my spine, cautious. My vision blurs.

"Casino printed this photo off." He taps a thick finger against the corner, damaging it ever so slightly, and I hold my breath. "I thought you'd want to have it."

I move for it, but Judge keeps it just out of my reach.

"I'm going to get him back, Minnie. I promise," he says, and I can't bring myself to look at him in fear of seeing lies in his eyes or waking up from this dream. "But we go when I say we go."

I'm ready to go now, injuries be damned. I sniffle. "H-how long?"

"It'll be weeks before—"

I flick my wide stare to his face. "Weeks? Damon—"

"I have to locate him first, figure out how many men he's got, and work out how to get Nicolás out alive. I'll be risking the whole chapter, Minnie. The whole club, even. I don't take that shit lightly." He takes a step, closing the distance between us. "You have to trust me."

A lot can happen in a few weeks. Elias thinks I'm dead. What's stopping him from hurting Nicolás? Or taking him to the other side of the world? The only comfort I have is in the belief he hasn't already hurt Nicolás.

He holds out the photo. "Do you trust me?"

Do I trust him? I look at his hand, then his face. The deep, woodsy smell of his cologne wafts over me, an anesthetic to my wounds. Damon Judge is a bad man and the list of his infractions is undoubtedly long…but I trust him. I nod my head.

Judge extends the photo of Nicolás, white side up. It's been so long since I've seen his face. I lost what little I had in the motel blast—my phone included. I'm not sure I want to see him, or that I'm ready to see him. I've held myself up as best I can, careful not to self-destruct under the pressure. I reach out, ignoring the shake in my hand, and take

114

the piece of paper from Judge's grasp. It's not paper at all. It's smooth and thick, like a photograph. I let out the breath I was holding and turn the picture over. My heart stutters painfully and sinks into the pit of my stomach. Sorrow and grief squeeze through my bones and constricts my chest. Even so, I can't help the smile that pulls at my lips. He's a good-looking kid, my Nicolás. He has dark, chocolate cotton candy-like hair that sits in a wind-whipped tuft on the top of his head. His big, brown eyes glisten like diamonds in the sun. His bright orbs are nestled under the longest lashes I've ever seen and above the cutest button nose. I look at his smile and the sliver of tongue that pokes between his lips. Nicolás has a lopsided smile that could melt even the coldest hearts.

Well, almost.

A choked sob cramps my throat and I clamp my hand over my mouth. Crying for Nicolás feels like something I should do alone, but...I'm tired of being alone, of doing things alone. Since I escaped Elias, Nicolás had been my only companion—and he's enough, he's more than enough—but I couldn't hold adult conversations with him. I couldn't vent, or cry, or shout. In his presence, I had to put on a brave, happy front, even though I was falling part inside.

Out of gratitude and desperation, I reach out for Judge and pull him in close. His thick, muscular body tightens as I wrap my arms around his neck and hold him tight. His thighs hit the bed between my legs, and I bury my face into the nape of his neck and cry. It flows through me like a tsunami. I expect him to pull away, to tell me to suck it up. What I don't expect is for him to put his arms around me and hold me back. I can't remember the last time someone held me and just let me cry. The gestures bring the tears on harder and I soak Judge's skin and his shirt, but it doesn't last. The warmth from his body seeps into my pores and soothes the cracks in my heart—albeit temporarily. Sniffling, I force myself to release the Devil's Cartel president and keep my attention on the picture of Nicolás.

"Sorry," I murmur, pushing a rogue teardrop off Nicolás's forehead before it soaks into the card. "I wasn't expecting…" I swallow the forming lump in my throat, letting the sentence go as I lift my gaze. Warmth spreads up my neck at the sight of him watching me, his expression hard and concerned. "Thank you."

He doesn't say anything. Why would he? Judge turns and walks out of the room, leaving me alone with the most precious gift anyone has ever given me.

Hope.

J U D G E

I didn't know what the hell to do when she grabbed me. My brain told me to pat her on the back and put as much distance between me and her emotions as possible, but the urge to comfort her wound through me. I wasn't easily moved by shows of emotion, but there was something about Minnie that reminded me of my old self, back when Nila was alive.

Not to mention, the woman survived one hell of a beating and an explosion that decimated an entire motel. If anyone deserved a hug, it was her.

"Are you listening, Prez?" Hawk snapped and Creed straightened in his chair, glaring across the table at our road captain. If I gave him the nod, Creed would jump the table and cut Hawk's heart out of his chest for talking to me the way he was. Good thing I wasn't a fucking tyrant. "I said, we can't fuck with Elias Vergara."

I rubbed my chin. He didn't get what I was saying. "You won't. I will."

They all looked in my direction, but it was Creed's stare I felt burning holes in my face. He'd follow me to the end of the world, if I went, so I knew he'd take a lot of convincing to stay behind. If he refused to listen, I had a Plan B and her name was Blondie. I was sure she could put on the waterworks and beg him to stay. Maybe jiggle her tits for him, for good measure.

"As in...by yourself?" Armi asked, scratching his head.

"That's what I said."

"Sorry, Prez," he exhaled, sitting back in his chair. "Can't let you do that."

"I wasn't asking for permission." I adjusted my position in my seat at the head of the table, drawing my shoulders back, lifting myself a little higher. "I'd ride 66—no colors. In and out."

"Do you know where he is?" Creed asked, leaning forward on his elbows, his cut creaking. "How many men he has with him? Whether the boy is even alive?"

"I know he's close." And that was about all I had.

The table erupted into conversation, one side arguing about coming with me, the other side shouting shit about suicide. We had to make this decision as a unit, I knew that, but whether they approved or not, I was going, and I was going alone. I dragged my stare to Modo, who was uncharacteristically quiet, those damn Ray-Bans covering his eyes.

"Modo?" I boomed over the discussion, and the men fell quiet.

Nothing. *He's sleeping? Again?*

Stoic nudged him with his elbow hard in the ribs and he jolted, grunting like a pig.

"I agree," he shouted, pulling his sunglasses from his face. "We do need more clubwhores and would it kill you to get mature-aged women? The little teenyboppers you've got running around here just ain't doing it for me."

Someone snickered. I stared at him. We all stared at him. First of all, the clubwhores were all twenty-one and over. There weren't any *"teenyboppers"* running around our clubhouse. Second of all, he looked like shit. His skin was oddly pale, and his eyes held the biggest bags I'd ever seen.

"What's going on, Modo?" Creed asked, reading my mind. "You look…"

"Like the underside of a nutsack?" Ayr joked, grinning wide.

"Oh, piss off." Modo lowered his sunglasses to the long, oak table. "Haven't had much sleep."

"Why?"

"There's…" He pursed his lips together, and glanced around the table at each of us, discomfited. "There's a spider in my room."

I rolled my eyes as multiple snickers made their way around the table and Modo shifted in his seat, huffing. Modo, the crazy British bastard, was over six-foot-tall and he was wide with thick muscle. A spider? He fed his parents to a fucking illegally acquired Komodo Dragon, for God's sake. To many, he was a walking nightmare, a psychopath

119

without a cause. In a way, he was our secret weapon. Every man at this table feared him in some way—except Creed—and he was scared of a spider? I shouldn't be surprised. He felt the same way about snakes, even though his room was filled with all kinds of scaly creatures.

I scratched the bridge of my nose. "So, kill it?"

He balked and fisted his beard, shivering in his cut. "Yeah, fuckin' right."

"Don't you have lizards and shit in there?" Armi said. "Make one of them eat it."

"Spiders aren't a part of their diet," he stated. "And also, that's fucking gross."

Laughter erupted around the table and I groaned. I didn't have time for this. A spider was the least of my worries. "Armi, when we're done here, take care of the goddamn spider in his room so he can get some sleep, will you?"

He nodded and conversation erupted once more. I grabbed the gavel in front of me and slammed it against the sound block with a bang. The room fell quiet, the men around the table focusing their attention on me.

"Back to the main topic of this discussion. Elias Vergara."

"I meant what I said. You're not going alone." Armi drummed his finger against the table. "You need me, and you know it."

"You need all of us," Casino chimed in, taking

me by surprise, given our disagreement when I tried to bring Yasmine into the clubhouse. "You've been there for us when we needed it, so if helping that broad is something you want to do then…we've got your back."

I nodded at him, a silent thank you. "Then it's settled. Our chapter will go up against Elias Vergara."

"The mother chapter won't like it," Creed pointed out. "There'll be repercussions if this goes wrong, since none of us have laid claim to Minnie."

I pressed my teeth together and dragged an inhale through my nose. If this goes ass up, the mother chapter will see it as a terrorist attack and end it all. "Then it can't go wrong."

I demanded Rah find out everything he could about Elias's location and to liaise with our road captain, Hawk, to find us the quickest way in and out. Then, he needed to speak with Armi about soldier numbers, and Armi would set us up with the best plan of attack. We had to follow Hawk and Armi's lead, no ifs, ands, or buts about it. I slam the gavel into the sound block one last time, ending the meeting. The men file out of the room and spill through the clubhouse, but Creed doesn't budge. When we are alone, he exhales and turns his whiskey stare on me.

"Why are you doing this, Damon?"

I pushed my chair back and lifted myself out of

it. "You'd do it for Izzy."

"Yasmine isn't Izzy," he pointed out, almost offended. "A few days ago, you didn't care about this woman and now you're ready to risk it all for her?"

Maybe I did care. Maybe I cared more than I wanted to admit. I grabbed my gavel and turned away from the table. "Atonement."

"Atonement?" Creed paused in thought. When I placed my gavel back on the bookshelf next to the thick binder of our bylaws, I turned around and realization lit his features. "You have nothing to atone for. Nila wasn't your fault."

The mention of her name made my heart stutter, then guilt sank in. When was the last time I went to the cabin? When was the last time I walked our favorite track down to the river?

"It's not about Nila." I swiped at my forehead. "Minnie's trying to get her son back and I wasted her time."

He shrugged his broad shoulders. "Such is life. You don't owe her anything."

"I don't owe her? I treated her like shit, James." A strange expression rippled across his face. I rarely used his first name because he didn't like it. Only Blondie could use his first name without incurring his anger. "I treated her like a nuisance, like a druggie, like a whore, like a servant. I let her go back to that shitty motel where she got beaten within an inch of her life, then nearly blown to shit. I wasted her time and called her a crazy, lying bitch when she told me nothing but the truth."

Yeah, I was an asshole, but I wasn't totally fucking heartless. Creed looked away. If he didn't get it, he didn't get it. He wasn't there when I told Minnie I'd help. He didn't see the way her eyes sparkled with hope, or the way her skin brightened, my words literally breathing life into her. He didn't see the look of total heartbreak when she saw the photo of Nicolás, either. Nor did he feel what I felt when she held me tight. It was…well, I didn't know what it was.

Yasmine Garcia was the most emotional woman I'd ever met. And I liked it. Every tear she shed chipped ice off my heart and pulled me further out of the emotionless tar pit my ex kicked me into. My heart didn't thump right, not since Nila's murder, but it changed its beat the more Minnie cried into my shoulder, her sweet tears seeping into my pores and changing my DNA.

Creed cleared his throat. "I said I would ride with you and that wasn't a lie. I just want to make sure you're doing it for the right reasons."

"What are the right reasons?" I asked, just as Blondie strolled into the room.

I flicked my stare over her small black boots and up her tight black jeans that clung to her thighs. I tilted my head as I surveyed her black lace bodysuit, and her little leather cut draped over her shoulders. She looked like a bad bitch, but her sweet face betrayed her secret. She was still Exeter's sweetheart and that'd never change. In her manicured hand, she held a clear, flat-lid cup with green juice. Yep. She'd always be the privileged princess she was when we took her from her father. I didn't mind it. Call her a spanner in the works, a colorful swirl of pink perfume in a sea of black stench.

Izzy beamed at me, exposing her bright white teeth. "Hey Judge."

"Blondie." I flicked my hand, a small wave. "What's with the get-up?"

She shrugged her slender shoulders, her attention on Creed and only Creed. "Thought I'd try something different."

I kept my eyes on her, watching her stroll toward the table, toward her lover boy. I rolled my eyes as he pushed out his chair and she sat in his lap, placing her drink on the table. The green liquid sloshed up the sides and ran back down.

"Are you ready to go home?" she asked him, caressing the sides of his face. "I can cook steak for dinner and run us a hot bath afterward. Then, if you're not tired, we can watch a movie in bed."

Her eyes sparkled when she looked at him, like he was her whole world. I guess he was. She threw her studies out the window to stay in Exeter with him, to be his old lady. They even bought a big house at the end of Burning Road, the same road the clubhouse was on, on a large slab of land by the secluded Mary River. It was a six-bedroom house and I knew for a fact four of those rooms were for the tribe of kids they were going to have as soon as Isabelle felt she was old enough for children.

"Fuck." Creed groaned and pulled his face out of her hands. "Can't. We've got something coming up and I have to stay here until it's sorted."

She tilted her head, and behind her ear I noticed a black smudge. "Okay. I don't mind staying here, like old times."

I stepped closer as they whispered to each other until I could make out the teeny-tiny motorcycle tattoo with the initials *J.C.* and a small heart tattooed beside it. I lifted an eyebrow. When did she get that done?

"It's bad luck, you know."

Izzy and Creed cast me the same irritated look.

"What is?" she asked.

"The tattoo."

"No, it isn't."

My lips quirked at the corners. "Am I behind the other ear?"

Blush ran up her neck and swirled in her cheeks. "Why would you be?"

I shrugged, relishing in the way Creed scowled at me. The other men liked to poke fun at him and his commitment to Izzy, but he had it good. At the end of the day, when all this club shit was over, he had her to keep him company. He didn't climb into bed with a different woman every night. It was the same woman, the same body, the same smells, and the same feelings. Lately, that weighed on my mind heavier than ever, and it was thoughts like that that contributed to my disinterest in Liv, and any other woman in the clubhouse. I teased Blondie and Creed a lot, but I knew, deep down, women like Blondie would never understand me. They hadn't lived the same life or made the same sacrifices. How could I be with someone who didn't understand the pain I lived with and, therefore, could never help me heal it? Blondie was good for my body, but meaningless to my soul. Isabelle and Creed were made for each other and they knew it the moment they met. I joked about it, but I'd never come between them.

Isabelle leaned forward and kissed him. She made a whole show of it too, kissing him hard and fast, pushing her tongue inside his mouth. She slid her small hands up his chest, neck, and into his hair, forcing him harder against her. I blew air from my lips and turned away.

As I passed the threshold of the meeting room, I called over my shoulder. "When you're ready for a real man, you know where my room is."

I heard their kiss break from out in the hall.

"Damon, you fuck!" Creed shouted, and I simpered.

I had to stop playing or he was going to shoot me dead one day. As I entered the main room of the clubhouse, I inhaled and held the smells of whiskey and barbeque in my lungs. I felt different—free, sort of—because I left that room without the usual worms of jealousy squirming through my insides. When I looked at Blondie, not a single thought I had was about wanting her.

I no longer envied Creed.

TEN

YASMINE

Two weeks later

Disturbed.

That's the name of the band whose music is thundering through the clubhouse. It's also a word that accurately describes how I'm feeling. Disturbed. These people don't stop. Life's a party. They ride, drink, fuck, and turn it up all day, every day, and well into the night. Harlei told me this is the way, especially when there's a big, dangerous mission coming up, and since that mission is because of me, I guess I have no right complaining. Since each party brings me closer to Nicolás, I should welcome it.

The guest room is situated at the beginning of the hallway, where it opens up to the main space. Naturally, the music hits my room first. By the time it gets to Judge's, one of the last rooms at the end of the hall, it's a dull drone and the bass sounds like the beating of a heart instead of the bashing of a drum. Can I go to his room, like I did on the first night? Or is that inappropriate? What if he has company? My stomach turns and I ease myself onto my side, tucking my knees higher.

Harlei is very happy with how quick I'm recovering, but I don't think I had anything to do with it. The woman has healing hands, it's incredible. Because of her, my bruises are faded, my cuts closed, and my swelling gone. The various burns on my body are still there, but they don't hurt, and she thinks if I continue to take care of them, they'll leave minimal scarring.

Giggling in the hall pulls me from my thoughts and I blink into the darkness, waiting for them to pass my door. When they do, I ease the blanket off my legs lift myself off the squeaky queen bed. Maybe I can make my way to the infirmary and get some more sleeping pills. I open my bedroom door as quietly as I can and I peer out into the empty hall. Then, I glance down at my loose, black tee and short, black bed shorts that Harlei gave me. The infirmary is on the other side of the building, meaning I'll have to go through the thick of the party to get there.

I'd rather not.

I turn my head left and stare down the long hall

to Judge's room at the very end. Is he in there? Would he spare me a tablet just for tonight? I haven't seen him in two weeks. I don't know how his plans are progressing or when he's leaving to get Nicolás. This could be a good opportunity to get more information from him. I step into the hall and close my door behind me. As quickly as I can, I tiptoe toward his room. When I reach his door, I swallow hard and blow air from my lips, wiping my clammy palms against the fabric of my shorts. Then I knock.

But there's no answer.

*I hope he isn't asleep...*I knock again and yield the same result. Holding my breath, I push on the handle and gently open his door.

"Judge?" I utter, slipping my head into his spacious room.

The glow from the big TV mounted on his wall is enough to light up his space. I say his name again and slip inside, closing the door behind me. I stand still, folding my arms over my chest, and I wait until silent seconds stretch into silent minutes. *He's not here.* I turn around to leave, but the paused video on his T.V. snags my attention. It's the blur of a little girl mid-spin, her arms outstretched, her head tilted down to watch her feet.

I glance at the door. *I really should go...*but I find myself moving toward the television, toward the black leather sofa in front of it. I take the thin remote off the armrest and sit down. Reason screams in my head, demanding I mind my own business and leave Judge's room, but I want to see her. I want a glimpse of Judge as a dad. I hit play and happy, childish laughter fills the room.

"You're going to make yourself sick, Nila," Judge's deep, amused tenor follows, complimenting his daughter's light laugh. "Or fall on your face."

It makes my heart swell and pound in my chest.

"No, I won't," she shoots back, her dark hair swishing around her shoulders. She stops anyway and beams at her dad, who stands behind the camera. "See?"

Tears spring to my eyes. She's so happy, and she looks so much like Damon. Nila turns and runs away, her pink party dress bouncing around her knees. The camera pans toward a large picnic table decorated in different shades of pink balloons and streamers. And a handful of bikers sit around the table, all wearing princess tiaras on top of their heads and pink feather boas around their necks. I smile as the camera follows Nila as she runs up to the table. One of them, who I recognize as James Creed, turns in his seat as she approaches, and she jumps into his arms to sit on his lap. *They really are a family here...*

Nicolás didn't have birthday parties. It was just me and him. If I were lucky, Elias would be out of town, so I could bake Nicolás a chocolate cake.

We'd dance and sing, wrestle, and snuggle. If Elias was home, I had to pretend Nicolás's birthday didn't exist.

"Another birthday down," Judge says, but the camera stays on Creed and Nila as Armi paints cake cream on her nose and she tries to reach it with her tongue. "What're we going to do for the next one?"

The men laugh and poke fun, even Casino—who does nothing but scowl at me—is happy. I guess these were simpler times for the Devil's Cartel Exeter chapter.

A woman chuckles, her voice husky. Judge's ex, I assume. "Think we can get the boys into tutus?"

The camera turns on Judge as he laughs, exposing his perfect, white teeth. He's so young, and his skin is clean. There are no tattoos up his neck or on his forearms and I wish I knew him then.

I exit the video and am led to a folder with a million more clips. I know better than to snoop, but I want to see Judge happy. I want to see what a functional family looks like. I watch another video, and another. With every laugh from Nila and warm, loving smiles from Judge, I fall deeper into my admiration for Judge's softer side. He's the most beautiful father I've ever seen, and I know, if I'm not careful, I'll hang all my hopes and dreams on him. I exit the video of Judge and Nila playfully arguing while covered in flour in the clubhouse kitchen, then I turn the TV off and sit in the darkness. My heart feels too big to fit in my chest and my tummy is turbulent. Quickly, I find myself romanticizing the idea of Damon and Nicolás, and it's wrong. I shake my head, lift myself off the couch, and exit the room.

"Lost, darling?" a deep, British voice asks, and I squeak, jumping a mile out of my skin as I whirl on my heel.

"Oh, you scared me." I swallow my panic with a hand over my heart as Modo, the friendly-looking biker, smooths his large hand down his copper beard, his eyes smiling along with his lips.

I need to come up with something and fast. I don't want word to get back to Judge and he thinks I was snooping around his room.

"Modo, right?"

His lips pick up at the corners and he adjusts his leather cut, all smug-like. "The one and only."

"I'm looking for Judge. Have you seen him?"

He tsks, feigning sadness. "The pretty ones are never looking for me." Then he grins and flicks his head down the hall, gesturing for me to follow him. "C'mon."

I follow him toward the party, where the strong smells of BBQ meat and beer emanate. I smooth my palms down my shirt and tug on the hem of my shorts, trying to pull them further down my thighs. I'm not dressed for a party, and my hair—I quickly rake my fingers through it as we step into the large area. Clashing glass, roars of laughter, and the chattering of conversation is almost deafening.

"He was in the garage, fucking around with a bike, last I saw," Modo shouts over his shoulder and I fight to keep my attention on his, instead of the skull printed on the back of his cut. "Are you in a hurry?"

I shrug and he snags my wrist in his big, warm hand.

"Have a drink with me." A demand, not a question.

I let Modo pull me toward the bar where a young man in a brown leather cut saunters closer, eyeing me curiously.

"Does Prez know she's out of her room?" he asks, drumming his tattooed fingers against the oak bar.

I frown.

"Mind your own business, Kace." Modo leans over the bar. "Get me four shots of tequila."

Kace shifts his attention to me, purses his lips, then turns with a defeated sigh and fetches Modo his order. *Tequila?* He wants to go straight to tequila?

"Am I not allowed to leave my room?" I ask Modo, watching Kace as he sets four small shot glasses in front of him and lifts a bottle of tequila.

"You're a grown woman. You can do whatever you want."

Modo excitedly drums his palms against the bar and I drop my stare to tiny specks of salt and liquid as they bounce with the vibrations.

"Do you know—" I pause as Modo cranes his neck, moving his ear closer to my mouth. "Do you know anything about Elias? About when you're going?"

He smirks at me. "You're really gonna ask me to divulge club business to you?"

"It's my business too."

I keep Modo locked in my stare until Kace brings the shots of tequila and turns around again. Without breaking eye contact, Modo pushes two shot glasses toward me.

"We're gonna get your boy back, Minnie," he says. "You've got nothing to worry about."

How could I not worry? No one tells me anything here—not even Harlei—and Judge hasn't visited me in weeks. He told me to trust him, but I'm hanging by a thread.

Sighing, I glance at the mini glasses. I'm not much of a drinker, but if I'm going to talk to Judge, I could use the liquid courage. I grab the shot of tequila and tip it down my throat with a quick swallow, pushing the lime and salt away. "Tell me, how'd I get the nickname Minnie?"

Modo laughs, picks up his glass, and drinks it down. Like me, he forgoes the lime and salt. "Because of me. I thought your name was

Yasminnie when I read it. The fellas found it hilarious."

I snicker and grab my second shot. "Yasminnie, huh?"

He grabs his too. "Don't you start."

We take our shot at the same time and bare our teeth because the second dose doesn't feel as smooth on the palate. I shiver and push the shot glasses far away from me. I zone out while Modo talks about the politics of a foreign country I know nothing about, and I glance over my shoulder, over the heads of bikers and women milling about. I'd put Elias up there as one of the most dangerous men on the planet, and it boggles my mind that these people aren't afraid of going up against him. I wish I had their bravery, their tenacity. It's no secret this chapter is going to lose some of its members. Nothing was fatality free when it came to Elias Vergara. He liked his enemies to suffer. For him, the more bloodshed there is, the happier he is.

"And that's why Harry stepping back from his royal duties is bullshit!" Modo booms, slapping his hand against the bar, turning his body toward me. "Want another drink?"

Shaking my head, I exhale and push away from the bar. "Sorry, Modo. I need to see Judge."

Modo points over his shoulder to the front doors. "Garage."

Smiling, I pat his shoulder and head toward the

big, black front doors. Outside, the cool air clings to my bare skin, but it fails to chill my warm blood, thanks to the tequila. Twenty yards ahead, the warm lights from the garage spill onto the gravel drive. A distant clang of metal sends my heart rate through the roof. What's he doing in there and why isn't he at the party? My mind drifts to the video paused in his room. Did viewing them drive him out here? To be alone? I lift myself onto the tips of my toes and ease across the pointy rocks toward the garage entrance. I follow the sounds of quiet rock music deeper into the building. Scents of oil and freshly welded metal assault my senses, lifting the hair on the back of my neck as I inhale it deep into my lungs. A fine layer of dirt and debris sticks to the soles of my feet as I brush by four neatly lined black trucks with blacked out windows. At the back of the garage, I see him, a topless Judge, hunching over a chunk of metal on a makeshift plywood counter, a spotlight swinging above his head. My throat runs dry at the sight of his broad, tattooed shoulders, and the defined shape of every muscle in his back. He swipes his hands against his jeans, drawing my attention to the black t-shirt tucked into his back pocket.

"Can't sleep?" he asks, and I startle, my lips parting to let out a rush of air.

Tingly nervousness runs down my arms and I fidget with my thumbnail before I step forward with an exhale, touching my finger to the grill of the truck beside me. I don't know why, but it grounds me, makes me feel less anxious.

"No." I walk closer to him, dragging my fingers along the cool, black metal.

I approach the counter and peer over his big forearms to see what he's working on. I don't know what I'm looking at. A small engine, maybe. Whatever it is, it's dirty and corroded. Judge stops what he's doing and peers down at me. His dark, ocean eyes flicker down my face to my chest, then back to the chunk of metal in front of him.

He points across the counter. "Pass me the wrench."

Thank God I know what a wrench is. I lean over the wood, feeling the warmth of Judge's gaze sweep down my side. I grab the wrench and slap the heavy steel into his open palm.

"You can't sleep either?" I ask, watching as he loosens something on the rear side of the engine. "Is it because...you're scared? Of what's coming?"

Judge snorts, dropping the wrench to the plywood. "Scared? Me? Not likely."

He turns and walks away from the counter. I turn too and watch as he steps around an engineless motorcycle and sits on a black leather backseat that's been ripped out of a car.

"I've been scared once in my life and my worst nightmare came true." He reaches into the empty orange frame and twists something with his fingers. "Nothing left in this world to scare me."

He's talking about the death of his daughter, Nila, and I understand what he's saying on a deeper level. The fear of losing a child—*your* child—is the scariest thing in the world, and I'm facing it.

"You were a good dad."

The words fall from my parched lips before I can stop them, and Judge pauses with his fiddling. Embarrassment warms my veins and heats my face. I didn't want to say anything, but since watching his home videos, there's a warm mass in my chest of admiration for him that I can't swallow down. I want him to know I saw him with his daughter, making her laugh and smile, making her feel loved, as a child should. I want him to know I think he's a good father in case he's never been told, like I've never been told I'm a good mother.

...perhaps I'm not.

"Yeah?" He continues to twist something. "How do you know?"

I open my mouth to tell him I was in his room, but I can't bring myself to utter the words as my brain shouts that I breached Judge's privacy. He didn't show me the videos, so I had no business viewing them. I don't want him to be mad at me.

I lower my gaze to the floor. "Just a hunch."

I lift it again as Judge sits back with an exhale and places his hands on his thighs.

139

"What're you doing?" I ask and he groans.

"I don't even know anymore." He taps the empty seat beside him, gesturing for me to sit. "I've been trying to repair it to surprise Kace for his birthday. Nothing's going right."

I sit beside him and trap my hands between my knees. Among the smells of oil and metal, I pick up on Judge's cologne and the gentlest hint of cigarettes. My mouth waters and my skin pebbles as the scents mix expertly together, taunting me almost.

"That's nice of you."

He gently kicks the motorcycle with the tip of his boot. "Creed thinks we should buy him a new one, but...your first bike has to be a throwaway, you know?"

I nod, but I *don't* know. I don't know the first thing about motorbikes or club life. We stare in silence at the empty orange frame for an eternity, it feels like, when he finally speaks again.

"Why are you here, Minnie?" he asks, turning his head. His stare heats the side of my face and I want to look at him, to see him up close for the first time in weeks, but I'm afraid what secrets his handsome face will draw out of me.

"Just checking up on you." I moisten my lips out of nervousness. "I haven't seen you in two weeks. I wanted to…"

Nothing. I can't do anything...because I'm

afraid. Afraid of men, of rejection, of failure. I'm afraid of falling into the wrong crowd—*again*. I'm afraid of being exposed, of creating new enemies. Of course, I can't tell him any of this.

"You wanted to what?"

I shift my gaze from the bike to Judge's hand. Dark, dry blood stains the ball joint on the side of his wrist and the skin is lifted, dirt and metal darkening the entrance to his wound. Without thought, I reach out and touch his wrist, smoothing my small fingers alongside the cut.

"You're bleeding."

He shrugs but doesn't shake me off. "Caught my skin on the bike."

I glance around the garage, looking for a place to clean it. On the left wall, a small, dirty white sink stands all on its lonesome. I lift myself off the chair and tug on Judge to do the same. He doesn't fight me as I lead him over to the sink where— thankfully—the water works. I pump the soap dispenser and collect two beads of soap. Judge isn't impressed as I clean his hands, then rinse them under the water. Black water runs into the basin. I wash them twice before the water stays clear and I'm happy with his clean hands. I inspect the cut and, since the dirt and debris has been washed away, it doesn't look so bad.

"Just a scratch," I murmur, looking around for a towel.

When I can't find one, I use my shirt to pat his hands dry and it feels…intimate.

"How'd you know I was in here?" Judges asks, his tone quiet and calm.

"Modo told me." I continue patting his hands, my confession on the tip of my tongue. He deserves to know I invaded his privacy. I'm sure Modo will tell him anyway. "I went to your room first. You weren't there." Our stares lock. "You left your TV on and I saw…"

I swallow hard. What do I say? How do I say it?

"You watched the videos?" He searches my eyes for the answer. "Is that what you meant when you said I was a good dad? Because you saw me smiling in a couple clips?"

His tone is suddenly venomous, and I absorb my flinch, trying not to internalize his frustration. I get it. I spied on the most precious, most memorable times of his life. I'd be annoyed with me too. I release his hands as irritation dominates his handsome face.

"Not because you were smiling. Because you played with her and made her happy. You took care of her." I straighten my shirt and smooth my palms over the damp wrinkles in the fabric as fire burns at the back of my neck. "And I love that."

I'm swept up in the flash of his deep blue irises as blush swirls in my chest and travels north. I see the weight of my words rest on him as he absorbs

142

what I said. I mean every word. I know what a bad dad looks like. They don't smile, aren't compassionate, and they certainly don't go out of their way to make their children laugh.

"I don't feel like a good dad," Judge admits, glancing down at his hands. "I don't think I've ever felt like a good dad."

My heart stutters and I step forward, only to stop when his arresting gaze hits mine again, and I'm lost to their turbulent, vulnerable depths.

"It's the curse of being a parent," I tell him. "We never feel good enough, even when we're doing our best."

I let my own words sink into my bones. More often than not, I feel like the shittiest parent in the world, but I'm doing my best with what I have, with what I've been left with.

"And that's what you came all this way in the middle of the night for?" He steps forward, and I tense. "To tell me you think I'm a good dad?"

"I…" The blush in my cheeks turns to hellfire. I glance at his lips and I stop breathing as the heat spreads through my veins. *Why'd I come out here?* "I…well, I…"

Judge moves forward and I suck air between my teeth, backing toward the sink until I'm flush against the partition the sink is mounted to and he's only a hairsbreadth away. He presses his slim hips to mine and his warm breath blows across my cheek.

"Tell me you wanted to see me," he says, and I tilt my chin higher, bringing my mouth closer to his. "Tell me this midnight call is because I was on your mind...like you were on mine."

I lick my lower lip. The thought of admitting it aloud sends tendrils of dread burrowing through me, as if speaking the words gives another man control over me. In response to my silence, Judge eases his large body harder against mine and smooths his hand up the wall beside my head, craning his neck with a threat to kiss me. Instead, he moves his head toward my neck, grazing his lips against its slope. Shaky air rushes from my mouth and anticipation prickles down my spine, lifting fine hairs all over my body.

"Tell me," he murmurs, touching his lips to my flushed skin.

Still, I hold the words deep in my chest. Judge continues to kiss my neck, moving north to my jaw. Every second kiss sees his tempo pick up. They become needier, more passionate, and he's threading his fingers through my hair. My eyelids flutter shut as I'm lost to the unbearable tingles his lips send shooting over my skin. They penetrate my pores, singe my nerve endings, and I swiftly become putty in his hands.

"I..." I purse my lips into bloodless lines. *I won't say it.* "Damon..."

He doesn't stop. He nips at my skin until it hurts, then he kisses it better. He does it over and over until my head spins, my breathing is labored, and my knees tremble under my weight. I let my head loll to the side, giving him more flesh to kiss.

"I wanted to see you," I tell him, taking the back of his neck and holding him to me. "I wanted to see you so bad."

I feel him smirk against my skin and he lifts his head. I only have a second to suck in a quick breath before he covers my mouth with his. Damon kisses me hard and heavy, and I'm helpless against him as he pushes his tongue into my mouth. His taste fills me, igniting a hunger deep in the pit of my belly.

I want more.

I need more.

I've never been kissed like this. I've never been kissed so hard my head swims and my bones liquify. Not even with Elias. I shove my fingers into Damon's hair and kiss him back with wild abandon, but it doesn't matter how hungry I am because he's hungrier and I struggle to keep up. I break the kiss to catch my breath.

"Jesus," I gasp, licking my kiss-swollen lips. *What the hell am I getting myself into?* "You're a lot to handle."

Judge's eyes flash and I gasp as he grips my thighs and lifts me into his arms. "Baby, you have no idea."

Baby. I don't think I've ever been called baby. I crush my mouth to his and plunge my tongue between his lips. I kiss him *hard,* claiming him for myself. A guttural groan releases itself from his throat, sending shockwaves of pleasure through my chipped soul.

Because he wants me.

And I haven't felt wanted in years.

Damon presses me against the cool wall and the rough denim of his jeans sparks goosebumps across every inch of the exposed flesh of my inner thighs. Using the wall to prop me up, he pins me against it with his hips and grips the hem of my shirt. He starts to tug it up, his intention to pull it off over my head, but a cool breeze blows into the garage, causing thin sheets of metal to knock together, startling me out of my daze. I break the kiss for the umpteenth time.

"Wait," I whisper, swiping a hand down my face, an attempt to sober myself. "Not here."

Cursing, Judge glances over his shoulder, pausing on one of the blacked-out trucks. Laughing under his breath, he pulls me close to his body and carries me toward the first truck. He yanks the door open and sits me inside. I slide effortlessly across the black leather backseat to the far door, making room for Judge's large frame. He climbs in and closes the door behind him as I sit sideways and draw my knees closer to my chest. I open my mouth to ask him whose truck it is, but he turns and grabs my ankles. I squeak as he yanks me hard, pulling me closer to him. I catch myself on my elbows as he pushes one of my legs off the seat, opening me up to him. Heat flares, swirling south to settle between my legs where Judge's dark eyes linger. I wait in the silence, hating the way my heart beats a million miles a minute under his gaze. Almost instantly, the temperature inside the car picks up, and a thin layer of sweat bubbles across my forehead.

Judge adjusts his position on the backseat to lean over me, bringing his face level with mine. I lower myself flat on my back and smooth my palms along my stomach. I must come across as nervous because his face softens.

"How long has it been?" he asks me, flicking his stare over me.

"Since I've been with a man?"

He nods. Though Elias hated my guts, he kept me in his bed. Once Nicolás was born, I didn't want to have sex with Elias, or sleep in the same room, but he's not the kind of man you can say no to. To spare myself, and Nicolás, further pain, I allowed Elias to steal my sleep and take whatever he wanted from me. Sometimes I enjoyed it.

Mostly, I hated every second.

"Willingly?" I ask.

Judge grimaces, his big body going rigid, and I worry I've killed the mood.

I touch my hands to his shoulders and gently caress him, making my way to his neck. "Years. More than I can remember."

I arch up and pull on his neck, drawing our mouths closer together. I flick my tongue out and touch it to his top lip and he releases a little rush of air. He slips his hand under my shirt and smooths his rough palm over my hip, lifting the fabric.

"You can say no to me," he utters, sliding his hand to my ribs. "I'll stop any time."

He's a good dad and a good man. My pulse quickens. *Somebody fucking catch me because I'm in danger of falling.* Keeping my stare locked on his, I withdraw my hands from his neck and pinch the fabric of my shirt between my fingers. Inhaling deep, I lift it over the rise of my breasts, exposing myself to him. His blue gaze falls to my breasts, and the way they darken stirs something wicked between my thighs.

"Fuck, you're sexy," he says, his voice a husky rasp as he takes my right breast in his hand.

I open my mouth to say…I don't know. Thank you? But Judge claims me with a kiss, rendering me senseless and breathless all at once. He bears down on me, pressing harder between my legs, and all I can do is lie there, completely incapacitated by his passion, by the quick, fervent pace he sets. I don't know how long he kisses me for, but when he pulls away, I gasp for air and my lips feel swollen. I purse them together and lick them as Judge places open mouth kisses down my jaw, my neck, and between my breasts while he drags his thumbs over my hardened peaks. He plays there for a while, not leaving an inch of my torso untouched, or unkissed, and it stirs an unrelenting ache between my legs. As if reading my mind, Judge releases my breast and snakes his touch down my stomach. Painfully, and achingly slow, he slips his long, thick fingers under the fabric of my bed shorts and pauses as he glides against my bare pubic mound.

He lifts his head. "You're bare?"

Embarrassment explodes in my face. I may have taken care of the hair that was growing. I can't stand it. I can't stand the feeling of hair against my underwear. "You don't like it?"

"I fucking love it." He pushes further between my legs, smoothing his palm against me, stealing the breath from my lungs, making my clit pulse. "I just wasn't expecting it."

Pulling his hand from my shorts, Judge plants his hand on the door's armrest above my head and the other on the seat beside my ribs, making it dip.

He lifts himself off me. "Take them off."

My shorts? I lift my hips and curl my fingers under the waistbands of my shorts and my underwear. I push them down a few inches, then pause and peer up at Judge, who watches intently. Noticing I've stopped, he flicks his dark eyes to mine.

"Quicker," he demands, sending my heart rate through the roof. "Or I'll rip them off."

I shove the scraps of fabric down my legs and work them down the rest of the way by moving my legs. When they reach my ankles, I kick them to the floor. Judge moves his hand to touch me *there*, but I catch him by the wrist and lift my chin. Warning flashes in his eyes, a silent demand I give him exactly what he wants.

"If you want to touch me *there*, you have to kiss me a little more."

His lips quirk and they hold all my attention. I love kissing him. He tastes amazing, *and* he's good at it. I don't think I've ever been kissed the way Judge has kissed me tonight and if this is the only time we do it, I want to get the most out of it. I want him to give me enough to commit to memory.

"Have to?"

"Yes." I release his wrist. "Unless you don't want to."

Judge lowers his head and teases his lips against mine, a gentle graze. "I want to."

He kisses me and, this time he keeps his tongue at bay, only letting it out to lick at my lower lip, a quick, teasing flick. Then, he cups me between my legs, making my breath hitch. I pull away from his mouth, earning a wicked smile from him. Warmth pools at my entrance, my wetness growing tenfold, my arousal ready to pour into his hand.

"You're so fucking wet for me," Judge rasps. "I bet I could slip right in, huh?"

He presses his index finger to my clit, and I startle, my stomach clenching, as vibrations rip through me. I lift my head off the seat only to be met by Judge's kiss. This time, he takes my mouth with his tongue and teeth, licking and biting so hard my head spins. Groaning, he sweeps his finger over my sensitive bundle of nerves in a circular motion and I squirm, unsure how to handle the sensations he effortlessly stirs in me. Without pause, he glides his touch to my entrance. I squeeze my eyes tightly closed as he breaches my opening with the very tip of his finger. Hot surges of arousal roll through me and I tilt my hips, urging him in deeper, but he stays at a teasing distance.

"I shouldn't be doing this," I whisper, a shiver trembling over me, sobering me.

How can I be doing this when everything in my life is going wrong? How can I be so selfish? Judge must feel the sudden apprehension in my body because he breaks the kiss, his heavy breath hitting mine.

"In a couple days, you'll be Mom again," he murmurs, and I open my eyes as my heart swells in my chest. "For now, you're *mine*. Enjoy it."

He pushes his thick finger all the way in. My breath hitches painfully in my throat and I arch off the seat. Pulling his finger out to circle it over my clit again, Judge cranes his neck and licks the column of my throat. A moan slips from my lips and I close my eyes, enjoying the pins and needles feeling his kisses, and nips of his teeth, leave in their wake as he makes his way to my breasts again. This time, he doesn't stop there. He continues his descent to my belly button, then to my pelvis, all while gently circling me, slowly building my pleasure. Pausing his rain of kisses at the apex of my thighs, Judge peers up at me with a devilish smile that makes my heart race.

"What?" I ask, breathless, fighting the urge to lift my hips into his hot breath as it blows against my most sensitive parts.

"Nothing."

"Nothing?"

Judge moves his finger out of the way to plant his hand on my thigh. He pushes it, opening me up, then closes his mouth over my core, thrusting his tongue between my creases. *Oh,* shit. One of my hands fly to his hair, the other to the car door above my head, and I moan—*loudly.*

"Damon…" I sigh, arching my back and flexing my hips.

He licks and sucks me harder, brushing his fingers along the crease between my thighs and my pelvis before pressing them to my entrance. The skin behind my ears pull tight as he breaches my opening and sinks right in. *Holy fuck.* With his fingers seated deep inside, he devours me with unbelievable confidence, like he knows my body better than I do.

Lifting my head, I peer down my body to watch his passionate assault on my most private part and our gazes meet—brown to blue—and the air is siphoned from my lungs.

"So good," he groans, licking me with the flat of his tongue as he massages me from the inside, minutely pumping his fingers in and out. "So fucking good."

I watch, enraptured by his movements, by his eyes that watch my breasts bounce and sway, and his lips that glisten with my arousal. My orgasm builds at the sight of him. His big body looks uncomfortably squashed up on the end of the seat, but he doesn't seem to notice. I slowly shuffle back, pulling my hips away to give him more space, and he grunts, grabs my hip, and pulls me harder against his face. I curse and let my head fall back against the seat. My eyelids flutter shut. I can't remember the last time I felt so…delusional.

"Oh, my god," I whisper, the pleasure he gives me robbing me of my voice. My abs clench and I grip his hair in both hands. "I'm coming. Judge—"

It builds inside me like the rise of a roller coaster. I grit my teeth and my thighs quake as I reach the height of my pleasure. I teeter on the edge, pushed over when Judge pinches my clit between his lips and sucks hard on it. I fall into my orgasm, my head spinning like I've hit a loop-the-loop. Warmth spreads through me as I explode into a million tiny pieces. I cry out—in pleasure and pain—as my left calf cramps. I clench it with one hand and try to rub it as best I can with boneless arms.

"Fucking hell," Judge swears, planting a kiss on my inner thighs. I tuck my legs up, drawing my knees close together, as he rears back and tugs on his belt, opening it up. "You went off quick."

I squeeze my tender calf and watch him, watch his gorgeous body, and lick my lower lip. In this light, his sweat glistens and shadows pool perfectly in the depressions of his muscles. Judge stares down at me with his hard eyes, eyes filled with lust. Then he grabs my knee and tugs on it. I let my legs fall open as he leans over me, planting one hand on the edge of the seat by my head, the other on the door.

"You're damn beautiful," he utters, and I press my palm to his cheek, caressing his skin through his stubble, blush blooming over my face. "Perfect, even."

"You don't have to do that," I whisper, and his eyebrows draw close.

I know better than to romantically involve myself with Damon Judge, but here I am, in the backseat of an unknown truck, my shirt around my neck, my pants on the floor, and someone else's saliva drying on my flesh.

"Do what?"

"Make me feel good about myself. Make me feel like I'm different, more special, than the other women you…" I rub my lips together, unable to say the word. "…you know."

Judge lowers his hips, pinning mine against the seat. His open zipper exposes skin low on his pelvis and the warmth of it increases the slickness between my thighs.

"I ate your pussy until you came," he states, as if that makes a difference. "I never—"

I turn my head and laugh. "You're such a liar."

He lets me laugh, his own lips quirking in response as he studies my face. "A liar?"

"Yeah, a liar." A final giggle bubbles out my mouth. "But it's okay—"

Growling, Judge shoves his arms under my body and scoops me into his arms. My breath hitches as he sits and yanks me forward. There's no space in here, and yet he manipulates my body so easy. In the blink of an eye, my thighs are slipping to either side of his, my knees pressed into the backrest of the seat. Wrapping one arm around my waist, he snakes the other up my back and into my hair.

"I'm many things," he says, and I inhale sharply, sucking air between my teeth, anticipating him yanking my head on an angle. Instead, he gently eases it, his dark, blue gaze falling to the slope of my neck as my hair tumbles to the side. "But I'm not a liar."

"So, you don't…" My voice melts to nothing as Judge shakes his head. "Ever?"

Embarrassed heat inches through my veins and I want to pull away from him, suddenly insecure. "Is it because you don't like it?"

His eyes flash. "I love it."

"Then I don't get it."

"You've seen the women in here, how often they jump from member to member. I'd die for my men, but it'd be a cold day in hell before I put my mouth where they thrust their cocks." He brushes hair out of my face, then drags his thumb along my lower lip. I smell the strange soap I used to wash his hands. "You…you are all mine."

I lift my eyebrows. My pulse quickens. "Yours?"

"All mine." Judge kisses me. He claims my mouth in a way that's so sinfully intimate, I feel I'm imposing on the moment, so I close my eyes. My heart pounds in my chest, my skin prickling with things I shouldn't be feeling. He breaks the kiss, leaving me drunk on him. "For the moment, at least."

My eyelids flutter open. "And when we leave the truck?"

"I think, when we leave this truck, it gets a little more complicated." He glances between my eyes and my lips. "It meant a lot…when you told me I was a good d—"

Hands slam against the window and we startle, whipping our heads in the direction of the two small palms pressed against the black glass.

"Keep your fucking hands there," someone orders, and the truck gently rocks.

Panic rises in my throat like bile and I yank my shirt down, covering my hardened nipples and heavy breasts.

Holding me tight against him, Judge shushes me. "They can't see us."

"They?"

Then I see it, her long, blonde hair, and his cropped hair style, the kind that's shorter on the sides and longer on the top. He towers over her, smoothing his big hands down her arms. I suck air between my teeth. *Oh no.* It's James Creed and Isabelle Laurent. *Don't they have their own room?*

She straightens her head, blows air out of her lips, and watches her reflection. Even through the dark tint, I can tell her skin is flushed pink and heated. I swallow hard, watching them. I should look away. I should open the door and let them know I'm here…but I don't want them to know I'm with Judge. I don't want them to know what we've done.

"You wore it," Creed grumbles, pulling her hair over one shoulder. He lowers his face into the nape of her neck, planting soft kisses there. "You knew they'd all look at you, all want you, and you still fucking wore it."

"You bought it."

He grabs her by the hair and pulls her head back. Isabelle's eyes flare with pleasure, her lips quirking with delight. "Yeah, I bought it. You're supposed to wear it for me. No one else."

Judge laughs under his breath and I look at him.

"We should tell them we're here," I say, but he shakes his head.

"No. In order to tell them, we'd have to stop. We'd have to leave this truck." He pushes my shirt back over the swells of my breasts and cups one in his large palm. He squeezes it, feels the weight of it, then pinches my nipple between his thumb and forefinger, forcing my hips to flex against him of their own accord. "I don't want to leave this truck. I don't want to fucking stop."

Judge cranes his neck and envelops my nipple with his hot tongue and groans heartily.

"Judge…" I sigh, tilting my head to watch him suck me into his mouth.

Sexual interaction with Elias was never like this. With him, it was a perfectly choreographed dance. He came in, knew what to do, then finished. I could predict how sex with him would go every single time. With Judge, tonight, it's different. I don't know what he wants to do next—or if he wants to do anything at all. I can't predict his next move, next touch, or the next words that are going to come out of his mouth. And I realize…I miss the spontaneity of a man.

I miss their smell.

Their feel—how they make me feel.

I turn my head and watch Isabelle and Creed make out against the car, his hand gripping her jaw, her head pulled to the side. They kiss passionately, hungrily, as if they'd just met and all they had was lust. It's amazing, considering they've been together for years. Creed's hand leaves Isabelle's jaw, and she turns her head back to the window, mesmerized by their reflection.

"After tonight, you won't wear this here again," he demands, his finger curling around the low neckline of her black lace bodysuit. "It's only for me. In our home. Got it?"

"Yes."

He yanks the lace down to sit underneath her generous bust. I look away, look to Judge, who no longer has his mouth on my nipple, and meet his heated stare. My lips tug at the corners.

"This is so awkward."

"More awkward than getting caught without pants on? I don't think so." He moistens his lips. "We'll wait it out. He doesn't last long."

I snort, and we stare at each other for ages, a silent game neither one of us wants to lose by looking away first. The only interaction between us is the facial expressions we make in reaction to the ridiculousness going on outside. Eventually, I turn my head. Isabelle's breasts pressed against the glass whenever Creed wasn't grabbing them. The car rocks side to side, shaking me on Judge's lap, then Creed slams his hand against the glass beside Isabelle's. Her hands are much smaller than his, much more delicate. Everything about her is much more delicate than him, but I get the allure. She's come from a controlling and strait-laced upbringing. Here, she can do anything. Here, she's not a princess. She's a queen.

Lost in my thoughts, I don't realize the rocking has stopped until Isabelle's soft laugh filters through the glass. I focus on them once more, watching as he helps her with her jeans, then her shirt. He smiles at her, a bright beam, then they share a chaste kiss. Finally, he rakes his fingers through her hair, smoothing her blonde locks all while staring at her adoringly. When they leave, Judge plants small kisses along my collarbone and I exhale, relaxing my muscles. I close my eyes and rest my head against his as he smooths his hands up my back, then down again. He caresses my hips, my shoulder, my backside, and lifts my shirt to massage my breasts. My skin still hurts and there's a deep ache in all my muscles I don't think will ever go away, but his touch works magic, drawing so much pain out of my body, like a painkiller. I don't know if it'll last, or if I'll feel as good tomorrow, but for now, I don't want it to stop.

I don't want him to stop.

I move in Judge's touch, wanting him to massage me harder, to grip me harder. I rock my hips, seeking the friction of his jeans that bunch around the open zipper, and he flexes against me. I open my mouth to tell him to take whatever he wants when another slam on the glass has me nearly puking up my skeleton. We whip our heads toward the window for the second time and Judge tenses against me, cursing under his breath. I feel the blood drain from my face and the tremble in my hands at the sight of Nicolás's picture taped to the window. Thick tendrils of dread burrow through my chest and stab me in the heart. *What the hell am I doing?*

"What the fuck?" Judge swears, and I push away from him as he twists his hips, slipping onto the seat bedside him.

He opens the door enough to stick his head out and I tug my shirt down, then reach for my underwear and pants off the floor. He talks to me, but I can't hear him over the sound of my broken heart beating in my ears. Weeks. I've waited weeks and for what? Because Judge told me to? And now I do this?

Where the fuck is my son? Gone. And what's his

mother doing? Messing around with the president of a biker gang. Bitter disappointment in myself socks me in the stomach. I'm despicable. Nicolás deserves better than me. He always has.

I slide into my underwear, then my pants, unable to get them on quick enough. As Judge shuts his door, I throw my side open and jump out, not bothering to close it behind me.

"Minnie?" Judge calls out, but I don't stop.

I hightail it out of the garage and into the cool night air, barefoot. The gravel drive digs into the soles of my feet, but I don't care. I barrel through the big black doors of the clubhouse and keep my stare downcast to my feet, afraid my eyes will betray what happened between Judge and me. I make it halfway across the room and see two scuffed black boots before I slam into another man wearing leather.

"Shit," I swear, as alcohol the color of whiskey spills over a rocks glass clenched in a giant fist and it hits my shirt.

Gasping, I lift my shoulders as it soaks in and kisses my skin. Then I lift my head. I survey his old belt buckle, then skim my gaze over his leather cut and the 'Vice President' patch sewn into the chest of it. Finally, I meet the same dark eyes I saw on the man towering behind Isabelle Laurent not too long ago. Heat climbs my neck and swirls in my cheeks. Creed stares down at me, his black and gold eyes flashing dangerously.

"Who're you running from?" he asks, uncaring that his drink has wet his fingers.

"No one."

A clang of the opening front doors catches my attention and I glance over my shoulder. Judge enters the clubhouse, pulling his black shirt over his inked abdominal muscles. He scans the crowd looking for me, and my pulse skyrockets. I look at Creed and realization lights his features.

"No point running from him. He always gets what he wants." He sips his drink, apparently delighted. "I saw you two, you know. *Watching*."

I feel my face turn beet red. Everything north of my neck heating to boiling point. My stomach churns like a violent sea, threatening to upturn the nothing I ate for dinner. Under his teasing gaze, all I can do is swallow hard and lift my chin.

"I don't know what you're talking about."

He tilts his head and, in his eyes, the intimate scene replays, causing volcanic heat to gather around my collar. "Of course you don't."

Scoffing, I push past him before I vocally condemn myself before Judge catches me and turns this—whatever this is—into a public spectacle. I hurry toward my room, pushing through the throng of leather and body odor.

"Hey, Minnie!" Creed calls, and the chatter in the room falls silent, the only sound coming from the bass of the speakers, Rage Against the Machine's *Bulls on Parade* playing loud.

I don't turn around in fear of what he's going to say.

"Your shorts are inside out."

And I fucking die.

ELEVEN

JUDGE

I avoided her like the plague for nearly twenty-four hours. I didn't know who put the fucking photo of her kid against the window, but somebody did. The sight of it turned Yasmine's body from lava to ice. She went from melting in my hands to rigid like steel in less than a second. I had my suspicions, but no definitive proof. This morning, I all but hung Casino from the rafters by his ankles, but he insisted it wasn't him. I believed him...maybe. I punched him hard enough in the face the other week, so he knew better than to cross me again.

I interrogated Blondie and Creed—who knew we were in Armi's truck the whole time but didn't say anything, the perverts—and they swore it wasn't them either. In retrospect, I had nothing...but I kept my eyes peeled. Whoever did it knew we were in the truck, and they knew what we were doing.

And they fucking sabotaged it.

I slammed the clean rifle down on the table and exhaled, earning a side glance from Armi.

"You okay, Prez?"

"Fucking peachy," I snapped, tossing down my dirty red cloth. "Why wouldn't I be?"

He shrugged, focusing on cleaning a smudge underneath the trigger of his own rifle. "Seem a bit agitated, is all."

I had no response for him. Of course I was fucking agitated. I hadn't had sex in weeks, and I didn't want to—not with anyone other than Minnie, who I almost had. The photo of her son sobered her, and she ran away from me, as if being with me was the most awful thing on the planet. As if me eating her pussy was the most shameful thing she ever had to endure.

Fuck her.

I never had to chase a woman. Ever. If she wanted to run away from me, then away she'd stay until I finished what I needed to do. When I did what I promised, when I hand her son over to her, I'd send her on her way. Then, I'd go back to my usual shit without wasting another precious thought on her. I wouldn't waste another second on something that had nothing to do with me, or my club.

"I don't know what her fucking problem is," I blurted, surprising myself.

I bit my tongue, not wanting another word to come out of my mouth, at risk of sounding like a goddamn bitch. Armi lifted his eyebrows but kept on cleaning his gun.

"It must be hard for her..." he uttered, not looking me in the eye. "Not having her kid and all that."

"Have you seen him?" I asked, probing whether he was behind sticking the photograph on his truck window. It was *his* truck. Made sense he'd want us out of it before I stained the leather.

He shook his head, his stupid manbun barely moving. "No, but Casino told me he was Down Syndrome."

"Yeah." I glanced over the top of the makeshift table and across the acreage that seemed to go on forever.

We had a little piece of paradise here on Burning Road. I couldn't imagine this land belonging to anyone but us. One day, I'd build each of my most important men their own place, so they were no longer confined to a single room. One day, I'd turn this entire property into our kingdom, turrets and all.

A hundred yards out, I watched Yasmine sit on the grass, her face turned up at the morning sun. Her olive complexion glowed as it absorbed the vitamin

167

D, the highlights in her brunette hair turning from black to gold, almost. She wore jean shorts, and an old *Guns and Roses* t-shirt, too big for her body, and it killed me I didn't know who it belonged to.

Which was probably for the best. As president, I couldn't shoot a member over a woman I laid no claim to. So, I gritted my teeth and tolerated it.

"Have you seen Creed?" Blondie's voice, her question, was a pin in my bubble.

I turned my head and dragged my stare up her toned, tan legs to her tiny, black cut-offs. Then I looked at her cropped gray hoodie and the long, blonde hair that draped over her breasts—breasts I tried hard not to look at when they were pressed up against the window last night.

I dropped my head back to peer around her at the clubhouse. Creed was busy negotiating a meeting time with the Ventillis for tomorrow night. Elias was hiding out in Vegas and we needed Marco Ventilli's permission before entering his territory—unless we wanted another war. A war with the Ventillis was on the cards, but not for tomorrow night.

"Why?" I asked, straightening my head.

"I need to go into town."

I blew impatient air between my lips. "So, go."

"I need Creed to come with me."

"Well, I need him here."

"Damon—"

"Why're you so clingy?" I snapped, cutting my eyes at her.

"Clingy?" She reared back, scrunching her pretty face as if I'd slapped it. "I'm not fucking clingy."

Isabelle's crystal blue eyes filled with water and she averted her gaze across the land. She rubbed her lips together, as if it helped keep her tears at bay. I sighed and flicked my chin at Armi. Without a word, he placed his heavy rifle on the table, pushed his chair out, and left. When he reached the clubhouse steps, I dragged my attention back to Blondie, who was till avoiding my eyes.

"You really can't go by yourself?" I asked.

I didn't get it. She was a grown woman. Did she really need Creed around every second of every day? She couldn't go to the grocery store without him? Couldn't sleep in a bed without him? Did the psychological scars her father still affect her *that* bad?

"They stare at me when I'm by myself, Damon," she said, finally bringing her stare to mine. Her words made me feel like shit. "When he's with me they don't dare stare and it's so fucking nice." She inhaled through her nose and quickly swiped at a tear that rolled over the rim of her eye. "I know you need him. I know he's your Vice President, and I know he's an important part of the club." She pulled her big, black sunglasses off her head and settled them over her bloodshot eyes. "But he's an important part of my life too and you have to learn how to share."

Learn to share? I shared Creed when she needed him most. What we were currently working on was the biggest thing I'd requested of my vice president in two years. She *owed* me this.

"The club comes first," I told her, and there were no ifs, ands, or buts about it.

Her lips fell into a disappointed pout. "Thanks, Damon."

Izzy turned away and heavy weights of regret hung from my ribs. *But I promised I'd take care of her too. I might not be able to give her Creed, but there were others.* I snagged her wrist and pulled her back to face me.

"Take Liv with you," I suggested. If she needed company, did it matter who from? "Or one of the other girls. I need my VP today."

"Liv? The other girls?" Isabelle pulled her sunglasses off her face and her blue eyes flashed. "Are you kidding? They hate my guts."

That was true. Not a single female in the clubhouse had love for Blondie. Because of her, Creed was off the menu and he was a fan favorite. A bad idea sprouted in the back of my skull and I flicked my head to where Minnie was sitting, still basking in the morning sun. She could probably use some girl time.

"Take Yasmine."

Izzy arched a brow. "Your prisoner?"

"She's not my prisoner. We're working together." I felt the need to point that out. Yasmine hadn't been my prisoner in weeks. I glanced at Isabelle. "And the townspeople don't like her either, so they'll gawk at both of you."

She laughed and tipped her head, her smile reaching her eyes. "I can't stand you, Judge. You know that, right?"

Smirking, I shrugged and released her wrist. Isabelle loved me. It might not be in the same way she loved Creed, but she loved me. I meant a lot to her. We all did.

"Fine, I'll take her out," she agreed, smoothing her hands down her cropped gray hoodie. "I hope she likes sushi."

I pulled a face as Blondie stepped around the table and walked toward Yasmine. *I hate sushi.*

Ten feet out from where she sat, Yasmine noticed Isabelle's approach, and I watched as discomfort visibly rolled through her. Blondie crouched beside her and Minnie shook her head, declining whatever she was being asked. A small eternity passed before Yasmine smiled gently. It socked me in the ribs, knocking the air from my lungs. She was beautiful and, if I were being honest with myself, I hadn't stopped thinking about the intimate moments we'd spent together in the garage and in the back of Armi's truck. It played on my mind, like a record, all day. I wanted to rewind time, to go back to that quiet space, and listen to her tell me I was a good dad. Her tone was sincere, her expression full of admiration. I could see myself believing her words if she said them enough.

Armi appeared at my side as Isabelle and Yasmine stood and turned toward the clubhouse. Blondie spared me a glance, but Yasmine kept her attention on the clubhouse, not letting it slip to me, not for a second.

"Send Ayr and Stoic to tail them," I told him. "They'll keep 'em safe."

Nodding, he did as he was told, and I went back to cleaning the guns.

***

Creed and I shifted uncomfortably in our seats, clenching our drinks in our hand, our attention on the front door. Neither one of us said anything about the time, about how late it was. The sun went down hours ago and it was nearing nine p.m. I wasn't worried since Ayr and Stoic kept in touch with me all day, but I was annoyed. Blondie said she needed to go into town. I assumed a trip to the nail salon and a quick stop for sushi was all that was on her agenda. I didn't realize she'd take Minnie and blow through town, then spend the afternoon at a day spa an hour's drive from Exeter.

"Ayr told me they were on their way back," I said to Creed, lifting my drink to take a sip. "They'll be through the door any minute."

He cut his eyes at me and hummed, unimpressed. He was pissed I sent Blondie off without him, but what was I supposed to do? He had work that needed to be done and it wasn't like I sent her without protection.

"You said that an hour ago," he shot back. "If anything has happened to her, I swear to—"

He abruptly ended his threat as the front doors were pushed open and Blondie stepped through, looking over her shoulder. Korn, *Coming Undone,* fades to nothing as the song ends, and the clubhouse fills with girlish laughter and hushed conversation. Stepping to the side, Blondie held the door open for Yasmine. When she walked into the room my whole world slowed down. She was the most beautiful woman I'd ever seen. I knew she was beautiful—too beautiful for her own good—but tonight, all dolled up? My throat ran dry as I dragged my stare up her long, golden legs to the hem of her dress, a dress so pale blue it almost resembled gray. I flicked my attention over the fabric, dotted with white polka dots, to where the neckline dipped at its lowest point, between her generous bust. She looked healthy and happy. Her long, shiny hair tumbled in waves down her back and framed her pretty, fresh face.

173

Ayr and Stoic entered the building behind them, their stares landing on Creed and I. Nudging Blondie, Ayr pointed to us and they headed in this direction. My stupid stomach flipped with every step Yasmine made as she closed the distance between us. She flicked her nervous stare over me before focusing her gaze on the table.

Creed finished his drink as Blondie pulled out a chair next to him and dropped into it, leaving the chair beside me the only place for Minnie to sit. I kept my eyes on her as she gently lowered herself into the seat. Blondie reached across the table and took my drink out of my hand, smiling sweetly as she batted her lashes. She took a big mouthful, then slid my glass to Yasmine, who finished it off and pushed it back to me. Creed and I glanced at each other.

Ayr cleared his throat and shifted his weight. "Might wanna get them some water, Prez."

"Have they been drinking?" I asked and he nodded, rubbing at the back of his neck.

"Izzy more than Minnie."

"You didn't mention they went to a bar."

"They didn't. They had mimosas at the day spa, then Isabelle made Mai Tais when they got back to her place."

Creed sat forward and grabbed Blondie by the face, pulling her close. She lifted her eyebrows and her eyes glistened with devilish excitement.

174

"Tell me you weren't driving?" he said, squeezing her cheeks together, making her lips pout.

She pulled her face out of his grip. "Ayr and Stoic gave us a ride here, actually. That was fun since Yasmine has never been on a motorcycle."

I straightened. Creed did too. Whistling, Stoic elbowed Ayr in the ribs and flicked his head toward the bar. It was best they put as much distance between Creed and I as possible. I had no right to be jealous, but Creed did. Blondie was his bitch—his property. By right, he could kill all three of them for breaking the bylaws and there wasn't a damn thing anyone could do about it.

"Are you fucking kidding me?" Creed growled, turning his body in Izzy's direction.

"Oh, relax." She giggled, and Yasmine spluttered, holding off her own. Isabelle cupped Creed's cheek and planted a chaste kiss on his lips. "It wasn't safe for me to drive. I had no choice."

"Who'd you ride with?"

"Not telling." Isabelle grinned and patted Creed's stubbly cheek before turning her head to Yasmine. "Gin and tonic?"

My lips kicked up. She had full control over him, and he fucking knew it. Yasmine nodded and Blondie lifted herself out of her seat and bounced toward the bar where Kace worked tirelessly. She slid between Ayr and Stoic, who shifted

175

uncomfortably as her slender biceps rested against theirs. Almost in unison, they inched over, giving her more space. I laughed under my breath. They weren't dumb. I bet they could feel Creed's glare burning holes in the backs of their cuts. Isabelle didn't drink often. I guess I was happy she found someone she could let loose with, even if drinking weren't what I had in mind when I told her to take Yasmine out. Speaking of which, I shifted my attention to Yasmine, who was playing with a tiny, loose thread at the end of her dress. She tugged on it, making the thread longer. I stretched my legs out and dug into the pocket of my jeans for my lighter. Over the years, I'd made a conscious effort not to smoke, but I may've had a couple stress cigarettes waiting for the girls to come back tonight.

"Come here," I said, grabbing the armrest of her chair. She gasped as I tugged it toward mine. "You'll ruin it if you pull on it."

I open the lighter's lid, ran my thumb over the spark wheel, and she flinched as the sparks ignited a flame. I burned the thread and closed the lid, extinguishing the fire.

"Thank you," she said, smiling at me.

I didn't tell her she was welcome because Creed was staring right fucking at me, like I was an alien, an imposter. If he weren't here, I'd tell her she looked good. I'd touch her. I'd lift her dress and smooth my hands over her soft skin. Maybe I'd tell

176

her I was low-key worried about her all day. Maybe I'd tell her I hoped she had fun, that she deserved time to herself.

Yasmine rubbed at her slender elbow and twisted her arm to look at the gauze taped to it. The white gauze was stained with fresh blood and it was the perfect opportunity to get her alone. She cursed and I pushed my chair back, lifting myself out of it.

"C'mon," I said, walking around her. "I'll get you some new dressing."

Nodding, she left her chair and followed me out of the main room and into the hall that led to the infirmary.

"I thought Harlei said you'd be healed by now?" I asked when the thumping sound of Pearl Jam faded enough for her to hear me speak.

Most of her injuries had healed. Her bruises were a faint yellow I could barely see, and her minor cuts were all scarred up, but there were burns that were still in the process of healing, some deeper cuts too.

Minnie shrugged. "Some injuries are in trickier places than others, I guess."

In the infirmary, Yasmine sat on the edge of the bed while I gathered what I needed to redress her wound. I washed my hands, put on gloves that were much too small for my hands, and I pulled away the old dressing. As I cleaned her wound, she watched my face.

"You smell good," she murmured, and I peered

at her as I rubbed down the edges of the occlusal bandage. "Like a motorcycle on an open road."

The corners of my lips twitched. "How much have you had to drink?"

She didn't look drunk. Her eyes weren't glassy, and her skin wasn't clammy. If anything, she looked relaxed. There was a calm about her as she gently swung her long legs back and forth.

"Enough. Not enough. I don't know." Yasmine twisted her arm to check out the job I did on her elbow. "Not bad, Mr. President."

I laughed as I gathered the rubbish and put it in the bin. I disposed of my gloves and washed my hands, like Harlei always demanded whenever I was in here touching stuff. After drying my hands, I turned around and leaned against the stainless-steel countertop. I wanted Minnie alone, but now I had her, I didn't know what to do, or what to say.

"What did you do today?" she asked, taking lead of the conversation.

I folded my arms across my chest and tilted my head. "Well, I didn't have half as much fun as you did."

She hummed, gifting me a lazy smile. "Yeah. I had a good day."

The curve in her lips drew me forward, like a moth to a flame, and her smile only grew the closer I got, until I stepped between her legs. Minnie looked up at me and I placed my hands on her thighs, pushing her dress north.

"I half-assed all my jobs today because I couldn't get you out of my head," I admitted. "You're all I thought about."

Blush bloomed in her cheeks and her eyes glistened with delight. She liked occupying my every thought. She liked being wanted and desired.

"I thought about you too," she said, placing her hands atop mine as I reached the fold between her thigh and her hip. "I shouldn't, but I can't stop."

I craned my neck and grazed her mouth with mine. "Good. I don't want you to stop."

Yasmine lifted her hands and I felt them at my belt. I was hard already, my cock straining against my zipper. I wasn't used to going this long without. I wasn't used to craving *one* woman, but I craved her with every fiber in my being.

Because I understood her.

And she understood me.

She undid my belt, then dragged my zipper down, all while keeping her stare on mine.

"Is it wrong?" she whispered. "To want to return the favor?"

I frowned, unsure what she meant until she reached into my jeans and freed my cock. *Return the favor.* We were on the same page now. I slid my hands to her backside and yanked her forward. Gasping, she wrapped her thighs around my hips.

"No. It's best you don't owe me anything."

"Why?"

"Because, sooner or later, I will collect." I flexed against her. I was hungry for her, so fucking hungry I couldn't breathe. "And if it's later, I won't be so nice."

She licked her palm and slid her wet flesh along the underside of my hard length. My breath hitched and her gold pools flared in delight as she traced every vein with her fingertips.

"You feel good in my hand."

Excitement tore down my spine and built in my pelvis. "Yeah? Try me in your mouth."

Yasmine chuckled under her breath, then swallowed the sliver of space between our lips and kissed me hard. I let her control it, let her fuck my mouth with her tongue as she wrapped her fingers around my thick shaft and jerked me off. Over and over she pushed me, pulled me, and slid her skin over mine, drawing more arousal from my body to help her slide. I grunted and groaned, and she reveled in the noises I made. I'd never come into a woman's hand before, but Minnie was close to making it happen. I didn't want to. I wanted to be buried deep inside when I came, but...*fuck*. I broke the kiss and hung my head back. She swiped her thumb over my tip, collecting slick beads of arousal.

"Oh, my god. You're so turned on," she whispered, spreading it everywhere, making it wetter, making her hand as smooth as velvet. "And that turns me on."

She squeezed me between her thighs, and I straightened my head. Her beautiful eyes were hooded and lusty, and I knew exactly what she wanted. I shoved her backward and she caught herself on the palms of her hands with a gasp.

"Judge—"

I flicked her dress over her stomach and grabbed my cock. With one hand, I palmed myself, but it didn't feel half as good. With the other, I brushed my finger along the edge of her black panties, where her thigh met the crease before her pussy started. My skin touched hers and she shuddered, lifting her hips into my touch. I pulled her panties to the side and she stilled. She was so pretty between her legs. And wet. Her arousal glistened on her bare, pink flesh under the warm lights. I touched the wet tip of my cock to the inside of her thigh and pressed my thumb to her clit. Moaning, she lifted her ass off the bed, forcing my thumb down between her creases to where her body opened up.

"Yes," she sighed. "I want you. Please."

I hummed. This wasn't the right place to fuck her. The door could open any minute and she'd be bared to whoever crossed the threshold. If that happened, she might never trust me again. No. I had to wrap this up and quick. I cupped her between her sexy legs, rubbing my palm over her clit. Yasmine flexed her hips again, shifting her ass further off the bed to get closer to my cock as I continued to stroke it against her.

"Damon," Yasmine pleaded, opening wider. "Please."

I clenched my jaw. I was of two minds. I could come on her thigh, call it even, and hoped it satisfied my hunger for her. Or I could put us both out of our misery and bury myself deep inside her. I dragged myself along her inner thigh and she watched as I moved my cock toward her pussy. I pressed my head to her clit and jerked myself against it. Yasmine sucked sharp air between her teeth and her thighs trembled as she lowered her upper body to rest on her elbows. Pressure built in my pelvis, in my fucking balls, and I couldn't stand it. I'd never been so wound up, so deliriously horny.

Fuck it.

I was going to take what was mine to take—what was owed to me since I was busting my ass for her. I was going to take what I'd wanted to take since that night she slept in my bed and pressed her ass against my cock.

Bang. Yasmine startled, crunching her body into a semi-seated position. I pulled back and strained my ears.

"Damn it, Justin," Harlei shouted, her voice muffled behind the door. "Again?"

Shit. I stuffed my still-hard cock back into my jeans as Yasmine adjusted her underwear and smoothed her dress over her thighs. I was uncomfortable, barely able to get my zipper up, and a snort from Yasmine had me cutting my eyes at her.

"You have it so easy, don't you?"

She shrugged, biting back her smile, and I just managed to get the buckle of my belt sorted when the infirmary doors opened.

"Go sit over there," Harlei snapped, pulling her blue hair into a bun on the top of her head.

Justin, the member she was with, stumbled toward the bed adjacent us. He flopped onto the bed with a groan, oblivious to us staring at him, and my gaze fell to the metal fork sticking out of his chest.

"Oh, hey, Prez. Hey, Minnie," Harlei greeted, and we waved as she moved toward the sink to wash her hands. "Is something wrong?"

I stepped back as Yasmine slipped off the edge of the bed and stood on the floor. "Judge was helping me replace the dressing on my elbow."

I looked at Harlei and saw the knowing smirk on her face, but she was smart enough not to comment.

"What happened to him?" I asked, changing the subject to the man with a fork in his chest.

I didn't know him personally, but I knew of him since he paid a ridiculous amount in club fines every quarter.

"Modo stabbed him above his clavicle with a fork. Idiot is so drunk I don't think he realizes." She dried her hands with paper towels and levelled me with her stare. "Mom wants to know why you didn't eat your dinner, Judge."

I rolled my eyes and took Minnie by her elbow. "Tell Pearl I'm a grown ass man and if I don't want dinner, then I don't want dinner."

I escorted Yasmine to the door and yanked it open.

"You sure you want me to tell her that?" Harlei called after me, and I paused as Yasmine crossed the threshold and into the hall.

No, I didn't want her to tell Pearl that. If she did, I'd be served vegan dishes for the rest of the month. I turned around and gripped the doorframe in one hand and the handle in the other.

"Just…tell her I'm sorry, will you?"

Harlei laughed and I closed her cackle inside the infirmary.

Walking side by side, Yasmine and I strolled down the hall. The music, Mötley Crüe's *Ride With The Devil,* grew louder the closer we got to the main room. Before we breached the archway, I turned my body into Yasmine's and pushed her against the wall. Her nervous breath skittered across my face as I craned my neck to speak in her ear.

"We're not finished," I told her, dragging my stare down the slope of her neck to her chest. I wanted to kiss her there, to lick between her full breasts. "You won't get away from me tonight."

And that was a promise.

TWELVE

YASMINE

My heart races as Judge rests his arm along the back of my chair, his firm forearm pressing against my shoulders. My cells are still in a flurry inside me, every fiber in my being still vibrating in the aftermath of our risqué interaction. I don't know what came over me—or him—but I won't forget how he felt in my hand for a long, long time.

Across the table, Modo talks, his British accent somehow stronger under the influence of alcohol, and everyone around him erupts with laughter. I haven't heard the sound in so long, and it's medicine to my sad, sick soul.

For no reason at all, I peer at James Creed, who relaxes in his chair, his arm around Isabelle, his handsome smile exposing his strong, white teeth. Sensing my attention, Creed flicks his stare to me, then to Judge's arm along the back of my chair. His full lips quirk at the corner, his dark eyes flashing, and my stomach sinks as heat spreads under the surface of my skin. I avert my gaze to the half empty glass of gin and tonic in front of me.

"And that's why I don't eat corn no more," Modo adds, earning more laughs.

I lift my attention to him—the funny British one with the copper beard. His smile reaches his blue eyes and his cheeks look like they could burst any minute with the amount of smiling he's done. He thrives off the attention and positivity. Making people laugh made him happy. If his skin were translucent, I bet you could see the gold rays of happiness traveling through his veins. Though rough around the edges, Modo is a handsome man. He's tall and broad shouldered, and as thick as a man should be. Best of all, I can tell he has a big heart. I don't believe for a second he stabbed that drunk man in the clavicle with a fork.

A gentle, skittering touch over my shoulder pulls me from my thoughts. I turn my head and look at Judge as he caresses my shoulder with his thumb. His slow, perfect circles causes the hair on the back of my neck to stand up. Speaking of handsome men, whatever is in the Devil Cartel's water supply needs to be investigated. I've never seen such a large group of gorgeous people. I flick my gaze to Judge's lips as he gently smiles at the conversation and their subtle curve sends my heart bashing through my ribs. It's genuine. It's not calculating or cruel and, honestly, I forgot what a real smile on a man looks like.

It melts me.

I place a subtle hand on Judge's thigh and smooth my palm along his huge chunk of muscle, until the tips of my fingers touch his inner thigh. He glances down at his lap, then meets my eyes, and a million things pass between us.

I want to go to bed.

He wants the same.

But there's no way we can both leave this table at the same time unless we want everyone in the room to know what we were going to do.

Sitting forward, Judge reaches into the middle of the table for the tall jug of water and pours the clear liquid into a clean, empty glass. Then he pulls the cup toward me and pushes my gin and tonic away.

"You've been nursing your drink for an hour." He sits back in his seat and brushes his thumb against me. "Don't have to drink it."

I smile at him, fully aware Creed is still watching, and I pat his thigh. I don't want to be disrespectful to Isabelle by not drinking my drink, but the alcohol I already drank today has worn off. I'm not in the frame of mind to start again.

"Thank you."

He offers me a smile, his eyes sparkling, then quickly diverts his attention to Casino, who adds his two cents about corn into the conversation. I sip my water, and as the refreshing, cool liquid touches my tongue, someone clears their throat. I swallow and turn my head toward the noise and—*oh, god.* The blonde woman, wearing a small, strappy black dress, puts her hands on her hips and glares down at me. Isabelle told me her name, but I can't remember. Whatever her name is, she belongs to Judge. I know he favorites her, that he chooses her over the other women. I remove my hand from his lap and take another sip of my water, wishing Judge would lower his arm from my chair. He doesn't. He doesn't stop drawing circles on my skin, either.

"Are you busy?" she asks him, crossing her arms over her chest, trapping her blonde hair against her bust.

I grip the edges of my seat and shuffle my chair, moving closer to Hawk, putting an extra inch of space between Judge and me. Finally, he drops his arm from the back of my chair.

"Excuse me," Isabelle barks, catching everyone at the table by surprise. "You're interrupting our conversation."

The woman snorts. "You're a Laurent. No one cares what you have to say."

Isabelle shoots out of her chair and it tips and crashes against the floor. "You are so fucking rude—"

I snap my attention to Judge, who lifts his

eyebrows, surprised by Isabelle's outburst. Most of the men around the table mimic Judge's expression.

"Okay, Terror," Creed sighs, pushing his drink away as he stands up. "Time to go home."

He bends low, grabs her around her waist, and lifts her over his shoulder. The men around the table slap their palms against it and make dog barking noises, quickening my pulse. Creed flips them off, continuing to carry Isabelle toward the front door.

"Yasmine! Come on," she shouts, using her palms to push off Creed's back in order to hold her head upright. She cuts her eyes at Judge. "Before you catch something."

Snickers sound around the table and Judge scowls. Maybe I shouldn't be here. Maybe it'll be easier for Judge to talk—or do whatever—to this woman if I'm not here. I ease my chair back and begin to lift myself out of it when Judge clamps his hand on my thigh, holding me in place.

I open my mouth. "Damon—"

"What do you want, Liv?" he asks, and the table breaks up into multiple small, stilted, conversations, giving us privacy.

"What I always want." I see her, out of the corner of my eye, bend toward his face. "You, baby."

She says it loud enough for me to hear and I want to throw up. I push my chair further back and lift myself off it, slipping out from Judge's heavy grip. I turn and step around Hawk, brushing my fingers along the back of his wooden seat to stabilize myself. The handful of members around the table spare me a glance as I pass by.

"Go bother someone else," Judge tells Liv.

A chair screeches against the floor and I don't need to look to know whose it is.

"Judge?" she shouts, and a deafening silence falls. "I miss you."

J U D G E

I scowled as Liv held on tight to my wrist, her volcanic pools glistening with need and desperation. She missed me? Was she fucking serious? Groaning, I turned my head and watched Yasmine get further and further away, the opposite of how tonight was supposed to end. I shook Liv off, then took her by the hand. I felt the excitement in her clammy palm as I yanked her past Casino, Armi, Stoic, and Amani. I stopped beside Modo, planted my boot on the edge of his chair, and forced it out, exposing his lap. Gripping her by her shoulders, I turned Liv's body so her ass was facing him, then I pushed her into his lap.

Swearing, he caught her with his thighs, and she slammed her palm against the table, spilling his beer.

"What the fuck, Judge?" she snapped, and I

looked at Modo.

He looked terrified and that amused me. He talked a big game, but I couldn't remember the last time I saw him with a woman. He had a tough upbringing. I knew through Ayr that Modo was uncomfortable with sex, but hey, maybe Liv did it for him.

"She's all yours," I told him, then leveled her with my gaze. "We don't fuck anymore."

Her heart broke in her face and I watched it shatter in her eyes. I tolerated her as best I could, knowing how she felt about me, but now she was fucking with my personal life. Maybe it was petty to throw her away because she was messing up my chances with Yasmine, but she signed a contract when she started here, one that stipulated she'd wouldn't interfere with the personal lives of our members. Fucking me wasn't a loophole and this was the price she'd pay for getting in my way. I had to make an example—and what respectable member turned a clubwhore into an old lady, anyway? Clubwhores weren't old lady material. That's why they're hired in the first place. They were throwaways.

"You're breaking up with me?" she shrieked, her eyes welling with tears, causing mascara to smear along her lower eyelids. "Giving me to this...this fucking *ape*?"

The men snickered. I imagined this was the best

entertainment they'd had in a while. I leaned into her face, so there was no mistaking what I was about to say.

"Fuck or leave. No one is holding you here against your will. You can end your contract at any time."

Liv swallowed hard and sniffled. Then she leaned against Modo's chest and made herself comfortable. She didn't think about it, not for a second. Of course she wasn't going to leave. They never did. The booze was free, drugs were cheap, cocks were hard, and the money was good. That was all that mattered to them. And that was why I could never fall in love with any of them—because they were weak, like my ex. The kind of woman I'd love would rather be homeless than let me put her on the knee of another man.

But Liv let me walk away and that told me more than words ever could. Not that it mattered. There's nothing she could do to stop me from pushing through the throng of drunk bikers to get to Minnie, who stood in front of Creed. I didn't like it. I didn't like the way he stared down at her, like a hungry goddamn wolf. I took as big strides as I could, but I wasn't quick enough. Creed touched her hair, a thin curl that sat against her breast and I felt her flush from here.

Motherfucker.

Between them, Blondie grinned at me and I

regretted ever toying with Creed's woman. I knew the moment I laid my arm over the back of Minnie's chair that I put a target on her back. Creed's gaze immediately fell to it and he'd found the perfect opportunity for revenge. I approached recklessly, barreling right up to them.

"Looks like you've got your hands full with that one, so Yasmine is going to stay at our place tonight," Izzy said, smiling smugly. "It'll give you and your *whore* some alone time."

My whore? Jesus Christ. She was drunk. I cut my eyes at my VP. "Get Blondie home before I take her over my knee for being so damn disrespectful."

Blondie stepped forward, squaring her shoulders. "Don't threaten me with a good time."

Creed laughed. I wasn't surprised he found it funny. He was so far up her ass it pissed me off. I blew impatient air out of my nose. I had enough. I snagged Yasmine's wrist and pulled her toward the hall. She followed, and somehow managed to keep up with my large, angry steps. I wasn't *really* angry, but frustration hung heavy in my chest. We stormed past the spare room and headed toward the door at the end of the hall: *mine*.

"Damon?" Minnie asked, slightly breathless as I pulled her along. "Are you mad at me?"

"No." But I bit the words out, and she dug her heels in, pulling against me.

"I'm not going in there with you."

I dragged her a few more steps before she ripped free of my grip. I whirled on my heel, leaned into her pretty face, and pointed at my bedroom door.

"You're gonna walk in there, or I'm gonna drag you—"

"Drag me?" She frowned and folded her arms across her chest. "Try it. I *dare* you."

I stared her down and she didn't budge. I raised my hand to swipe at my face and she lifted her shoulders with a flinch. She thought I was going to hit her? Guilt twisted through me and dug its barbs into every muscle. Why was I being aggressive toward her? She didn't do anything wrong. I just hated unexpected events, and I hated I lost control the moment she entered my clubhouse and demanded I throw her out on her ass myself. I should've left Armi to deal with her. I should've...there were many things I should've done but I didn't.

Yasmine Garcia was a spanner in the works of my life, and I didn't know why I needed her as bad as I did...

...I just did.

She symbolized everything I wanted, everything my daughter needed, and I guess I clung to the illusion I subconsciously developed. Minnie was a mom, and I adored mothers—*good mothers*. Maybe finding a good mother made the guilt in my chest less heavy, maybe that's why I coveted Yasmine so much.

I straightened my spine and moistened my lips. I had to apologize, but I hadn't said sorry in a long time, not for anything. Last time I said it was the day we lowered Nila's casket into the ground. Exhaling, I turned toward my door and twisted the handle. I pushed it open and looked at Minnie. She glanced inside, then at me. Her face softened, as if accepting my silent apology, and she stepped forward, entering my room. I followed, closing the door behind us.

Inside, Yasmine slipped out of her shoes, then made her way toward my bed to peer up at the night sky through the skylight. The light of the moon drenched her, making her skin and flyaways glow.

"It's a full moon," she said as I took off my boots and socks.

I stepped toward her. "Yasmine—"

"You don't owe me an explanation," she cut in, avoiding my gaze. "I'm not here to judge you or tell you how to live. I'm here for my son. That's all."

I sauntered closer, closing the distance between us, and I stood close behind her. "That's all?"

I touched her wrists as she hung her arms by her sides, and smoothed my palms up her forearms to her elbows, making her hang her head.

"Damon…"

"You don't like it?" I asked, sliding my palms up her biceps to her shoulders, then onto her neck and, finally, I pushed my fingers into her hair to massage her scalp.

"I love it," she whispered, tilting her head, guiding me to where she wanted me to touch her. "It feels good."

I stayed there for a small eternity, massaging her scalp, and touching her long, perfect hair. She smelled of coconut and raspberries. Nothing in this clubhouse has ever smelled of coconut and raspberries, and the sweet scent made my mouth water. I brushed Minnie's hair over one shoulder, then eased her flush against me, her back to my torso.

"Liv upset you," I said, lowering my mouth to her neck. I kissed her behind the ear, loving the way she shivered against me. "It won't happen again."

"I don't need your assurances, Damon." She lifted her arm and wrapped it around my neck. "Just your hands, and your lips."

I kissed her again and she sighed. I moved my hands to her sides and caressed her from her ribs to her hips, until her blissful sighs morphed into cute, little moans. Yasmine lowered her arm from my neck, and I wasted no time pushing the thin straps of her dress off her shoulders.

"I got rid of her," I told Minnie, for no reason at all. "I don't want her anymore."

"I don't care, Judge."

But she cared. I knew she did. Otherwise, why

would she leave? I felt the way her body stiffened when Liv approached, and how quick she pulled her hand from my thigh.

She cared. She just didn't want to care, to protect her feelings.

I grabbed Yasmine by the shoulders and turned her to face me. Her bare breasts swayed with the movement, only snatching my attention for a second, then we made eye contact.

And I stared at her, *into* her.

"You don't care?" I asked, my voice a husky whisper. "Or maybe you care too much?"

I wanted her to look at me while I touched her. I wanted her to see me and to see that I was making room in my life for her. Short term, or long term, I could accommodate her—and her son. I could take care of them.

I touched her waist and followed the curve of her body to her hips. She was softer here and around her belly, and it drove me crazy. I hooked my thumbs around the band of her underwear and pushed, but she stopped me as I was about to push the fabric over the curve of her ass.

"Maybe you're right," she said, flicking her gaze between my eyes and my lips. "Maybe I care too much."

Yasmine pushed her underwear down to her feet by herself and kicked them to the side. Stepping away from me, she turned and crawled onto my bed. Her bronzed body glowed in the moonlight, like that night on the lake, and it took everything I had in me to stay rooted where I stood.

"Are you going to stop at my scalp?" she asked, peering over her shoulder before lying flat on her stomach. "Because there are other places I liked to be massaged."

I shrugged out of my cut and it fell to the floor. Then, I yanked off my tee and my pulse quickened at the thought of finally putting my hands on Minnie's naked body. No one could interrupt me here. She was mine. All night.

And I was going to make the most of every second.

YASMINE

Judge holds my body between his thighs, the rough feel of his jeans causing goosebumps to erupt along my sensitive flesh. Digging in with the tips of his fingers, then following with the heels of his giant hands, Judge kneads my muscles with surprising skill and grace. I hum, struggling to hold my heavy eyelids open.

"What'd Creed say to you?" he asks, running the pads of his thumbs down each side of my spine until he reaches the curve of my backside. "When he touched your hair."

Warmth blossoms in my cheeks. "Nothing."

He makes a low noise in his chest, like a growl, and I feel his hand in my hair as he snakes it across my scalp. He lifts my head off the bed, and I tuck my elbows underneath my chest, lifting my upper body as he twists my head to the side.

"You wouldn't lie to me, would you?"

I turn my torso and Judge lifts his weight off my backside, allowing me to turn my body underneath him. He releases my hair and settles on my pelvis as I lie on my back and stare up at him. He's as gorgeous as ever from this angle, and I flick my attention over the ridges of his abdominals to his face.

"He called me bait," I confess, folding one arm underneath my breasts, the other across my middle, shielding myself from his heated gaze. "You're newest little plaything."

Judge arches a brow. "That all?"

The fact he doesn't deny it makes my pulse race.

"He said he was going to have fun with me." I moisten my lips. "Why would he say that?"

He glances across the room and lets out a heavy exhale. "Long story short?"

"Preferably."

"I slept with Izzy."

He meets my eyes and I lift my eyebrows, my mouth falling open. A pang of jealousy hits my gut. "And he knows?"

"He was there."

Oh. For some reason, embarrassment spreads up my neck and builds in my face. I know they're close I just didn't realize they were *that* close. "The three of you?"

"Yes." Judge leans on the bed, his palm beside my head, and moves his knee to the space between my legs. He forces them open, then settles between them, and the rough denim fabric of his jeans elicits goosebumps on my inner thighs. His lips quirk. "And I've made his life hell since."

"Why?"

"Because I thought I knew what I wanted."

"Her?" I ask, my stomach tying itself into painful knots. Judge dips his head, bringing his mouth toward mine. "Him?"

He pulls back, and I smirk as he screws up his face. "Are you serious?"

"What? It's twenty-twenty."

Sighing, Judge rolls off me and lies flat on his back. I turn my body toward him and rest against his side. We lie in the silence, staring up at the inky, star-studded sky that douses us in cool moonlight.

"You wanted her?" I ask, unsure I want the answer.

"Thought I did." He keeps his attention on the skylight. "I only wanted what Creed had—what I never had with Nila's mother. Thought Blondie could fill the emptiness, or something."

"Wanting the best for your child is a heavy

burden to carry," I whisper. "Failing to give it to them creates a void I don't think ever goes away."

"You called me a good dad. That made the void a little smaller." Judge turns his large body in my direction and brushes hair off my neck. "You're a good mom, doing everything you can to help Nicolás...even if it means being with me."

"You think I don't want to be with you?"

"Jumping from one criminal to another? It weighs heavily on you. I know it's not what you want—not for yourself, or your son."

Every word that falls from his perfect mouth is the truth and I can't remember the last time I had a conversation so raw and candid. Isabelle and I spoke a lot today, but it wasn't deep. I avoided talking about my son, my past, and Judge as much as she avoided discussing her past and Creed.

"I don't know what I want," I tell him, propping my head on my hand. "What should I want?"

Judge shrugs a shoulder. "Aren't you tired of men telling you what you want?"

I straighten my spine and swallow hard as his words strike a chord in me. "I...I am tired. Every day spent with Elias was on his terms. Every decision was his to make and all I did was follow. He chose my meals, my clothes, where we travelled, and who I spoke to. I woke every morning to a schedule I didn't design and obligations I didn't choose. In his control, I lost myself."

I'm a shell of the woman I once was. I keep the thought from falling from my tongue. Once upon a time, I was confident and steadfast. I knew what I wanted, when I wanted it, and how I was going to get it. If I'm going to survive out here, a single mother with a special needs child, I need to rebuild myself, to be strong and self-assured. I glance at Judge's mouth as he licks his lower lip. I know sleeping with him isn't going to rebuild me overnight, but it's a good first foothold. *Right?*

I lean forward and I kiss him. I kiss him because I want to.

Because I *need* to.

Judge reciprocates with as much vigor as I give, and I feel the heat of every flick of his tongue all over my body. I inhale him as deep as I can, getting so fucking high on my need for him. He brushes his tongue against mine, and bites at my lips, driving me insane. Judge groans and rolls in my direction and covers me with his body. He breaks the kiss by trailing his mouth along my jaw and down my neck where he bites my tender flesh and flicks his tongue against my pulse.

I reach between us and unfasten his belt, then work on his jeans. I manage to get them over the curve of his muscular ass and halfway down his thighs when his hard arousal springs free, his hot flesh scorching against my core. I smooth my hand against Judge's shoulder blade, feeling the shape and power of it as he holds his heavy weight off my body. I wander my fingers up the back of his neck, then grip the short hair at his nape and pull, lifting his mouth from my flesh as he hisses. I bring his nose to mine and his dark, chaotic blue eyes flash. I open my mouth to say…*something*…but words fail me. How do I ask someone I don't really know to keep his mouth on mine? How do I confess kissing him is my new favorite thing in the world without sounding like a psychopath?

As if reading my mind, Judge kisses me, and I release his hair and melt into it, into him. In a second, his kiss turns rough and possessive as he crushes me under his weight. Hot flushes bloom over my body and flare with every flick of his tongue. I'm lost in his mouth and the way a strange buzzing vibrates under my skin, travelling across my face and down my neck to warm my chest. Judge presses between my legs and I lose my breath, knowing how good it'll feel to have him deep inside me.

Holding me captive in his kiss, Judge reaches between us to grab his length and glides the head of his cock through my creases, covering himself with my heated flesh. I hold my breath as he braces at my entrance and eases inside. I gasp, breaking the kiss, and he slows, not pushing any further than the tip. It's been a while since I've been with a man. After Elias, I had no desire to be intimate with another man again, but Judge…he makes it feel right. Nothing in my life has felt right in a long time.

Exhaling, Judge's warm breath skitters across my cheeks and he grazes his lips across mine. "Want me to take it slow?"

"No." I smooth my hand down his bicep and he lifts, giving me access to slide my palm against his. "Don't go slow."

Judge threads our fingers together and rests our hands above my head. Blood pulsates in my skull, covering my head like a throbbing helmet, and my heart races, battering my lungs. Keeping his eyes on mine, Judge slides his free hand under my backside and grabs my ass. I hold my breath as he angles my pelvis and pushes all the way inside with a husky groan, using his big thighs to push mine wide open. Slick sweat builds between our naked bodies, and I writhe beneath him as he stretches me, inch by inch, until he can't anymore. Then he pulls out, only to plunge right back in—harder this time. His grip turns vicious, his gentle lips a hungry demand against mine, and I try to keep up, to return his energy, but *god*, he's a force. Where Elias is lean and suave, Judge is thick and reckless, and somehow, he fills the cracks, a soothing glue to the painful holes Elias left in my soul. With every thrust, he makes a tight noise in his throat and it sets fire to my blood. Every push of his body creates friction and electricity. It creates a freaking supercell of energy deep in my pelvis.

And we don't speak.

What's there to say? I fear if one of us opens our mouths, this will stop. I don't want to stop. I don't want a single whisper to bring either of us back to our senses. I wonder if our words can even be heard over the passionate sounds we make. With one hand, Judge keeps his fingers tightly threaded through mine. With the other, he uses it to roam my body, exploring every inch of me, and every fingerprint left in his wake is left with purpose. He may never know it, but his touch is healing. He makes me feel like everything will be okay, like my son is safe even though he's not in my arms.

I'm pulled from my thoughts by Judge's thick arms as he digs them underneath my body. Crushing me to him, he rolls onto his back and pulls me on top. His length probes deeper inside me, reaching its maximum point, and I plant my hands on his wide, muscular chest. I sit back, straightening my spine, and peer down at him as arousal throbs mercilessly between my legs. The cool moonlight from above brightens his features and casts light over the rises and depressions of his body, adding silver highlights to his moody black ink. I rock my hips, moving us together, as Judge smooths his rough hands along my thighs. Heat blooms under my skin in the wake of his touch and I shiver, opening my thighs wider, rocking faster.

"You're a sexy bitch," Judge says, dragging his dark, hungry stare to my face.

His esteeming gaze almost has me believing he hasn't had a woman in a while. It almost has me believing he hasn't had a woman his whole life.

I arch a brow. "Bitch?"

He plants his wide palm on the back of my neck and pulls my face to his. Kissing me roughly on the mouth, he turns his head and drags his lips along my cheek to my ear.

"Yeah. *Bitch*." I feel his lips quirk and he moves his face in front of mine. His eyes flash. "What, you don't like it?"

I don't know much about their customs, but I know the term "bitch" isn't necessarily a bad thing. Still, it burns my ears. "I'm not enthusiastic about it."

"Are you my woman?"

I stop moving, not anticipating that kind of question. "I…"

I don't know what to say. Judge grabs my hips, thrusts his, and pins me on my back, driving hard and deep. Seemingly irritated, he hooks his hands underneath my knees and pushes them toward my chest. I gasp flies from my mouth, along with the air from the deepest parts of my lungs.

"You're in my head, in my bed, and I haven't thought twice about not wearing a condom," he rasps, digging his fingers into my flesh. "I'm feeling every deep inch of you, and I think that makes you my woman." He leans forward and I moan as wild lust surges through me. "My *bitch*."

"That's not how it works."

Judge releases my legs and I let them slide flat as he drops his torso against me, grinding his pelvis against mine. "That's how it works around here."

Before I can open my mouth to protest, he kisses me, plunging his tongue between my lips. He groans into my mouth and alternates his thrusts between shallow and deep, soft and hard. Every cell in my being hones in on the sensations exploding from between my legs. *So what if I'm his? Is that such a bad thing?* I break the kiss and wrap my arms around his waist. I arch my back, smooth my palms to the tight muscles of Judge's shoulders, and crunch my body, moving my face into the nape of his neck. I lick him there, where his shoulder slopes, and feel him shiver against me.

"You feel good," he murmurs, tilting his head, giving me more skin to lick and kiss. "So fucking good."

Judge picks up his tempo and I dig my nails into his back, holding on for dear life as he pounds into me over and over, bringing my orgasm to the forefront of my mind.

"Yes," I sigh on exhale, falling back against the pillows. I grip one in my hand. "Yes."

With my other hand, I grip his powerful bicep and relax my tightening thighs. With the newfound space, Judge dives his hand between my legs and drops his head to my chest with a groan. He fists himself, feeling how well we fit together, then circles my tiny bundle of nerves. It doesn't take me long after that. The heat of my orgasm crashes into me with all the power of a solar flare and scrambles every cell in my body. He talks to me, but his words fall on ringing ears, his hot breath on buzzing skin. It isn't until he pulls his hand from between my legs to grip the headboard, I realize what he said. Ragged gasps fall from his lips and his rhythmic thrusts become stilted and jerky. Then I feel heat as it spreads through me and into...*nothing*. The feeling causes tears to spring to my eyes, a bitter reminder nothing will ever grow inside me again, I suppose.

I turn my head, expecting Judge to leave me on the bed and shower. Instead, he holds his softening length inside me and lowers his head to my cheek. He purses his lips and tries to regulate his breathing through his nose, before planting a soft kiss on my cheekbone. The gentle act tightens my chest.

"I want you," Judge says, matter of fact, and it stirs a nostalgic apprehension in my stomach. "You are mine."

I don't turn my head to look him in the eyes. "Last time someone said that to me, they ruined my life."

"Me too."

I inhale and turn my head. Our noses graze. Although we're different shapes, maybe we're cut from the same cloth when it comes to relationships.

I lick my lower lip. "You have to promise you won't hurt me."

"I promise." The words leave his lips without hesitation and his gaze remains steadfast and serious. His lips quirk, and although shadow covers his face, I see the shine in his eyes. "Easiest promise I've ever made."

"Then…" I swallow hard, praying I don't live to regret the next four words that fall from my lips. "I am yours, Damon."

He buries his head into the space beside my neck and exhales. Letting out an anxious breath of my own, I stare up into the lightening sky and chew the inside of my lip. It's dangerous uttering those words to him, knowing what secrets I'm keeping. If he ever finds out, he'll have no choice but to break his promise.

THIRTEEN

JUDGE

I felt the late morning sun on my face, bright and warm, but it wasn't enough to coax me into opening my eyes. I knew if I did, I'd have to slide into my cut and get on with the day. I wasn't ready. I wanted to stay in bed with Minnie until the sun sank over the horizon. I brushed my thumb along the underside of her breast, and she shifted her naked body against mine. She sat perfectly against my thighs, our bodies aligned, her long goddamn hair in my face. I blew air out my mouth, an attempt to get her light strands off my lips, but it fell back, tickling my lower lip. Exhaling, I shifted, turning away from her, and made the mistake of opening my eyes. The smallest glance was all it took. I paused at the sight of five of my men in my room.

"What the fuck?" I swore, swiping my hand over my face as I sat up.

They stood there and stared, all of them dressed in their leather cuts, all of them invading my private space. None looked happy. Their presence cut sharply through the bliss and stuck like a knife in my spine. *Something's happened.*

"She's a fucking cop, Judge!" Casino boomed, fisting a stack of paper. "It's no wonder Elias Vergara wants her dead."

I frowned and glanced at Creed, who leaned against the doorframe, a mix of anger and sympathy on his face, his arms folded tightly over his chest. Scoffing, Casino threw the papers onto my bed and they scattered, some hitting the floor.

"Read it," he demanded. "You fucked up, Prez."

Beside me, the mattress dipped, and I looked at Minnie as she sat up, gathering the white sheets at her chest. I didn't need to read the papers. Her face said it all. *She's a cop.*

And I've fucked up.

A thick tendril of regret burrowed through me, along with a sickness I'd never felt. It was a chill, almost, and I hated the way it made my skin feel. I looked to Creed again, for answers, but all he gave me was a tilt of his head and a drum of his fingers against his bicep. It was my call. I had to deal with it.

Minnie's warm, slender hand pulled me from my thoughts as she smoothed it up my back, to my shoulder. Her touch cracked my shock and rage shone through.

"Damon—"

I shrugged her off and flicked my head in her direction. "String her up in the fucking barn."

"The barn? Damon, please. Please, you have to hear me out—"

I tuned out Minnie's protests, her pleading as she begged me to hear her out. Casino stormed around the bed and grabbed her. She thrashed against him, desperately clinging to the sheets that covered her body. Creed and Armi had to help him, and the three of them had no trouble ripping her from my bed, as naked as she was when she fell asleep.

"Wait, wait! I can explain—Damon!" she shrieked from the hall, her shouts a fading noise.

Exhaling, I dropped against my pillow. This was just my luck. I knew it was too good to be true because it always was. That was how my life went. Finally fell in *like* with a woman and she turned out to be the bane of my existence. I should've sent her away the first night she came, made Wrench repair the bikes on his own. I should've left her to die on the drive the night she blew up a motel…

…but that was never gonna happen.

I was intrigued by Yasmine Garcia the moment I met her down by the lake. The more I thought of her, and her betrayal, the tighter my chest got. I cleared my throat and shifted on the bed with a groan. My pulse quickened, my heart palpitating in my chest. I tried to moisten my dry mouth as my skin prickled all over. Was I having a stroke? I drew deep breaths through my nose and out my mouth as the off feeling quickly passed. *What the hell?*

"Did you know?" Creed's voice infiltrated my ears and I stilled, stuffing the shitty apprehension deep down in my gut.

I only knew what Rah and Casino told me. This was on them as much as it was on me.

"You think I would've let her into the clubhouse if I knew? Or have her in my bed?" I shook my head. "They brought me pictures of her kid, but not her badge? Un-fucking-believable."

"Do you love her?" he asked, not letting the silence grow for a second between us.

"No." But I wanted to love her, and I could love her, eventually. Just not at the cost of my club. "No. I don't."

"Then what are you worried about?"

I blew air from my lips. I was worried I was gonna walk into the barn and turn on my brothers...for a woman I clearly knew nothing about, for a goddamn pig. I sat up and turned my body, swinging my legs over the side of the bed to plant my feet on the soft, plush rug.

"I'm not worried," I lied.

"What're you gonna do?"

I dropped my head back, tired of the damn questions. "She's a cop, Creed. I'll do what I have to, to protect the chapter."

***

I smoothed a hand down my cut before I grabbed the rusted handle of the giant, black barn and pulled the door open. Everyone was inside—everyone who mattered, at least. Creed, Armi, Casino, Stoic, Ayr, Modo, Hawk, Rah, and Amani. The rest of the members were in the clubhouse and out doing God knows what. They were none the wiser to what was going on down the back of the property. I entered the rustic building, hating the smell of dust and dry grass, and let the heavy door fall closed with a slam behind me. I dragged my attention over Modo and Ayr who stood at the back by the broken-down tractor, their heads hung as if I interrupted their whispers. Everyone else stood far apart, flanking each side of the long room. I felt their stares on me as I walked the thin, white line on the floor, courtesy of the swinging lights above. At the end of the line, Minnie sat, naked and roped to an old wooden chair. I clenched the roll of paper in my hand and swallowed hard. She was still on my skin.

Her love. Her fucking lies.

"Damon," she said, her voice broken and tired. "Damon, please."

Six feet from her, I turned and handed the papers to Casino. It was all there, printed in black ink. She was Detective Yasmine Garcia of Oakland, California. She was handpicked by the FBI to infiltrate Elias Vergara's life and deliver him on a silver platter once she gathered enough evidence to back up the allegations against him. I saw a picture of the day she was sworn in and she was as beautiful then as she was now, and the thought made me sick. A lot of thoughts made me sick. Was she still reporting to her superiors? Would fucking me make an appearance in her report? I thought back to the nights she was here at the clubhouse. Were any of us doing anything we'd get nailed for? The FBI just finished up on their never-ending investigation surrounding our chapter and it nearly crippled us. Fuck going through that again. Maybe this time there wouldn't be much of an investigation. Maybe she gave the evidence they needed to put us all away.

"Judge, listen to me—"

"Shut your mouth, *pig!*" Casino barked over my shoulder and I absorbed my flinch.

Angry heat spread up my neck, but there wasn't a damn thing I could do. She was the enemy and I had to treat her like it.

"Did you get to the end of the report?" she snapped back. "I fucking deserted! I'm not a cop anymore."

Casino snorted. "Once a cop, always a cop."

We've had defected cops in the fold before,

difference was we knew about it and they jumped through hoops to join us. Yasmine sniffled and I turned away from Casino before I punched him again. Why was he so riled up? It wasn't like she strung him along like an idiot.

"You should hear her out, Prez," Armi uttered as I approached him. Like he always did whenever we had someone tied up on this chair, he handed me my knife. "No sense in killing her if she no longer bleeds blue."

"Got a soft spot for pigs, Armi?" I asked, in fear everyone in this room saw right through me.

"Got a soft spot for innocent human beings," he shot back. "You do too."

I licked my lips and turned toward Minnie. She kept her head down, her long hair covering her face. The warm light that swung on a cord above her head cast bright highlights over her exposed, damp skin and dark shadows everywhere else.

I carried many burdens on my shoulders, many regrets, and many bad deeds. This was just another stone to add to the pile. I'd learn to carry the weight, like I always had. I wish it were different, but it wasn't, and I'd demand any of my men to murder their love interest if she betrayed them the way I'd been betrayed. I glanced at the knife in my hand. It was impeccably clean despite its past. How many traitors had I killed with this blade? Too many, so many I couldn't remember anymore.

Creed snatched my bicep as I passed by, pulling me out of my head.

"Sorry," he murmured, his eyes displaying the sincerity leaking through his tone. "Really."

"For what?"

He tilted his head and the disappointment in his stare was more than I could stand. He was sorry Yasmine wasn't the woman I thought she was. He was sorry she couldn't be mine.

I was sorry too.

I shrugged him off and rolled my shoulders to adjust my hoodie and cut. I approached Minnie and stood under the flood of light that drenched her naked body.

"You promised," she whispered, and I flinched.

She was stupid to hang her life on a promise after the information she withheld from me. What was I supposed to do? Turn around and tell my men, *sorry, I pinky promised some bitch I wouldn't hurt her?* I was fucking president of this chapter and I swore an oath to be as cold as ice and as hard as stone. I was the judge, the jury, and the executioner, and she'd die by my hand. Clenching my jaw, I pressed the blade to her chin, and she hissed, lifting her head as I guided it. When it was straight, I used the sharp tip to push her hair out of her face, and I met her dark eyes. My heart pounded and sweat gathered on my forehead.

I parted my lips to speak. "You—"

"Damon! Stop!" A frantic and familiar voice squealed through the barn and bounced off the walls.

Frowning, I turned to see Blondie storming down the center toward me. What the fuck was she doing here? Like a decayed tooth, this clusterfuck of a hole grew deeper the more it was opened. She stomped her little white flats, her pale blue summer dress bounced around her thighs, and no one made a move to grab her. I had a handful of America's most ruthless men under this roof and every single one of them feared their VP's little blonde nightmare because of the shadow that followed her.

Blondie closed the distance and shoved my chest before Creed finally intervened, grabbing her by the waist and cussing her out. He covered her mouth before she said anything that could get her tied to a chair beside Yasmine, and he dragged her ass out. Modo whistled and snickered and I'd reached my limit for one morning.

"Get the hell out," I boomed. "All of you."

"I'm not going anywhere," Casino said. "Not until she's dead."

I cocked my knife back and sent it flying in his direction. Lucky for him, it embedded itself in an old wine barrel beside his neck. My nostrils flared. If he refused to leave, I'd kill him. Armi grabbed Casino by the cut and dragged him out, trailing behind everyone else who had no problem leaving.

When the barn door closed, I waited a beat, then hung my head and exhaled. In the silence, I was free. There was no pressure to deliver the swift and brutal punishment my men expected.

"You lied to me," I said an eternity later.

"I never lied to you," she replied, the words quick to fall from her lips, as if she knew what I was going to say. I slowly turned to face her. "Not when we first met, not the night in the backseat of that truck, not last night when we…" she moistened her lips. "I've never lied to you, Damon."

"You're a cop."

"I was. In another life, it feels like." Her eyelids fluttered as tears welled. "I loved my job, and I was good at it, but that's not me anymore. I'm a shell of the woman I once was."

"A shell?"

She shook her head as if clearing her thoughts. "I'm less. Just less."

My heart pounded in my chest and I clenched my fists against the urge to grab her shoulders and shake her hard. She wasn't less. Less would never be enough to hold my attention—and she had all of it.

"I want to know everything."

"You read it."

"I want to hear it."

She pursed her lips. I waited and waited for her to say something, to give me a fucking reason to let her walk out of this building, to let her live. I waited some more. *Nothing? She had nothing to say?*

"You betrayed *me*!" I shouted and if Minnie weren't tied down, she'd have hit the ceiling.

"I didn't," she sobbed, shaking her head. "I wouldn't."

I stayed rooted in my spot as she hung her head and cried. Every sniffle made my temple pulsate, and every sob sent a chill down my spine.

I gritted my teeth and spoke through them. "I said I wanted to know everything. So, speak."

She dragged air through her nose and out through her mouth before she glanced up at the ceiling. "I was assigned to Elias Vergara and it blew up in my face."

"How?"

"Elias figured out I was a cop pretty early on, but I was none the wiser. He went above and beyond to make me fall in love with him…and I fell so easily. After months of having no information to give my superiors, and after the news of our engagement broke, they stripped me of my titles and my badge." Her stare found mine. "They turned their backs on me when I needed them the most, Damon. I have no loyalty to the law."

Do I believe her? I don't know. Turning away, I crossed the floor and yanked my knife out of the empty wine barrel. Yasmine kept her attention on the blade as I approached, visibly deflating with every step I took. If I let her live and it ever got out, it would put me on shaky ground with not only my chapter, but every chapter. There was only one way around this clusterfuck.

"I could kill you," I told her, pressing the tip of the blade into my index finger. "Or you could prove your loyalty."

Her plump, lower lip trembled. "H-how?"

As I opened my mouth, an ear-splitting bang sounded not far off in the distance and it shook the ground, seemingly tilting the world off its axis. My gaze met Yasmine's terrified eyes.

"Was that—"

Another explosion roared, followed swiftly by the sound of shattering glass and hoarse shouts of my men. Adrenaline tore through my veins, as aggressive as heroin, and I dived at Minnie to cut her ropes.

"Hide," I told her, glancing around the barn as I crouched to cut the ties at her ankles. "there's an old tornado bunker down the back of the barn. Get in it."

"Do you think it's him? Elias?" she asked and the panic in her voice stood the hairs up on the back of my neck.

"Could be anybody." As she lifted herself out of the chair, I shrugged out of my cut, pulled my hoodie off, and handed it to her. "Here."

Without thanks, she grabbed it and slipped it on

over her head. I picked up my cut and pulled it on over my black tee, then I stormed to the nearest gap between two wooden slats. I peered toward the clubhouse and caught black smoke billowing over the hill. *Fuck!* The barn door flew open and crashed into the wall. I whipped my handgun from the waistband at the back of my jeans and pointed it at Blondie as she stumbled through the door, Creed hot on her heels.

"Iz? Creed?" I started forward as he slammed the heavy door behind him. "What the hell is happening?"

"We're under attack. They've got rocket fucking launchers, assault rifles, and at least fifty men."

Shit. "Where's Armi?"

"Went in through the back of the clubhouse to get to the armory."

"Good." The sooner we got him on a weapon, the better our chances. I looked at Isabelle, who stood beside Creed. She was as stiff as a board, her face a sickly pale shade, and her chest rose and fell a million miles a minute. "Put her in the old bunker with Yasmine."

Creed took Isabelle by the wrist and tugged her closer to him. "No."

I didn't have time for this shit. I shouldered past him. "It's her funeral."

YASMINE

I stare at Isabelle's blank face. I don't think I've seen anyone so pale. Her blue eyes are dark and stormy, as if she's watching scenes from her past play on her retinas.

"Isabelle," I whisper, pushing strands of her long, blonde hair out of her face. I'm worried for her. I've said her name eight times since Creed brought her down here and I've got nothing back. "Are you okay?"

"I'm sorry," she finally responds, her eyes welling with tears. "I can't right now."

I let out a gentle sigh and sit back on an old milk crate. I'm thankful Judge's hoodie covers my backside since there aren't any comfortable places to sit save for the mesh cot where Isabelle resides. I startle as the sound of close gunfire punctuates the silence, sending my heart up my throat. It goes on and on until my knee aches from bouncing my leg so hard, and I've bitten my nails down as far as they'll go. *Screw this.* I can't just sit here and do nothing. If it *is* Elias's men out there, then they're here for me.

I lift myself off the crate and move toward the rickety shelf against the back wall. Cans line most of the shelves, their labels faded and illegible. I grab the old pair of men's sneakers and bang them upside down against the cracked concrete floor to make sure nothing sinister is hiding inside. Then I slip my feet inside and wiggle my toes in the extra space before pulling the frayed laces tight. Nerves eat away my stomach lining, but I need to do something. I refuse to die in the bunker of an old barn, like a sad mouse in a shoebox.

"I can't sit here and wait," I say to Isabelle, spotting a lead pipe against the bunker's stairs, and straighten my posture. "I can close the hatch, but you'll need to lock it."

She doesn't budge, not a nod of her head or a flicker of her eyelids to acknowledge what I've said. I feel bad for her. Whatever happened between her and her father must've been bad. I saw her feet when we went to the spa, I saw how scarred they are. Right now, she's as shut up as a clam, as if there's nobody home. Exhaling, I make for the stairs and grab the lead pipe. As I climb the stairs, I spare Isabelle one last glance before I push on the hatch and slip into the noisy darkness. I gently close the hatch behind me and shuffle forward, crouching as low as I can. The bulbs that previously hung on cables from the rafters are out, and deep, pounding thuds of flesh slamming flesh sounds in the near distance. Masculine and pained groans fill the air, a sickening symphony in my ears.

"Fuck off," I hear Creed growl, followed by the snap of a bone and a howl of pain.

Then a bang and a flash of light to my left.

Finally, as my eardrums ring, my eyes adjust and Creed is storming toward me, a plank of bloodied wood in one hand, and a handgun in the other.

"What the hell are you doing?" he booms, towering over my crouched form. He points toward the hatch with the gun. "Get back in the bunker!"

I stand tall, clenching the cold lead pipe in my clammy palm. "No."

Creed leans in close, so close I feel his warm, labored breath skitter across my cheeks. "If you die, you die. I'm not helping you."

As the last syllable leaves his lips, the barn door is thrown open and a handful of men dressed head to toe in black rush in. The door falls closed behind them and they gasp into the darkness. Creed takes me by the wrist and squeezes, a silent demand to remain quiet and still. In Spanish, one of the intruder's commands to know if anyone is in the barn. Another requests light from a flashlight. *Where's Damon?*

I swallow hard, and whisper, "Is it just you and me?"

"Yes. Scared, little piggy?"

When was the last time I fought multiple people? Or the last time I disarmed someone? I haven't worked out in years, so my muscle mass and endurance levels are minimal at best. The sweat in my palms multiplies tenfold. *Maybe I should've stayed in the bunker.* "Yeah."

The dark barn flashes with blaring golds and blinding whites before I feel the heat at my back and a deafening bang cracks through the air, making my ears ring louder than ever.

"Shit!" Creed shouts, pulling me to the floor.

He crushes my small body beneath his, the pit of his arm shielding my face. I squeeze my eyes shut, but the bright light of day intrudes on the darkness as splintered wood and shrapnel cascades over us, mimicking heavy rain and hail on the old concrete floor.

I let out a rush of air as Creed lifts his body off me, every movement dropping pieces of wood on me, and rushes forward, his arm outstretched. I roll onto my side and draw in a large breath, inhaling dust and God knows what. It tickles my throat and burns the sensitive lining of my lungs, and I cough until my lungs hurt as I lift myself onto my hands and knees. I focus on regaining my balance, my equilibrium, as gunfire tears around the room— short trigger bursts, then long, automatic roars. The world around me hisses and crackles, and sparks flicker around the barn as bullets hit rusted metal objects.

I turn my head and peer through the gaps in the ancient rowboat frame to my right. Creed fights two men, both now disarmed, and he's getting the beating of a lifetime. *Shit.* I grab my lead pipe and force myself to my feet. I head toward Creed as quick as I can. Ten feet out, he shoves the smaller attacker off his feet, sending him sliding along the floor in my direction, and focuses on fighting off the bigger guy. The one on the floor spots Creed's handgun to the right and scrambles for it. My heart leaps into my throat, pumping me with so much adrenaline my fingers tremble.

And I freeze.

The goon grabs the handgun and lifts himself to his feet. My lips part, my world slows as he points the gun at Creed, his forearm perfectly extended. He waits for his chance, waits for a clear shot at the club's vice president and I watch, helplessly, as Creed growls, his handsome face contorted with a mix of anger and exhaustion. He thrusts forward and the fabric of his attacker's hoodie splits in half. Whatever Creed pushes through his chest rips out his back, dripping blood all over the floor. Creed lifts his dark gaze and spots the gun. He looks at me, then shoves the impaled body away. I'm already moving. As if my body is on autopilot, I shoot forward and grab the guy's lean arm and he shouts as I yank it to the side. He squeezes the trigger and the vibration from the shot ripples up his arm and into my palm. I gasp as the smoking bullet embeds in an old plank of wood beside Creed's head. The vibration from the shot ignites something in my veins—something I haven't felt in a long time. It bubbles along, mixing with the adrenaline already coursing through me, and—*God*—it's powerful.

Addictive.

I shove him forward and lift my pipe as he whirls on his heel. Our eyes lock and my lead pipe meets his face. His body hits the floor with a thud.

"Jesus," Creed says on exhale, then flicks his head in my direction. "They're all yours."

All mine? I turn as two more of Elias's men enter the barn through the massive hole blown in it. Thankfully, they don't carry any guns and the smug relief on their faces when they see me without a gun myself tells me the feeling is mutual. I gently swing the heavy pipe in my hand, feeling more like myself than I have in a long time, then I bring it up around my head and bend my knees as if I'm going to bat.

"Elias isn't happy with you," the lanky one on the left says, his foreign accent thick.

"What's new?" I reply, clenching my pipe.

They dive at me, gaining more distance in a single bound than I anticipated. Shocked, I drop my pipe and duck a flying fist as it's thrown toward my face. My stomach drops, but my heart picks it back up again and I ball my fist, push down on my legs, and drive my knuckles into my attacker's ribs. He stumbles back, clenching his side. Surprised, the second guy whips a handgun from his waistband and points it at me. Creed booms my name, but I'm already on it. I zip to the left, then the right, before gripping the thug's hand and wrist. I snap it back, turning his gun on him and I push forward. Trapped, he squeezes the trigger and unloads two bullets into his chest. I take the gun as he falls like a tree and turn it on the other guy. He dives forward, grabbing me around my thighs, driving me back with his powerful shoulder. My feet come off the floor and I'm slammed onto my back. The back of my head hits the ground, and shooting stars disable my vision as air is forced from my lungs. He climbs on top of me, his weight too much for my frame, and wrestles me for the gun. If he gets it, I'm as good as dead. I shoot at nothing, emptying the clip before he can use it on me, and it makes him mad. My vision returns just as I catch a fist to my mouth. My lip splits and burns against my teeth, my head is tossed to the side, and my vision goes again.

"Minnie!" Creed shouts, and the weight on my body is lifted.

I roll onto my side and cough, hating the way my mouth throbs and my lungs burn. I lift myself onto my hands and knees as flesh pummeling flesh thumps around me. Blood drips from my mouth and darkens the concrete beneath me. I spit, then purse my lips and lick my teeth. They're there—*loose*—but there.

I sit back on my heels. *Click*. I freeze as the awful sound of a hammer being pulled back ticks by my ear.

"Shoot him," Creed demands, his tone firm, but kind.

Relief seeps through my bones and I lift myself to my feet and turn around. Creed extends a gun toward my chest and I take it, then look at him. His whiskey eyes soften, their gold hue a soothing liquid swirl. In his other hand, he holds a dazed enemy. I take the gun and Creed kicks the man behind his knee, dropping him to the floor.

"Will it change anything?" I ask, not wanting to kill the man unless it makes this whole morning go away.

"I can't speak for everyone, but you'd be okay in my book."

Good enough for me. I tread forward, my legs slow, my hands shaky, and I press the barrel to my enemy's temple. Without pause, I pull the trigger. The gun fires and its powerful frame kicks into my palms. I drop the gun, suddenly nauseous as my spine quivers under my weight. I try not to think about the tightness squeezing my chest or the pain seeping up the back of my neck as I swipe at the scalding blood on my cheek. Creed touches my shoulder, but I can't bring myself to look at him.

"Stay in the bunker. Keep an eye on Iz."

He brushes past me and heads toward the smoking hole in the side of the barn. His big boots echo around the space, crunching wood and glass under his soles, grinding debris into the concrete floor. I turn toward the bunker only to be stopped by a heavy slam hitting the side of the barn, and a grunt. *Damon?* My heart rate spikes as a gross prickle spreads under my skin. I whirl on the spot, looking for a gun, or something. Tucked underneath a slab of plywood, I spot the skinny barrel of a rifle and I rush for it. I shove the plywood away and grab the gun by its body. I tuck the butt of it against my shoulder and exit the barn. Outside reeks of gunpowder and smoke, making the heavy stone of anxiety grow heavier in my chest. If this chapter of the Devil's Cartel falls, where do I go? What do I do?

I peer around the sharp corner. Judge is pinned against the decaying wooden wall, a knife at his throat, and I recognize his opponent the second my stare finds the side of his pointy face. *Antonio*, Elias's brother. It's strange seeing him unkempt and wild, his straight, jet black hair a mess on his head instead of his usual slicked back look.

My heart drops into my bare feet. Judge's nostrils flare and his breathing is labored.

"Where is she?" Antonio demands, pressing the blade into Judge's skin.

Judge spits blood in his face and smirks when Antonio straightens his long, wiry body. Although Antonio is skinny, he's incredibly strong. He spends most of his time in his expensive foreign villas fucking trending supermodels, only coming to his brother's aid when he absolutely has to. Antonio is the last resort before Elias does it himself.

Growling, Antonio pulls back his fist and Judge holds firm, not even bracing for impact.

"Antonio, stop!" I snap, pulling the rifle harder against my shoulder. I line him up.

Antonio turns his head and his thin lips pull into a wry smile. He drags his volcanic glass stare over my face and down the length of my body, seemingly amused by the baggy hoodie draped over me. I don't look at Judge in fear of what Antonio will see in my expression.

"There she is, my darling sister-in-law." He seethes in Judge's face as he lowers his fist but keeps the knife firmly in place. "You lied."

Judge clenches his jaw.

"Let him go," I say, my voice wavering as fear creeps over my vocal cords.

There was once a time I could command a criminal to do whatever I wanted, and out of fear, they listened to me. Elias took that too, the confidence I was able to wield with a certain tone.

"No," Antonio simply says, paying me no attention. He leans closer to Judge. "You really weren't going to tell me where she was, huh?" Judge doesn't answer. He doesn't have to. "She has you wrapped around her little finger—"

"I ain't wrapped around shit," Judge swears, trying to shrug Antonio off.

Judge hisses and stills as a drop of blood rolls down his neck, disappearing under the collar of his worn, black shirt.

"If you're smart, you'll surrender her before any more of your men die."

Any more? My stomach twists.

"I had to leave Elias, Antonio," I interject, and he looks at me. "I had to protect Nicolás."

The corner of his lips twitch. "You *still* want to protect that retar—"

Cursing, Judge shoves Antonio backward and it's all the space I need. I shoot. I fill his thin body with bullets. Lots of them, until the gun runs dry and there are more holes in my ex-brother-in-law than a slice of Swiss cheese. Even then, I keep clicking, willing one more bullet to enter his flesh, then I'll be satisfied.

The rifle continues to click.

Growling, I toss the gun to the grass. There isn't a word I hate more in the English language than the 'r' word. Elias and his grossly uptight family walk around with their noses held high, as if their addiction to murder isn't an atrocious birth defect.

Judge stares at Antonio and his bullet-riddled black suit, then looks at me. I tremble all over— with rage, exhaustion, sadness, and nervousness. It's a messy mix in the pit of my chest and I don't know how to make it stop. Or if it ever will.

He steps closer, and it's calculated and

threatening. I straighten my spine, preparing for the worst. Damon's dark, stormy eyes narrow, his full, firm lips pursed into an angry line. Blood splatter paints his face and it sends a chill down my spine. Maybe he wants to kill me. I am the reason his clubhouse is under attack, after all. He stops a foot away and, for a moment, I regret tossing the rifle. His expression is authoritarian and demanding. He wants me to prove my loyalty, but I don't know how, or if I even want to.

I lift my chin. "I'm not here for you, or anyone else in his chapter," I tell him, though it's nothing new. "All I *want* is my son."

Judge flickers his gaze over my face, looking for something. A lie, perhaps. I flinch as he closes the distance and wraps me up in his arms. His hug is far from gentle. It's strong and protective, tighter than any hug I've ever had. He holds every ounce of himself against me, as if he's desperate to keep me from crumbling. I close my eyes and focus on the tension in my muscles and how it melts into the warm, smokey air. I part my lips and let out an exhale. Despite the chaos hurtling around us, the sounds of rapid-fire weapons, and the shouts of men fighting a battle I dragged them into, peace swirls through me. Because I'm safe.

Releasing me from his bear-hug, Judge cups my face in his big hands and forces me to look at him. "You're gonna go back to the bunker where it's safe until we've cleared out the property, all right? Then we'll talk."

I nod and he turns me around and nudges me in the direction I came.

FOURTEEN

JUDGE

I pressed my boot to the slick bastard's back and held his tired body to the gravel drive. Blood seeped from his lips as he groaned, blowing dust around his boyish face. I extended my arm, lining the barrel of Stoic's sawed-off shotgun to his head, and I shot him. The bang was deafening, but it made my mouth water. The gravel splashed with blood and the pieces of his skull were hard to distinguish against the small rocks. I stared at the mess below me, a gross mess that reminded me of a red paper mâché moon Nila made once. Exhaling, I lifted the shotgun, rested it against my shoulder, and stepped off Elias's goon. *I'm getting too old for this shit.* I turned as Armi sauntered close, his chest rising and falling like he'd run a mile.

Puckering his lips, he spat on the ground and planted his hands on his hips. "That the last one?"

I nodded, flicking my gaze over my approaching men. "Think so."

Cursing, he gathered his blood and dirt stained hair and pulled it behind his head. "Elias really wants her dead," he said, fastening his tangled locks into a bun.

My gut churned at the thought of going up against someone like Elias Vergara. He had power—and not just in America. He had international power. All I had was this damn chapter. Armi suggested I call our sister chapters, but it'd be a cold day in hell before I asked any of them for help. They wouldn't help anyway, not even if I begged. We ran different ships, believed in different things.

I handed Armi the shotgun and sauntered past him. "Don't touch any of the bodies. No doubt the cops will be here soon, and I don't want them pinning this shit on us."

I looked at Casino as he strolled in from the right, cupping his bleeding neck. His leather cut was burnt, and his black shirt ripped.

"You dying?" I asked, and he shook his head.

"Just a scratch."

"Good. Move the weapons, diamonds, and the drugs." I flicked my chin toward Ayr, who was covered head to toe in blood and wielded a splitting axe. "Ayr can take Kace and Iris and spray down warehouse three and four."

Casino cursed. "You reckon they'd search there?"

"There's fifty dead men on our property. What do you think?"

I kept walking, crossing the expanse of burnt and smoking grass toward the barn—or what *was* the barn. One whole side was blown off and there was no way it was repairable. I entered the barn as Creed was pulling Blondie out of the bunker. He guided her gently across the floor with one hand on her forearm, the other by her elbow, and his fingers pressed into her tiny bicep. He spoke to her in soft, soothing tones, but her face was a blank canvas, her eyes glassy and vacant.

"Is she all right?" I asked, and Creed shrugged it off.

"She will be."

I glanced past him at the open bunker, its entrance partially covered by debris. "Yasmine in there?"

"Yeah."

He eyed me as I walked past, and he didn't like whatever he saw on my face. Stepping away from Blondie, he snagged me by my bicep and held me in place. I peered at his grip with a frown. If it were anyone else, there'd be hell to pay, but Creed was my person—my brother. He'd been my best friend since I saved him from a gang beating in the detention center when we were kids. There was no one I trusted on this planet more than Creed.

"Go easy on her," he said, his golden eyes softening. "She did good."

Did he think I was going to hurt her? Whatever he thought my intentions were, I didn't plan on causing her anymore grief or harm.

"Did good?"

"Let's just say my brains would be amongst the debris if it wasn't for her." A strange swell of pride swirled in my chest and Creed released my bicep. "Not saying you have to forgive her but take what I've said into consideration before you punish her."

Punish her? I had no intention of punishing her, but I nodded anyway. If Creed were in her corner, I could use him to get her out of the mess she made when I sat down to talk with the others later. I'd goad him into doing most of the talking, then it wouldn't look like I was pussy whipped by Yasmine. In hindsight, she saved my life too. Somehow, her creepy ex-brother-in-law got the upper hand over me. If she hadn't come, I'd be dead.

But I'd never admit that.

I walked away from Creed and descended the bunker stairs. My gaze zeroed in on a pacing Yasmine as I reached halfway. She froze when she saw me and dropped her hand from her mouth to fidget with her nails in front of her stomach. Her big, dark eyes showcased every emotion she felt, their watery depths holding every shred of concern and regret. I continued down and stopped at the bottom of the stairs. I flexed my fingers at my sides as I surveyed her. Her almost black hair was wild around her face from the night we shared and from the fight. I bet she still smelled like me. I bet she smelled like gunpowder, blood, and sweat.

Yasmine parted her lips, then closed them again. She looked so fucking sorry.

So miserable.

"How—" Her voice cracked, and she swallowed hard. "How many men did you lose?"

My jaw relaxed and I pressed my tongue to the roof of my mouth. I didn't want to tell her. I already saw the heavy boulders of guilt she carried on her small shoulders.

"By the looks, eight…" I cleared my throat. "But an official tally hasn't been done."

She nodded, slowly at first, then it got quicker, more anxious. "I'm sorry."

Yasmine averted attention to the moldy roof and pushed her tongue to the side of her mouth, as if licking her teeth. The longer she tried to hold on to whatever she was holding back, the more agitated she became. Her eyes grew wetter, her face paler, and the tremble in her hands took over her whole body. I approached her and that made it worse. She tried to turn away, but I snatched the hem of the hoodie she was wearing—my hoodie—and pulled

241

her back. A rogue tear spilled over the rim of her eye and I had enough of seeing her cry. Exhaling, I pushed my fingers through her messy hair and lifted it off the back of her neck. It was hot down here, the air heavy and unclean.

"Death isn't scarce here. My men wake up every morning expecting it."

"They didn't have to die today. If I never—"

"They're dead," I cut in, releasing her hair. I cupped her pretty face in my hands and smoothed my thumbs under her eyes, pushing away her tears. "They're gone. It's done."

What the hell was I doing? I watched my tattooed hands as I cupped her face and did my best to catch whatever emotions seeped through her cracks. It wasn't like me to care, but here I stood, hating that she felt so burdened, hating that she was so sad.

"You need to shower," I said. "And eat and rest."

"I can't—"

"You can and you will." I smoothed my palms down her neck and onto her shoulders. "You need to be well-rested for your son."

Minnie's eyes lit up and it warmed my chest. "You're still going to help me? After everything?"

I knew better. I fucking knew better than to continue down this path after today's events, but I was a man of my word. Always had been. It helped that I was attracted to her, that my feelings for her snaked their way around each of my ribs and hung heavy in my chest, like a growing infection.

"I said I'd help you and I meant it. We leave for Vegas at sunset."

She made a tight noise in her throat and shot forward, throwing her whole body against me, wrapping her arms around my neck. I hugged her back, tightening mine around her waist.

Once Yasmine gathered her composure, we climbed out of the bunker and left the barn. Bodies were scattered across the grass and, in the distance, the sound of sirens finally made an appearance. I wanted her inside before they got here, and I got the feeling she wanted the same.

We approached the smoking clubhouse side by side, and the crowd of men that stood around the front steps, protecting their castle. I blew impatient air out of my nose, too tired and fucking sore to fight them too.

Casino was the first to step forward. He straightened his posture and crossed his arms over his chest. In a bid to intimidate her, he stood on the second step and towered over us. *The fucking nerve...* I cut my eyes at Creed, who stood off to the left, Blondie resting against him. She glanced awkwardly between Minnie and I and offered her a sympathetic pout.

"Get out of my way," I demanded.

"Can't let her in, Prez. She's a pig."

Out of the corner of my eye, Minnie lowered her head to look at the floor, and it made rage burn in my blood.

"*Was*," Creed said, coming to her defense. "So was Sora when he came to us."

"Sora didn't keep it from us. *She* did."

"She came to me as a townie with a problem. She wasn't looking to join the chapter, so her past was irrelevant," I argued, keeping my cool.

Casino barked a laugh and shook his head. Blood trickled from his neck and rolled under the collar of his shirt. "A townie with a problem? Are we the fucking boy scouts now?"

I clenched my teeth and my nostrils flared. I stepped forward only to be stopped by a small hand on my forearm. "You're whatever the fuck I tell you to be."

Casino dropped his gaze to the hold she had on my forearm, then lifted it back to my face. The challenge in his irises was clear. He wasn't going to drop it and I didn't expect him to. My men knew what they stood for and I admired it, even if it'd come back to bite me in the ass.

"It's you against us, Prez." He dropped off the second step and landed on the third one. "No pigs allowed."

I held my teeth tightly together and felt my pulse in my jaw muscles. We were at an impasse and I really didn't know how to end it without bloodshed.

I didn't want to hurt him, but I would if he didn't rethink his stance on letting Minnie pass.

A second ticked by.

A couple more ensued.

I straightened my spine, ready to end it for Casino when Creed pushed away from the building and stood beside Yasmine. Casino shifted his attention to Creed and his tense expression faltered. One by one, the men dropped down the stairs and stood on my side against Casino. Whether they were on my side, or just wanted Casino to shut up and let us pass, I didn't know. Casino peered over his shoulder at Modo, the last brother, who drummed his fingers against the base of his axe. I narrowed my eyes at him, silently demanding he make the right choice, or I'd kill them both.

"Well." Modo sighed and lifted his axe off the ground. "The lady is all right, Casino. We all gotta start somewhere. Shit, you worked for Ventilli in Vegas, remember?"

Modo dragged his feet to stand with the rest of us. Other members lingered, knowing better than to get involved in our *"upper management"* beef— even our prospect, Kace, who stood off to the side, kept his attention on the ground.

Realizing his defeat, Casino pushed his fingers through his cropped hair and looked at me. It was hard not to act smug. *Fuck Casino.*

"I gave you your orders," I said. "You should be

on your bike."

He licked his parched lips and planted his hands on his hips like he had more to say. Knowing better, he flicked his chin at Kace. "C'mon."

I let out the breath I didn't know I was holding as Kace and Casino sauntered up the drive, an excited Iris hot on their heels.

"Prez," Armi said, drawing my attention as he slipped his phone into his jean pocket. "Cops are a minute out."

Shit. I grabbed Minnie by the wrist and tugged her toward the stairs. "Go shower."

She started forward without hesitation, only to be stopped by Creed's call. "Take Isabelle with you."

We both looked at him with a raised eyebrow.

"To the shower?" Minnie asked, sparing a look at Isabelle, who made her way toward the steps, her movements more fluid than before.

"Yeah. I've given her valium. It'll kick in soon and she'll need supervising, maybe some help."

"And you've got the same parts, so…" Modo said, causing laughter to erupt.

I shook my head. I was in charge of a bunch of idiots. Looking uncertain, Minnie held out her hand and helped Blondie up the stairs. Peering over her shoulder at me, she opened the door and slipped inside the damaged clubhouse.

"So, she's your bitch then?" Modo asked.

I turned to face him, turned to face all the curious

stares pointing in my direction.

"There gonna be a problem with that?"

Heads shook, and Modo's lips quirked. "Nah, Prez. No problem here."

"Good." I pointed at him. "You can help Armi and Hawk prep the bikes for tonight. We leave for Nevada at sunset."

YASMINE

The water is hot. It billows so much dense steam I feel it in my lungs whenever I inhale. The glass walls encasing three sides around Isabelle and I are so fogged it barely registers when I draw a smiley face on it.

"I don't know what happened," she says, clutching Judge's black loofah to her chest. "It's like I was a prisoner in my own mind. I wanted to move, but…" I look at her as she stares at the slate gray tiles, focusing on nothing but the images in her head. "I couldn't."

"You're safe now," I tell her, taking the soapy loofah out of her hands. "It's over."

"With men like them, it's never over."

I press the loofah to her arms and continue the cleaning she started. As I reach the top of her shoulder, I lift her bra strap and clean under it. I wash off the dirt, dust, and mold spores that gathered on her skin while she was in the bunker.

She stays silent as I wash her body. Her underwear remains on, covering her most intimate parts from view.

I admire Isabelle Laurent on a whole new level now. The way she stormed into the barn for me...she didn't care it was her against the Devil's Cartel. She knew what they were doing was wrong and she wasn't going to sit by and let them hurt me.

"Can I ask you a personal question?" I ask, thinking about the events that unfolded between her and her father.

I've heard awful things. She nods, her face falling like she knows what I'm going to ask before I ask it.

"Did your father really—"

"Have me beaten half to death, then trapped me in a wooden box and tried to burn me alive?" She turns away from me, offering the small, smooth expanse of her back. "Yes."

I purse my lips and press the loofah to her shoulder blade. I circle her skin, wishing I could wash away my invasive question. I see her feet and the heavy scarring that remains. I should've known better than to pry.

"I've never seen Judge act like that before." she says a few minutes later, changing the subject. "He would've killed Casino for you."

I play dumb as I push her hair over her shoulder and wash her neck. "I don't think it would've gone that far."

But it could have. I felt the tension in his arm, the furious energy that wafted from his body. I have no doubt Damon would've ripped Casino's head from his body, but it wasn't all for me. Casino was challenging Damon's role in front of everyone. I don't know much about club life, but I know Casino was lucky to leave unscathed.

Humming, Izzy presses her white teeth into her lower lip and closes her eyes, apparently enjoying the way I scrub her. I let my gaze wander as I clean her, admiring her soft, curvaceous physique. Her body is perfect, unmarred by age and the gift of carrying a child. Her breasts are perky, her tummy flat and tight. My mind drifts to Judge and his confession. Until recently, he wanted the blonde I currently share his shower with. How often did he think about her? How often has he touched himself to thoughts of her? Something sinister pulls tight in my belly and I don't think it's all bad. It's a chaotic mix of intrigue, jealousy, and arousal.

"You're lucky," she murmurs, her tone husky and heavy. "He's a good lover."

I lift my eyebrows and part my lips as jealousy licks me all over. I wish she didn't know that. I wish those memories she shared with Judge were lost to a random bout of amnesia.

"And Creed?" I goad, forcing her train of thought to where it should be—on James, not

249

Damon.

"He's perfect." She turns around and flashes me a gentle, loving smile. "I love him so much I could die."

Good. I move the loofah under the hot stream, washing away the bubbly suds, contemplating how I'm going to wash my own body underneath Judge's black Iron Maiden t-shirt that clings to me like a second skin.

"You don't have to wear the shirt," Isabelle says, as if reading my thoughts. She steps under the stream and smooths her hands down the flat of her stomach, rinsing the soap down her body. "We have the same parts, after all."

I snort at her mocking use of Modo's words, but he isn't wrong. I've been naked in front of other women before. I drum my fingers against the hem that hangs low against my thigh. It'd be nice to clean my whole body...I drop the loofah to the floor and peel the shirt from my frame. Freeing my hair from the fabric's folding confines, I drop it and it hits the tiles with a gross squelch. I look at Isabelle and she flickers her curious gaze down the length of my body, lingering on the silver stretch marks pregnancy carved along my soft belly. I wish I can say the change in her eyes makes me uneasy, but it doesn't. Heat, hotter than the shower, spreads down the back of my neck, following my spine to scatter in my pelvis and pool between my legs.

"Would you have another baby?" she asks, reaching behind her back and unclasping her bra.

I absorb my flinch and the empty space where my uterus once was—before it was stolen from me—throbs painfully. "No."

"I would like to have a few."

I shift my weight as she lets the thin, pink fabric fall down her arms, exposing her bare breasts. I can't help my attention as it falls to her pebbled nipples, and her areolas—which were much bigger in circumference than mine.

"Five boys," she continues, curling her fingers around the thin hem of her matching underwear. "Three girls."

Eight? I often felt greedy for wanting two. Nicolás loves babies. I would've liked to give him a sibling, even if I did hate his father more than anything else on the planet.

"What's stopping you?" I ask as she bares her lower half.

She's beautifully smooth. Water runs over her body, making her look like a goddess, her body perfectly carved from wet marble. It's no wonder Judge wanted her, lusted after her. The longer I remain in the shower, the deeper I seem to slip under the same spell, entranced by her physical beauty.

"I want to get married first." Isabelle bends over and picks up the loofah. Squeezing the remaining soap out of it, she lathers it up again. "He hasn't asked me yet, but I suspect the question isn't far off."

"How do you know?"

"Because he asked me if I prefer yellow gold or white gold."

Stepping out of the stream, Isabelle takes me by my wrist and soaps up my forearm, her scrubbing technique a gentle massage for my pores.

"Which do you prefer?"

"Rose gold." She smiles, exposing her straight, white teeth. "He left a Google search open for rose gold engagement rings last week."

My lips quirk. Cute. Elias never proposed to me. He simply tossed a diamond ring in my lap and told me to wear it. It was nothing more than a ploy to force my superiors to abandon me, a shackle holding me captive to a man who hated me.

When I'm covered in soap, she drops the loofah, opting to use her hands instead. I stand still, watching her slender hands as she rubs up my arms and onto my chest, her fingers on my clavicles, her palms just north of my breasts. We stand almost identical in height, but we had around a decade gap in our age, and it'd be a lie if I said her youth didn't leave me feeling a little insecure.

"You know, if you're going to be Judge's old lady, you'll have to fuck Creed."

I blanch, my eyebrows lifting to my hairline of

their own accord. "Excuse me?"

"It's a promise," she says. "An agreement that someone else will take care of you in the event of Judge's death."

I swallow hard as she shoots me headfirst into a commitment I've barely thought about.

"I'm here for my son," I tell her, and the way she avoids my stare tells me she doesn't believe me. "I'm not going to be anyone's old lady. I'm leaving as soon as I get Nicolás."

Isabelle shrugs her shoulders, moving onto my breasts. She's gentle at first, her palm kissing my hard nipple as she skitters it over the top. "Does Judge know that?"

I purse my lips. I think so. I think he knows. A part of me doesn't want to go. I want to stay with Judge under his protection but how can I shun one criminal for another? Judge isn't cruel in the ways Elias is, but their work is the same. How can I raise my son in such a volatile place? Judge has enemies—too many of them. He said so himself.

She presses her palms firmer against my breasts, feeling the slippery weight of them in her hands. I let out a shaky exhale as she eases closer, mesmerized by her own touch and the way my nipples strain, reaching into her grasp. I love that her hands are like silk, so different to Judge's rough and firm hold.

"Tell me, if I did stay, what makes you think I'd

choose Creed?"

Her blue eyes meet mine, her lids heavy with whatever is happening inside her body. "Judge would make sure of it. He'd guide you in Creed's direction because the pair are inseparable."

A quick flash of a powerful and naked James Creed crackled through my mind and the thought of having him excited me more than it should, more than I'd ever admit.

"And you'd be okay with that?"

Izzy steps forward, easing her body against mine. She releases my breasts to touch my waist and glides her soapy hands to my back, holding us together. I spare a fleeting thought to her mental state and the Valium Creed said he gave her, but she doesn't seem heavily affected by it. Her eyes are clear, her body steady. If anything, she's calm, not off her head.

"I don't know," she admits, her breath blowing onto my lips. "I haven't lingered on the thought because it consumes me with an insane amount of jealousy." Tilting her head, she draws her lips closer to mine until they graze. "I'm aware being jealous isn't fair since I've already had Judge, but you're just so pretty." She smooths her hand over my backside, then up my thigh to dip low between my legs. I gasp and tighten my thighs around the fingers she presses against my center. "Your body drips with life experience and it makes me feel

254

inadequate."

What is she doing? How is she making my insides coil with such a gentle touch on my most sensitive part? Stepping forward, Isabelle eases me against the cold glass and pulls her hand from between my legs. She continues to wash me, pretending she didn't arouse me, that she didn't make me weak in the knees.

I admire her features as she washes me, our bodies still pressed firmly together. A lock of her blonde hair sticks to her plump lower lip, but she makes no move to brush it away and there's something about the wild look that stirs a strange longing deep inside me—something I've never felt toward a woman before. How can a girl like her feel inadequate? She eases forward, her sights set on my mouth, and she kisses me. It's innocent at first, a curious press of her mouth to mine, then she slips her tongue between my lips. Unlike the men I've kissed before today, Isabelle's isn't consuming and demanding. It's tender and sensual, a calming caress that makes my muscles lax and my mind foggy. I let her pull me under her spell, lost in the way her lips don't overpower mine and her hands remain on the small of my back.

"You're so soft," she whispers as she breaks our kiss, leaving my lips tingling, not swollen.

Isabelle glides her hands up my sides to cup my heavy breasts and a zip of morality penetrates the sensual mist I've been trapped in.

"What would Creed say," I ask, swallowing hard. "If he saw us like this?"

Tilting her head, Isabelle stares off in thought, then brings her gaze back to mine. "Creed isn't the one I'm worried about."

Her words sober me. Does she mean Judge? I place my hands over hers, stopping her from massaging more soap into my skin. And she gets the hint. Smiling, she pulls her hands back to her own person and angles her glistening body, offering me time in the hot stream to wash myself off. As I push off the glass, there's a knock on the bathroom door.

"Izzy?"

I stiffen as Creed's voice jams a steel rod in my spine. Isabelle shivers and turns toward the door. "Come in."

"What?" I blurt.

I bend and snatch Judge's wet t-shirt off the floor. I slap it against myself, hiding as much of my intimate parts as I can before the door opens. Thanks to the fog on the glass, Creed is nothing but a mass of dark blurry shapes.

"I brought you clothes. I figured you and Yasmine are similar in size, so I brought her clothes too," he says. "Are you finished?"

"No." Isabelle bends over and grabs Judge's bottle of men's shampoo. "Still need to wash my hair."

Creed mutters something, then leaves the bathroom. I keep the shirt against my body until five long seconds pass, then I drop it to the tiles again. As if the last ten minutes never transpired between us, Isabelle extends the blue shampoo bottle toward me.

"I'll wash yours if you wash mine?"

J U D G E

I turned my back to the group of policemen who stood by a far oak tree, talking in hushed tones and planning God knows fucking what. It was only a matter of time before the forensic team got here and combed through the property. Thankfully, we were running on minimal activity since the FBI investigation associated with Blondie wrapped up. Our clubhouse was clean—*almost*. Whatever they found, I was sure I could throw money or threats to make it go away.

"I want shotguns in my sidesaddle," I told Armi. While the cops sniffed around, I'd continue to plan our next run. "If you can spare a few grenades and a flashbang, that'd help too."

Nodding, he headed toward the garage. I brushed my hand through my hair and kicked gravel as I turned to face the clubhouse. The fires were out, and the damage was clear. We had some long days ahead if we were gonna repair this shit. It was due for an upgrade anyway. It still held the stench of our old president.

The sound of the screen door on the side of the clubhouse screeched, pulling my attention. Creed and Blondie strolled out, leaving the door to slap closed behind them. Ayr, Modo, and Hawk eyed them with irritation as they stood off to the left, engaged in quiet conversation.

The wind blew Blondie's hair around her face and carried her pale pink summer dress around her thighs. Creed kissed her on the top of the head and headed for the steps as Izzy leaned against the bannister of the porch, brushing her fingers against the burned wood. I frowned. What the hell were they looking at? And why was Creed so damn smug? We were surrounded by carnage and he didn't care. Not to mention, Blondie would have to face the consequences of her actions. She stormed the barn and interrupted official business. I should take one of her pinky fingers off her hand for the disrespect.

"What's with the smirk?" I asked as he closed the distance between us.

He opened his mouth and I wasn't prepared for the words he spoke. He told me about Yasmine and Isabelle and what they got up to in the shower. I listened intently, then I checked the date on my phone, and it wasn't April Fools Day.

"Minnie and Blondie?" I said, hating how much

Creed was enjoying my reaction. "In my fucking shower?"

I was pissed—turned on too—but mostly pissed. I headed toward the clubhouse, stopping next to Isabelle on my way to find Yasmine. "Giving you my VP wasn't enough, you want my woman too?"

"Your woman?" Isabelle reared back and smiled as if it was news to her. "I wasn't aware anyone claimed her. I was just being friendly."

Friendly? You can be friendly without sticking your tongue down someone's throat. I knew exactly what she was doing. She's deduced that Creed would be the one I shared Minnie with—if she ever became my old lady—and Isabelle was trying to get in on it. She didn't want to be left on the sidelines while Creed, Yasmine, and I sealed the deal.

I stepped forward, sneering at her. "What's the verdict?" I asked and she frowned. "Do you think Creed will enjoy her?"

I watched my question drop a bomb on her. It hit a sore spot and ricocheted through her system. Absorbing her flinch as best she could, she shrugged. "He won't enjoy her as much as he enjoys me, but he'll suffer through it to make you happy."

Suffer through it? Please. When the time came, Yasmine would make Creed forget all about Blondie—albeit temporarily. She'd make him come and that'd put me and him on even ground for the

259

first time in years. I turned my back.

"She's a good kisser," Blondie called after me, her pretty voice a song in the wind. "And so soft between her legs."

Modo, Ayr, and Hawk looked in our direction, their eyebrows raised. *This Bitch.*

"Who is?" Modo asked, shouldering past Hawk as he approached.

I glared at Blondie over my shoulder.

"If James didn't show up, who knows how far she would've let me go." Her lips quirk at the corner and her blue eyes flash with wicked intent. "All the way, I bet."

Creed was there? In *my* bathroom while Yasmine was naked? My nose twitched and I cut my eyes at Creed who climbed the steps.

He bared his palms to me. "I didn't see nothing."
Motherfucker.

"Where is she?" I demanded, storming toward the screen door.

"Still in the shower. Probably finishing what I started."

I flipped Blondie off, hating the way her laughter dug under my skin. It was official. The Devil's Cartel had turned her into a monster. The Blondie I knew two years ago would die of anxiety at the thought of kissing another woman. Now, that was her being *friendly*.

I ripped open the door and barreled through the

clubhouse to my room. Once inside, I closed the door behind me and rested against its cool wood. The pattering sound of the shower filled the room and the air was warm and damp. I reached behind me and turned the lock, shutting us in. Yasmine wouldn't leave until her shower with Blondie was a pale comparison to what I could do for her.

I slipped into the bathroom and sauntered toward the defogging glass box that encased her willowy body. Her back was to me, her long, dark hair wet against her spine, a dark ribbon between her delicate shoulder blades. It was hard for me to imagine she was anything other than a doting mother. I couldn't picture her with a badge, kicking down doors or shooting her gun, but that was her. I read her file. Yasmine Garcia was an ambitious badass, the pride of every precinct and agency she ever worked at. That should piss me off. It should disgust me that she was so damn good at her job, but it didn't. A strange sense of pride licked at me.

She was unstoppable.

Until she met Elias Vergara.

The shower door clanked as I grabbed the handle. Yasmine startled with a shriek and whirled around as I yanked the door open.

"What are you doing—"

I stepped into the shower, swallowed the distance between us, and pressed my clothed body to hers. Cold water seeped through the fabric of my t-shirt and goosebumps prickled as it kissed my skin. The jets beat against her back and I caught the cold off spray.

"Water's cold." I reached behind her and turned the handle toward *heat*. "Isabelle was right. She turned you on, huh?"

Minnie balked. Her eyes went wide, and she scoffed. She was surprised I knew, but she hadn't been around long enough to know Blondie tells Creed everything. Normally, Creed doesn't share the details of their quiet whispers, but today, he just couldn't help himself. Minnie shook her head, but the blush in her cheeks deepened the warmer the water got.

"I didn't start it," she said, her arms draped by her sides. I watched water drip over her cupid's bow and onto her pink lips. "She kissed me. She did more than kiss me."

Pulling back, I shrugged out of my cut and threw it over the top of the shower. "You want her?"

"No."

I closed the distance again. "She make you come?"

Minnie scowled a gorgeous scowl and blood flushed her face. "No."

"Good." I grabbed her by her soft hips and pulled her against me. "You are mine and mine only."

"That's not true."

I frowned. "Yes, it is."

"Isabelle told me what would happen if I stay."

I blinked. She was referring to *the DCMC Exeter Chapter Bylaws – section five – old ladies.* Isabelle knew better than to scare her with that shit so soon, but I guess payback was a bitch. I wasn't going to touch that topic. Not right now.

"*If* you stay? Do you plan on leaving?"

Her eyelids flickered, her long lashes fluttering with uncertainty, and it made my heart race. Last night she agreed to be mine and I didn't take that shit lightly. She was the first woman I ever wanted to be mine. I made my ex mine out of obligation, not love. I protected her because she was the mother of my baby—a baby conceived by accident. Yasmine was different and I wanted her to stay. I enjoyed her company. I enjoyed having something else to think about, something other than work. Mostly, I enjoyed not feeling bitter threads of jealousy carve through my stomach whenever I saw Blondie and Creed together.

"I don't know, Damon. My top priority is my son's safety and trading one criminal family for another is..." She licked her lips. "I just don't know."

She raised a good point, but we were different from Elias Vergara. Hell, we were different from other chapters in the same club and we worked damn hard to be different. It was too early for her to decide what she wanted anyway. Even through the water and soap, I smelled smoke in the air. I smelled blood, and it was enough to turn anyone off this life.

"Last night you said you were mine."

"And I meant it. I want to be yours, and as long as I'm here, I am." She licked her lower lip and lifted her arms to drape them over my shoulders and caress the back of my neck with her fingertips. "But I'll have to make some decisions in the next twenty-four hours and those decisions might not be in our favor."

I pressed my tongue to the roof of my mouth, doing my best to hold back my demands. I wanted to demand she stay. I wanted to tell her she held all my attention, that she was mine whether she wanted to be or not. I didn't want her to see me in the same light as Elias, who didn't give her a way out. All I could do was choke down the tight grasp my natural possessiveness had on me and hope she was as drawn to me as I was to her. I felt like an idiot for wanting her as much as I did, but I couldn't deny it. Her existence was a pull on my body, a strange twang in my soul that sprang up the second she called me a good dad.

Maybe I felt it before then too.

I didn't know.

I did, however, know that tonight we were leaving for Vegas, where Elias currently resided.

There I'd kill him and rescue Minnie's son. So, if this was the last time I was going to have her alone, I wasn't gonna waste it. I leaned closer to her.

"For as long as you're here, you're mine?"

"Yes."

As if on cue, we both moved forward, our mouths coming together with dangerous urgency. I kissed her passionately, letting my concerns for the future dissolve. There was nothing on my mind, nothing coursing through my veins, other than my desire for her. I stepped forward, my boot on the tiles between her legs, and I pushed her out of the stream. I kept pushing until the bulk of the water sprayed down my back and I had Minnie pressed to the wall—where I wanted her. Breaking the kiss, I attacked her neck. I licked and nipped at her flesh while my hands roamed her slippery torso. She gripped my belt as she sighed and undid it in record time, then moved on to the button of my jeans.

I didn't know what the future was gonna bring, but I knew there was no stopping what was about to happen, not until we were finished. I let out a heavy exhale when she freed my rock-hard dick from my jeans. I pressed into her, sliding my sensitive head against her smooth belly.

Minnie pressed her hand to the top of my cock and lifted herself onto the tips of her toes, pushing my hard length lower. I bent my knees, wanting to be lower, wanting to be between her legs. I gripped her behind her knee and pulled at it. She gasped, falling to the flat of her foot as I lifted her leg high around my waist.

"Shit. We're gonna fall," she said, her voice light with humorous tones.

"We're good," I replied, bending my knees. "I got you."

I lowered my hips and put my cock between her spread legs. I grabbed her soft hip and pulled her off the wall, only to push her back against it as I drove into her wet heat. She grabbed me around the neck and dug her nails into my flesh as water continued to fall along my back and down my sides.

And I loved it.

Minnie slid against the wet tile with every upwards thrust and every retreat, the slippery tiles making it effortless. She moaned and it echoed around the confines of my bathroom. The sound of her pleasure, the feel of her slick softness, consumed me in an instant. Everything outside these glass walls no longer mattered. I wanted to stay here where I had no responsibility, no army at my feet, and no lives in my hands. I think that's why I liked Minnie so much. She made me feel like I was more than a motorcycle club president. More than a criminal. She made me feel youthful and carefree, and reminded me that there was life to be lived outside our chapter. I could never live a normal life again, but it'd been nice tasting it on her tongue.

Sighing, Yasmine dropped her head against my chest, and I bent my knees, desperate to fit more of myself inside her, but this position sucked ass. Growling, I gripped her high on her other thigh, digging my fingertips into her ass and I lifted her onto me.

"Holy f—" she gasped, wrapping her legs around my backside. "Damon…"

I shoved every inch of my cock inside her and felt her tight walls spasm as they stretched to accommodate me. I thrust into her. In seconds, my steady thrusts turned erratic. I buried my face into the nape of her neck and against her wet hair as my movement lost all care and coordination. A nagging in the back of my head told me to take care, to be gentle and careful of her spine against the hard tile, but it had no control over me. I was too damn horny to listen.

And she was enjoying it too much to stop me.

Her thighs quivered. Her body squirmed in my grip, her moans turning from short and sweet, to long and gasping. I kissed along the nape of her neck to her jaw. She dropped her head back and I claimed her mouth as hot breath from her nose blew across my cheek. I kept kissing her, my tongue deep in her mouth, her tongue desperate to taste mine, and I kept thrusting my hips.

Harder. Faster.

Until she broke the kiss to shout, but no sound left her mouth. Tightening her grip on my neck, she forced our foreheads together. Our breaths clashed as our open mouths opposed each other.

"Yes," she says on a breath, then sharply inhales. "Yes, Damon."

Fuck. I wanted her bad and not just like this. I wanted her to be mine. The fullness of her breasts slid against my chest as I kept my fast pace, fucking in and out of her. I wanted her to feel good. I wanted to make her feel better than any man had ever made her feel. She shuddered against me and her pussy tightened around my dick.

"Oh, shit," I swore. "You feel so good."

I tried to slow down to give her time before I ended the show, but the tight contractions of her body, and the sounds that left her mouth, dragged me to the edge of my release. Her moans became cries of pleasure, and with every thrust I lost self-control. I clenched my jaw and fucked her harder until the sound of my body crashing into hers was heard above the roaring shower. She shouted my name, God's name, and every swear word under the sun as I slammed into her, chasing the pressure that burned at my thighs and bubbled up my shaft.

"Yes," Minnie called, her voice a sonnet through the euphoric fog. "Give it to me."

That was all she had to say. I groaned as pleasure seized my entire body, and spilled into her with thick, powerful jerks. I pinned her to the wall, my hips spasming, my cock twitching as my orgasm ran its course and filled her with everything I had to give.

Exhaling, I lifted my head and looked her in the face. Smiling, she ran her fingers over my scalp, down my neck and across my shoulders, igniting tingles in her wake.

"If I leave," she said, her voice raspy. "Will you visit me?"

Tension spasmed in my shoulders. Visit? Could I visit her and not take what was mine? How could she respect me, knowing I'd be here, playing with the women I employed, wishing for them to be her? Even if I didn't touch another woman, who's to say I wouldn't rock up one day and find her with someone else? Something long distance with Minnie was a recipe for disaster. If she was gonna leave, that was it. I lived my life in absolutes. It was all or nothing.

"No. Not even once."

Disappointment swam in her dark eyes, the blush in her cheeks deepening. "So, that's it?"

All or nothing. "That's it."

She offered me a small smile, then unwrapped herself from my body. I slipped out of her and lowered her onto her shaky legs. Softly patting me on my chest, she stepped around me and I turned, making space for her to step under the water again.

No, that's not it. I swung my arm over her head and pressed my palm into her chest. She gasped as I pushed her back and she stumbled, but didn't fall, as I eased her against the wall once again.

"You don't have to worry about me when you're gone," I told her as I smoothed my hand between her breasts, down her soft tummy, and between her legs. I parted her lips and touched her clit, making her hips twitch. Then I felt the warm, sticky gift I gave her as it leaked from where I left it. "But while you're here, you're mine, and there'll be consequences if you let anyone in this building touch you again."

Her golden gaze flickered over my face, her expression morphing from shocked to hungry. She snapped forward, crushing the distance between us to kiss me hard on the mouth. I parted my lips as her tongue probed me, taking without asking. When the shock wore off, I kissed her back. I kissed her with everything I had, a kiss I knew I'd never given anyone prior. Before long, she had me out of my shirt, out of my shoes, socks, my jeans, and I was butt naked and deep inside her again. Over and over. We made good use of the shower, the bathroom, my bedroom floor, my couch, my walls, and my bed.

And I knew.

I was going to drag her husband out to Humboldt River and burn him alive in a metal barrel.

Then I would make Minnie stay.

FIFTEEN

YASMINE

I can smell him. I can smell the leather, the denim, and the whiskey. Enticing hints of burning wood and oil tickles my nose, adding to the smells that make up the man I can't get enough of.

Judge drapes his arm over the back of my seat and draws circles on my bicep with his thumb. It fills me with a warmth I've never felt. We sit at the head of the first of four long, wooden tables, the legs of our chairs kissing.

Today has been a hard day. For the most part, I spent it in Judge's room, alone, while he sorted the mess outside. I don't know what happened with the bodies of Elias's men, or what the police plan on doing in retaliation to the mini war that unfolded on the Devil Cartel's property this morning. Whatever the outcome, it's a problem for the future and I'll be long gone. The main factor contributing to the

272

anxiety, panic, and excitement that overwhelms every fiber in my being is, tonight I will *finally* hold my son in my arms. I can't stop thinking about it. Will he be heavier than the last time I saw him? Lighter? Will he be the same sweet kid, or has Elias broken him?

When I left Judge's room in the afternoon, I walked about the clubhouse. The men and women of the chapter strolled around, talking and laughing, as if they didn't lose eight of their own. They casually discussed weapons and tactics as they went about their day. They kept the beer flowing as if they didn't have to ride to Vegas in the evening.

By the time the sun sat low in the sky, many of them were drunk, but I learned those who were, weren't coming on the ride anyway. Those who were coming sat at long wooden tables, a single beer in front of them, and that's all they'll have. They call this the last drink…because some of them won't make it home. Guilt stabs my heart.

I eye my own beer and watch condensation drip down the clear, cold glass. My nerves are heightened, buzzing under my skin like tiny drills, and I'm not the only one feeling overwhelmed and worried. I flick my attention to Isabelle, who sits with Creed to the left of the head of the table. No matter how many times Creed makes her smile by kissing her face or whispering in her ear, her worry creeps back and she chews her lower lip. She's worried he's going to go and not come back. Elias is a dangerous man, there's a good chance none of them are coming back. I press my palm to my stomach, hoping to ease my apprehension. I hate I could be the reason Isabelle loses him…but I want my son. I asked Judge to keep Creed home, but he laughed it off as if it were a stupid request.

Creed toys with Isabelle's long, blonde ponytail and whispers in her ear again. She turns her body in his direction and he tugs on the front of her pink sweater, pulling it tighter around her chest. I can't hear what he's saying over the animated conversation surrounding us, or the laughter, but he makes her smile. It's a big smile, showcasing all her white, perfect teeth. She leans into him, burying her face into his neck, and he wraps his big, tattooed arms around her, holding her tight.

"He'll come back," Judge speaks into my ear and I startle, whipping my head in his direction. "He doesn't know it, but I've put him on lookout tonight. I'll take Armi and Modo in. The rest will follow, but not him."

He listened to me? Relief floods my chest. "He'll be safe?"

Damon nods and finishes the last mouthful of his beer. He swallows with an exhale. "Unless he does something stupid."

I smile at Damon, flicking my gaze over his handsome, refreshed face, then I look at the men and women who sit around our table. They don't know me or Nicolás but are risking their lives to help me get him back. How can I ever repay them?

"Just so we're clear," Judge says, pushing his glass away. "I'm going to kill him."

He's talking about Elias. I've imagined his death more times than I can count. It's hard to believe the time has finally come…and I've never been surer about anything in my life.

I nod, hating the way my scared pulse pounds in my neck. "Elias's death is what I want. We'll never be safe as long as he lives."

The thought of being involved in conspiring to murder another human being sends gross chills down my spine, but I'll do anything to keep Nicolás safe. I made a promise to him, and myself. And that promise is the reason I need to leave Judge and this chapter behind. As much as I care for Damon, he isn't safe. This lifestyle isn't safe.

Laughter roars from our table, startling me, and I peer at the center of the attention—Modo—who grins, wide and wolfish, through his crimson beard at his brothers. I can't help my own smile as his eyes glisten. He really loves being the center of attention, the one who can make the whole room laugh.

"And that's why you shouldn't use hair removal cream on your balls," he announces proudly before sculling back his beer.

Beside me, even Judge vibrates with laughter and it stirs a chuckle of my own. I take another sip of my drink and, out of the corner of my eye, Armi approaches James Creed. He bends and mutters into Creed's ear, who then pulls away from Izzy. He turns his whiskey stare on Judge, then flicks his head, gesturing Judge follow him.

Sighing, Judge drops his hand from the back of my chair and leans in to kiss me on the temple. It's a chaste kiss, quick and dry.

"I'll be back," he says, pushing the chair back. It squeals against the wooden floor as he lifts his large body up.

Creed does the same. "Blondie, keep my seat warm, will you?"

She slides into his spot without protest and wraps her arm around mine. She says something, but I don't hear it. I'm too focused on Judge, Creed, and Armi, who make their way to the back of the building, toward the dark room I recall being filled with provocative dancers and topless women.

"Is something wrong? Do you know where they're going?" I ask Isabelle and she catches her lower lip between her teeth.

She knows something, but all I get from her is a shrug of her shoulders. "Club stuff. Who knows?"

"Club stuff…" I frown and grab my beer.

I sip at it, trying to put my curiosity to rest, but my attention keeps drifting from the conversation at hand to the back room. What are they doing?

J U D G E

Darkness spread under my skin, thirsting for revenge, for penance from whoever interfered with my life and fucked up my night with Minnie. I entered the club room and it took a second for my eyes to adjust to the darkness. The LEDs that line the room transitioned from green to red and I saw it.

I saw her.

Liv.

She was tied to a wooden chair in the middle of the room, dressed in cut-off jean shorts and a blank tank top. Behind us, Armi locked the doors and split. Sauntering to the bar, he disappeared behind a wall of red lights.

I looked at Creed. "Her?"

He nodded. "She told one of the other girls. They told me."

I licked my teeth as irritation prickled under my skin. I should've fucking known it was her who put the photo on the window, ruining my night with Minnie in the backseat of Armi's truck. Liv sat in the chair, her wrists and ankles bound to the wood by rope that was much too tight. I stepped forward, slowly, purposely making it menacing and torturous. She knew better than to fuck with me— *me, of all people!*

"So," I started, closing the distance. "*You* were the one who ruined my night?"

Liv lifted her head and stared me down. She put on a brave face. It was the face of a woman who wanted to go toe to toe with me, but I knew her. She was scared. I bet her spine was shaking.

"I stopped you from making a mistake."

I paused in front of her and laughed. It was a bitter sound in the silent room. The fact she thought she had any control over me pissed me off.

"Stopped me? No, darlin'. You didn't stop anything. I got what I wanted. Over and over again." I smirked and crouched, coming face to face with the woman I used to fuck. She pouted her full lips and batted her eyelashes. "Where did you think I was all day? I was with her, in a bed I never let you sleep in."

Growling, she bared her teeth and seethed. "Yeah? Well, you downgraded."

Creed snorted and my lips twitched at the corners. He disagreed. I did too. I mean, any idiot with eyes could see Liv was sexy. She was tall, slim, and physically fit. She had big, fake breasts, wide hips, and a tiny waist. She was a Barbie doll on crack, and I knew there were men out there who'd sever the limbs from their own bodies for a taste of her.

But she wasn't for me.

She wasn't what I wanted, or what I needed. Liv

was here, and she was easy, but I didn't crave her with every cell in my body. I gave no fucks about her emotions, or her thoughts. She was expendable and easily replaced. While Minnie was *many* things, she wasn't a downgrade—in any capacity.

"Why're you so hung up on her?" Liv asked, her tone quiet, meant only for me. She eases forward as much as she could in her chair. "Why're you doing so much for a kid that isn't yours and is so fucking weird to look at?"

An angry snarl ripped through my chest and I clamped my hand over her mouth. If she went any further, said anything more venomous, I'd kill her. How uncomfortable in your own skin did you have to be to pick on a child who had no control over their creation? A kid who didn't ask to be different? Who was already hated by his own father?

"You want to die?" I asked, my index finger twitching against her cheek.

Liv's breath left her nostrils, quick and scared, and blew across my hand. Minnie's brother-in-law offended her by speaking ill of Nicolás earlier today and she shot him to pieces. I saw her face and the satisfaction that spread over it when he collapsed to the ground. Made sense to let her deal with this one too. It was her kid, not mine. I lowered my hand from Liv's mouth, but never broke eye contact.

"Get Yasmine," I told Creed. "Bring her to me."

He obliged without hesitation. When he returned,

Yasmine's sharp intake was as loud as a gunshot in my ears. I stood and turned toward her. She looked as edible as ever in Blondie's white tank top that hugged her torso and accentuated the curves of her womanly figure. Flicking her gaze over my face, then to Liv, she smoothed her palms down the front of her tight, black jeans.

"What are you doing?" she asked, pushing hair from her high ponytail off her shoulder.

"Found out who used the photograph of your son to torment you." Her whiskey eyes darkened, noticeable even in the dimly lit room. "I won't repeat what she said about his appearance."

Yasmine's eyelids flutter, her jaw set tight. She sauntered forward, toward the stupid girl on the chair. She didn't say a word, didn't lift a finger. She looked at her, even leaned forward, bringing her face close to Liv's, who simply lifted her chin. I wanted Yasmine to hurt her for what she said...because that would put me on a clear path. It'd make us cut from the same cloth and re-cement the fact Yasmine was made for me—sent by divine intervention, or some shit.

"I wish you never came here," Liv whispered, her eyes watered in the changing lights. "I wish you—"

She swallowed her words as Minnie straightened and stared down at her. "Let her go."

I tensed. Creed sensed it and stepped forward on

my behalf. "Not how it works around here, Minnie."

"I don't care how it works." She turned her head and looked at me. There was resolve in her eyes. "Let her go."

"No," I said.

"She's in love with you, Damon," Minnie pointed out, as if I didn't know. I knew. I've always known Livia cared for me more than I ever cared for her. "It's cruel to keep her here."

The fact she didn't understand why Liv was tied up, and refused to get her revenge, didn't sit well in my bones. Maybe she wasn't mine. Maybe she wasn't sent by the universe as a reprieve from my never-ending pain. Anger boiled in my blood and burned my bones because she wasn't even trying. I felt stupid, like a jealous child. I tried to swallow it down, the words I knew better than to say, but they came out anyway.

"You're leaving," I said, as calm as bay water, and I shrugged my shoulders. "Maybe I'll keep her after all."

Creed cursed under his breath. Yasmine's eyelids briefly trembled, but the hurt I expected never flickered across her face. She was so good at shutting out the hurt. "Suit yourself."

She turned and stormed toward the door.

I looked to Creed, who pushed his fingers through his cropped hair as he scowled at me.

"What?" I snapped as the door slams behind Yasmine.

"You're no good at this, are you? You've got no fucking clue."

"And you're an expert?"

"I'm better than you."

Fuck. I blew air from my lips and turned on Liv, who cowered under my glare, regret plain on her face. "Pack your shit. I want you out of my clubhouse before I get back."

She lowered her head without argument. She wronged me. If she kept her mouth shut and minded her own business, she could've stayed, but she broke my trust. I had none left for her. I stormed toward the door and exited into the hall. Up ahead, Yasmine continued her stomping, stewing in her own tempest.

"Yasmine," I called out, and she ignored me. "Yasmine!"

I stomped forward, closing the distance between us with my big strides. Before she could round the corner, I snatched her by the elbow and tugged hard, forcing her to face me. "Woman, will you just fucking wait—"

"What?" she demanded, her ponytail whipping across her face, then falling flat over her shoulder.

Her face was pinched tight with anger. Her pretty eyes were fiery slices of frustration, her lips pouted pillows of disappointment. I hated I chased her up the hall. I hated the words that were about to leave my lips. All of it was an admission. An admission that she had me in her tiny palm and wrapped around all her slender fingers.

"What I said…I didn't mean it." I glanced at the wall. "Stay, Minnie. I want you to stay."

Her anger melted from her face, softening it into a look of pity. "I can't."

Goddamn it. Anger sliced through my chest and I clenched my jaw as panic tightened the muscles around my heart. The last time I was in such a vulnerable position, my life was ruined. The best thing for me, as president of this chapter, was to let her go and forget all about her. I knew I had to…but I couldn't. I wouldn't.

"I'm not asking you. I'm telling you," I seethed, tightening my hold on her elbow.

Minnie stepped forward and lifted herself on the tips of her toes, bringing her face closer to mine. "I am not your prisoner, Damon. I never was and I never will be."

I released her arm and towered over her, until she stood flat on her feet. "You're whatever I tell you to be. You *owe* me."

"I won't stay."

"You don't have a choice. I'll fucking chain you up."

She smiled at me and it was sympathetic because I was being pathetic. Because, deep down, I knew there was nothing I could do to make her stay. It was me or her son and she wouldn't choose a man over him again. Nicolás had Minnie's whole heart. I only held a fragment of it.

I exhaled and hung my head to look at my boots. I would let her go. What's another loss on the tally board that was my life?

Yasmine touched my hand, then gently cradled it. Her touch soothed the lava in my veins. It lowered my blood pressure and took the tension out of my shoulders.

"You can visit me any time, but I can't raise my son here. You know that."

My jaw ticked. I wanted to concede, but I wasn't fucking wired that way. "I said I wouldn't visit you."

"Shame. I'd make it worth your while." Lifting herself on her toes once again, she cupped my face, my stubble spikey against her palm. My set jaw softened under her gentle touch and she placed a soft kiss on my lips. "Please, can we go get my boy?"

I swallowed. There was nothing I could do to make her stay. Some things weren't meant to be. Yasmine deserved her fresh start with her son. And I...I didn't deserve anything.

I cleared my throat. "I'll meet you out front."

With a pat on my cheek, Yasmine turned away. I watched her disappear around the corner and, *damn it.* I pinched the bridge of my nose. I was gonna make time to visit her. I'd visit her every weekend and I didn't care how far I had to travel.

"Why her, Judge? Why the fucking complicated one?" Creed asked from behind me, throwing the question I asked him all those years ago back in my face.

And I finally understood.

SIXTEEN

YASMINE

The ride to Nevada was long and they didn't stop for anyone. My thighs ache from clenching Damon's thick body between them and the vibration from the ride remains a dance in my veins. Out front, a biker named Hawk leads the pack in a path he deems the quickest, and safest, way into the Vegas sands where we'll meet with a man called Marco Ventilli. If I recall my days at the Exeter precinct correctly, Marco Ventilli is head of the largest mafia family in Nevada. I heard The Devil's Cartel and the Ventillis had a score to settle, but I guess Marco has been too busy fighting his own enemies—enemies that live within his borders. As my trail of thought ends, I spot a line of black SUVs along the desert horizon, their shapes a silhouette in the bright moonlight. At a steady pace, we follow Hawk along the aged asphalt and pull over around eighty-five yards out from the intimidating shadows that block our way.

Creed rolls to a stop beside Judge and I and lowers his hands from his bars. "How do you wanna do this?"

"Grab the briefcase." Judge lifts himself off his motorcycle and I plant my hands on the warm seat in front of me to keep myself steady. "You're coming with me. Tell the others to wait."

Creed leaves his bike and saunters toward the rest of the crew while Judge extends his hand to me. I take it and he eases me off the motorcycle. I sigh in relief. It feels good to stand, to stretch my muscles and feel them firm under my weight.

"How was the ride?" he asks.

I blow air from my cheeks. I would've appreciated the ride more if anxiety wasn't eating me up inside. "Long."

Even though it's dark out, the moon casts a beautiful light and I see him smile. He grabs me by the teeth of my zippers on my black jacket and I gasp as he tugs me closer. He rubs his full lips together while he zips me up, protecting my chest from the rapidly cooling Nevada air. Then, he pushes my ponytail off my shoulder.

"We'll take the truck on the way home. You can sit with your boy on the backseat."

Excitement inflates my chest at the thought of holding Nicolás in my arms. I long for it, to have him in my personal space, to hold the most precious thing in the world to me. It's painful, how much I miss him.

"Thank you for everything you've done for me."

His face turns uncomfortable and he angles his body away, glancing over the sand dunes to the right. "Thank me later, when it's over and we're back on home soil."

The unease in his tone tilts my stomach, filling it with worry. *I hope we make it back to Exeter.*

"They're not happy about hanging back," Creed says as he approaches with the suitcase.

"Too bad." Judge shrugs his large shoulders and pulls his cut tighter around him. Flicking his head at me, he turns toward the SUVs. "C'mon, Minnie."

I blanch as a metal rod jams my spine and my heart sinks into Isabelle's boots—boots that are a little too small for my feet. "Me? Why?"

"You don't leave my side," he orders, and Creed takes my bicep in his giant hand.

He pulls me along, forcing me to walk between them. I stuff my hands into the pockets of my jacket and walk fast, trying to keep up with their big strides. I glance at both of them. Their handsome faces are set tight, their dark eyes focused only on the SUVs ahead. I feel safe between them, safer than I've ever felt, but a teeny tiny part of me won't settle. A nag in the back of my mind demands I stop being stupid. It demands I protect myself because they're going to betray me. I stop, so does Judge and Creed. They both glare at me and there's such a beautiful resemblance in their features. If they told me they were brothers, I'd believe them.

"What?" Judge demands and I lift my chin.

"Can I have a gun?"

He frowns. "What for?"

"To protect myself, if needed."

They glance at each other, then Judge flicks his head at Creed who reaches behind his cut and frees his handgun from the waistband of his jeans with an offended laugh.

"If we were gonna throw you under the bus, sweetheart, you'd be there already."

He extends his gun to me and I take it, slipping it into my own waistband at my lower back. "It's nothing personal."

It's only to silence the automatic thoughts before they run rampant in my brain. We walk, closing the distance between us and the men who begin to exit the SUVs. They're tall and statuesque, and dressed like they're attending a business meeting at the very top of a high-rise building. There's something unsettling about their formality compared to The Devil's Cartel men who spend their days doing business in washed out band t-shirts, leather cuts, and faded jeans. Maybe it's because I link their sleek attire to Elias, who's always dressed like he's on the cover of an elegant men's magazine.

Out of the front passenger seat of the third SUV in the line of five, steps a pudgy man in a pastel blue polo and white pants. Without a glance in our direction, he reaches inside and pulls a white jacket off the seat. He shrugs into it, and signals to three men on his right. They lift their big, black rifles and flank him. Judge stops, snagging my elbow, and I wait with bated breath as they stroll closer, as if they have all the time in the world.

"Damon Judge," Ventilli calls, stopping eight feet out. "It's been a while since you've shown your face at my border."

Judge hums and I ease closer to him, our arms brushing. "Wouldn't be here if I didn't need to be."

An awkward silence falls between us. They simply stare, all of them, and I can't take my attention off the rifles. A creeping suspicion that Elias has already paid off the Ventillis snakes through my mind. Will they shoot us? I didn't come all this way to be shot dead on a back road.

"How's Seraphina?" Creed voice cuts through the silence, and everyone looks in his direction.

Everyone except me. I keep my stare on Marco, whose expression gives away his irritation.

"Married. Just gave birth to twin girls."

"Married? To who?"

Marco points to the tall, broad shouldered man standing on his left. "Ben Campbell."

The man, Ben, stands taller by squaring his

shoulders and glares down his nose at Creed. He's big, as big as Judge and Creed—if not bigger. His index finger twitches as he rests it alongside the body of his rifle, not far from the trigger.

"I'm disappointed," Creed says, and I hear the taunting tones in his voice.

What is he doing?

"Why? I heard you robbed a different cradle." Marco's thin lips quirk at the corner.

Judge snorts as Creed scowls. I don't think he appreciates the implication. I don't know the exact age gap between Isabelle and Creed, but I know it's at least a decade.

Marco stuffs his hands into the pockets of his slacks and leans to the side, peering between us. "Casino back there?"

Judge stiffens. "Don't worry about it."

The mafia boss straightens and watches Judge down the bridge of his crooked nose for an uncomfortably long time. "I hope you haven't forgotten we still have our war to fight."

The air surrounding us is palpable, thick enough to cut with a knife, but Judge is uncharacteristically placid.

"There's a long line of people who want to kill us, so you're gonna have to wait your turn." He flicks his wrist. "Give him the money, Creed."

Money? The briefcase is filled with money? Creed lifts the briefcase and walks forward. Ben

Campbell lowers his rifle and steps forward to receive it. The briefcase clicks as Creed opens the metal clasps. I lift myself onto my toes and lean forward, trying to see inside.

Ben eyes it suspiciously. "I heard you were operating at minimum capacity since the FBI investigation."

"Don't believe everything you hear," Judge tells him. "It's all there. Two hundred and fifty thousand for a temporary ceasefire, as requested."

Two hundred and fifty thousand? Blood drains from my face and my legs wobble. Ben glances over his shoulder at Marco and nods. Satisfied, Marco nods back and Creed closes the briefcase.

"How're you liking the family business?" Creed asks, but Ben ignores him, turning his back.

"I'll give you six hours," Marco says. "Overstay your welcome and my men will hunt you down and bury you beneath the sand." He steps forward, toward Judge. "You can spend eternity with your friend, Mayor Laurent."

I suck in a sharp breath and peer at Damon. I've heard the rumors about Jonathan Laurent's disappearance. All of them circled The Devil's Cartel, but the authorities have never found any hard evidence to hold them accountable. Isabelle was badly hurt by her father and I have no doubt Judge and Creed took care of him. Marco all but outed Judge as a murderer, but Judge stands strong and firm, unphased by the accusation. Dare I say, he's even a little proud.

I peer at the cool sands surrounding us for miles. Laurent is buried out here? A chill sweeps up my spine and I shudder. Does Isabelle know? Would she even care?

"Six hours is more than enough," Judge says after a small eternity has passed.

"Then you get four."

"Four?" I gasped, stepping forward only to be caught by Judge's palm on the flat of my belly.

"Four will do," he says, flicking his thumb over my mid-section.

I look at him. Four hours isn't enough time. What if Elias has changed his location? What if Nicolás needs medical treatment? What if any of us need medical treatment? If the wounds are bad enough, we won't make the drive back to California. My chest tightens.

Without a farewell, Marco turns, and they walk back to their fancy SUVs. Judge, Creed, and I stand in silence, watching until their taillights disappear into the night.

"Tell the others," Judge says to Creed. "Clock's ticking."

Creed saunters off as Judge turns his body in my direction. He glides his palm to my hip and clasps it, before gently turning me to face him. He surveys my face and I know he can see the concern etched deep into my skin.

"Trust me," he utters, and I rush air from my lips. "Just trust me."

I peer into his ocean eyes—eyes that are as black as space right now. I should trust him. I do trust him.

"That was a lot of money." I rub my lips together, hating the way my anxiety reaches my voice, making it shake. "More money than I can ever repay..."

"You don't have to repay it. It wasn't from the club's fund, so there's no paper trail, no contract."

I frown. "If it didn't come from your fund, where did it come from?"

I pray it isn't his money. If it is, I'm a goner. I can't walk away from a man who'd give so much without wanting anything in return.

"It's Blondie's money."

Oh. "Isabelle? Why would she do that for me?"

"She's got a big heart." He inches closer until our bodies press together. I crane my neck to look up at him and he peers down at me with a gaze full of esteem, making my tummy flutter. "And deep pockets."

Thoughts of her money lead me to thoughts of her father, Jonathan. He's a missing person still—assumed dead, but not declared.

I lift my arms and wrap them around Judge's waist, holding his thick body against mine. "What

Marco said...did you really kill her father?"

Judge purses his full lips and his eyes gloss over in thought. He stews on my question for longer than I anticipated. I assumed he would brush it off and tell me to mind my own business, but I can see the gears turning in his eyes.

"I asked you to trust me and you have, wholeheartedly. Now I'm going to trust you." He cranes his neck, bringing his lips to my ear. "I've scattered Jonathan Laurent all over this desert, and tonight, Elias will join him."

He lingers by my ear, his lips the gentlest graze, lifting the hair on the back of my neck. He's confessed to murder...and I feel nothing. Not even fear. I know now, without a doubt, that Damon Judge is dangerous. He's a criminal. A murderer. He's everything I once swore an oath to destroy...but his charming lasso remains tight around my soul.

"I..." I swallow hard, noticing my mouth is suddenly dry. Images of Elias shaking Nicolás as a newborn—images of every wrong he's committed against our son—assault my mind. He deserves to die. He deserves to rot in hell. "I want to be there when you bury Elias. I want to see it."

"Nah. Let me shoulder all the evil shit." Judge touches my hair and cups my face in his warm hands. "How can you raise Nicolás with those visions in your head?"

He lowers his head and presses his mouth to mine. The touch stuns me with its gentleness. Judge's kisses are normally conquering and plundering, leaving his mark so I won't soon forget it.

But not this one.

I part my lips and his tongue is right there, slipping between my lips to taste me. I dissolve into him, my leather jacket melting into his cut. As if the ticking clock he previously mentioned has paused to allow us one last unhurried moment, he uses his tongue to patiently memorize my mouth. I touch his arms, then slide my hands up to hold onto his shoulders and a husky groan vibrates his chest. He wraps his arms around my waist and squeezes me to him, kissing me even deeper, until my head spins…

…until an ear-piercing whistle zips through the night air, penetrating our bubble to remind us that the clock is still ticking.

Judge pulls away and our gazes lock. His lips are wet and shiny from our kiss, making me want more, and there's a sad, disappointed look in his eyes. For a second, it feels like he's going to ask me to stay, but he already knows the answer.

"I hope you know I want to stay with you, more than anything…" I drag a subtle inhale through my nose, expanding my lungs. "But I need to put Nicolás first."

"I get it." He plants a chaste peck on my lower

lip and releases me from his hold. "I'll visit you. No motorcycle. No colors."

Something deep in my soul brightens. "You changed your mind?"

He glances over the desert, genuine happiness tugging at the corner of his lips. "Yeah."

Does this mean we're dating? Are we exclusive? I'm too scared to ask, but whatever he means, it's enough for me. Smiling, I hold out my hand and he takes it. We walk side by side back to his motorcycle and I feel good about what's coming. The universe owes me a win, and I feel it. This is it.

"There was no time for me to stop at McDonald's for a cheeseburger, but there's plenty of time for you two to play tonsil tennis?" Modo shouts, sitting atop his bike, his big arms folded tight in front of his chest. "What a crock of shit."

Ignoring him, Judge lifts his leg over his bike and settles on his seat. I take his extended hand and step onto a tiny metal plate welded to the side of his motorcycle. I grip Judge's thick shoulder for balance and straddle my seat, pressing my thighs around him.

"You can get your cheeseburger on the way home, Modo, you fat shit," Creed calls, turning his motorcycle on.

"Then let's fucking go!"

The motorcycles roar to life—all of them—and I inhale, my body filling with renewed confidence. I can't fight the smile on my lips at the powerful sound the bikes make. It's like a kingdom of lions or raging oceans at the center of a tropical storm. A powerful surge of emotion swells in my chest. I'm no longer a desperate and powerless mother trying to move mountains on her own. I'm not alone anymore.

Now I have an army.

SEVENTEEN

JUDGE

Elias Vergara was exactly where Sora said he would be. In a fortified lodge hidden in the woods by Mount Charleston. His security was minimum because he was an arrogant bastard who believed no one had the balls to attack him. We're gonna do more than attack him. Tonight, we were going to smash his legacy into pieces, until there was nothing left to salvage.

Our approach to Elias's hideout was simple. We peeled off the secluded road just under a mile out from the long, steep decline of the white gravel drive that carved the way to the main entrance. Our bikes were many and we pushed them into the dark thicket, haphazardly hiding them from the road. Amongst the sounds of crickets, and whatever else scurried through the Nevadan hills this time of night, my men murmured and prepared their guns.

Clicks of metal and a gentle hint of gunpowder invaded my senses, eliciting goosebumps across my flesh. It'd been a long time since we were all out on a run like this—and we were all here for Nicolás. Even our prospects.

Minnie sat on my bike and quietly watched as I dug through my saddlebag. From its depths, I took out a handgun and placed it on my seat in the space between her legs. Then, I reached inside the bag and grabbed a busted packet of cigarettes.

"Is that to calm your nerves?" Yasmine asked, and I looked at her as I pinched the butt end of a cancer stick and freed it from the pack, along with a skinny blue lighter.

"Something like that."

I put the cig between my lips, lighted it, and dragged on it. I held the smoke in my lungs until it burned, then I blew it out and licked my lower lip. She looked the part of a bad biker bitch and I was falling for it—for the daydream of always having her on the back of my bike.

Holding out her fingers, she silently asked for my cigarette. I gave it to her and watched as she held it between her full lips and inhaled, the cherry on the end glowed bright red.

"I gotta tell Creed he's on lookout." I cleared my throat and glanced over at Creed, who admired his AR-15 as he wiped over its army print barrel. "I promised Blondie I'd keep him safe."

Blowing the smoke from her lips, she gently coughed. "He's not going to like that, is he?"

"No."

"Well…" She took another drag, blew more smoke from her lips, and handed my cigarette back. "Good luck."

My lips quirked. *Good luck.* When it came to telling Creed *no*, I needed more than luck. I needed a damn miracle. I touched Yasmine's leg. It was a small touch, the tip of my index finger against her thigh. I brushed it up and down, a soft caress, and she watched it. Then, I left my packet of cigarettes and the lighter on my seat and I headed in Creed's direction. I flicked my head at Armi as I passed him, and he followed me with his sniper rifle against his shoulder. Creed lifted his attention to us as we approached, and he smirked.

"I've been waiting a long time to try out my custom trigger," he said, lifting his gun to show us, but it didn't look any different to me. "Finally."

I dragged on my smoke and blew it out before it hit my lungs. "Give Armi your rifle."

Creed thinned his dark eyes as he frowned, but he did as he was told. He handed over his rifle to Armi, who stepped forward to take it. Armi was my best marksman and it was a risk not to have him on the sniper, especially with this much surrounding foliage, but for Creed, being up here on the incline was safer than being in the middle of the shitshow.

Before today, I would've told Blondie to shove it. Creed was my right-hand man and I never entered a fight without him, but Blondie was ready to start her family and she needed James alive for that. I told her I couldn't keep him on the sidelines forever, but for the time being, I could surrender him. God knows he wanted a baby, and he wasn't getting any younger.

"Sniper is yours," I told him, dropping my cigarette to the ground, no longer liking the taste on my tongue. I stomped it out in the dry leaves under my heavy, black boots. "You'll be on lookout."

Armi extended the rifle to Creed, but Creed didn't reach for it. Instead, he cut his eyes at me, and if looks could kill, I'd have dropped dead. Leaning against his bike, Creed crossed his arms over his chest.

"I'm not coming down the hill?" he asked, and I took the slim, but heavy, sniper rifle from Armi's grip.

"You're not coming down the hill."

Armi turned on his heel and sauntered away with Creed's pride and joy. The silence between Creed and I was palpable, but it went deeper than anger. He was disappointed and I knew why. He worked his jaw, processing the fact I was leaving him on the sidelines. He couldn't stand being idle, not when the whole chapter was out for the first time in years.

"Blondie put you up to this?"

I didn't react, not a nod or a shake of my head. I wasn't following Blondie's orders entirely. I didn't want him down there because I needed someone I could trust—a good man—to take over the chapter should something happen to me.

And, also, Isabelle was pretty fucking scary when she demonstrated what she'd do to my balls if Creed were hurt tonight.

"Keep your distance. Stay up on the hill," I growled at him, shoving the rifle into his chest.

He didn't take it. "Or what?"

"Or I'll shoot you myself."

His stare didn't leave mine. He didn't back down, and I didn't expect him to, but I expected him to have enough respect for me, as president to do what he was told. He usually listened without argument, but Blondie had been a spanner in the works from the moment he met her, and I no longer trusted him to comply. I pressed the rifle harder against his arms and chest, and clenched my teeth. *Just take the fucking gun.* I didn't want to hurt him, but I'd shoot his foot if he didn't obey.

Exhaling, Creed uncrossed his arms and snatched the gun. The thick tension in the air melted away and I let out a breath I didn't know I was holding. The last thing I needed was to fight him. For Creed, one of the most stubborn fuckers I'd ever known, to give up without much of a fight, meant he must've already had this argument with Blondie. He knew

303

what she wanted. She wanted him to come home as healthy as he left.

"I won't be able to see shit through this foliage, Damon." He placed the gun on the back end of his motorcycle, muttering something that ended in *"boring as hell."*

I shrugged and held out my hand. "Should've brought a book."

Cussing, he dug into the pocket of his cut and freed a silver pair of cuffs. I didn't dwell on the betrayal emanating from Creed's person because I had another heart to break. Stuffing the cuffs into the front pocket of my jeans, I made my way back to Minnie, who stood behind my bike admiring my handgun. She rolled it in her small hands, appreciating every crevice, pausing when I entered her personal space. Her lips curved gently as she turned to face me.

"What gun do I get?" she asked, extending my gun—handle first—toward me. I take it and slip it into the back of my waistband.

I didn't answer. Behind us, the chapter was ready to go, and they melted into the greenery. The air changed when they left. The wind turned ice cold and the insects held their breath. As I stood with Yasmine under the trees, I was no longer president of a motorcycle club. I was a friend. A lover. I was someone who cared deeply about the outcome of the fight.

The problem with caring so much for someone was the distance I was willing to go to keep them safe. Even if it hurt them. I knew the pain of not doing enough, of not being protective enough. I knew better now, and I'd do everything in my power not to suffer through it again. Even if they hated me for it.

I touched Minnie's soft wrists, then her dry, cold hands. They trembled.

"It's been a while since I've stormed a building." She smiled at me, but it didn't reach her eyes, and fear etched her features as clear as day. "Eight years ago, I would've been in my element."

While she spoke, I reached into my pocket and freed my cuffs. Yasmine looked at them, confused and unresponsive as I trapped one of her wrists with the metal.

"Wh-what are you doing?" She lifted her gaze to mine and it'd be a lie if I said the look of her didn't sock me in the guts.

She didn't even fight me as I leaned around her and handcuffed her to my bike. Gasping, her eyes went wide and her skin paled. She looked like she was in pain, as if I violently drove a knife through her chest a million times. Tears welled, but she squared her shoulders and lifted her chin. Yasmine was driven and prideful. She had this vision of being her son's hero, of being the one who delivered him from his evil father, and it was clear in her stance, and her expression, that she hated me for taking it from her. But I was keeping her safe, and up here with Creed and Iris, she was as safe as she was gonna be.

"Uncuff me," she demanded, her voice miraculously controlled for someone with such turbulent eyes. "If you don't, I swear to God—"

She swallowed her words as I grabbed her face in both my hands. I cupped her cheeks and pulled her forward until her body hit mine, then I smoothed my hands over her hair. I wrapped her ponytail around my knuckles, feeling the soft, thick strands slip between my fingers. Her body bubbled with anger and betrayal. She was so mad I was certain steam would billow from her pores any second. I crushed my lips to hers and kissed her. Minnie's body went rigid against mine, but I felt her grip on the front of my cut, pulling me further into her, into her kiss. Her pride didn't want her to kiss me, but I felt the desire in her soul tugging at me.

I touched her face and broke the kiss. "I won't be long, baby."

I turned and stormed off, cringing at the sound of the metal cuffs scraping the metal of my bike.

YASMINE

Judge disappears into the thicket without a glance over his shoulder and I purse my lips, biting down hard to prevent the scream that bubbles at the base of my throat from tearing out of my mouth. How can he do this to me? How can he drive me all the way to Nevada only to string me up on the sidelines? Here I'm helpless. Useless.

Judge knows how bad I want to be there. Nicolás needs to see my face first. He needs to know I'm leading the charge. He needs to know Mommy is here fighting for him, risking it all for him. How else will he forgive me? How else can I forgive myself? I spent so long begging for help, doing nothing but waiting for Judge to get off his ass and give me the manpower I needed to get my boy. And now I'm here. I need to be at the forefront, only then would the risks I've taken be worth it. Only then will I be able to rid myself of this guilt threaded deep inside me and clear the heavy cloud of uselessness hovering over my head.

Ten minutes pass before I growl in exasperation and slump my shoulders.

"He wants to keep you safe," Creed says, irritation thick in his voice. I lift my head and peer at him as he slings his sniper rifle over his broad shoulder and slips his phone into the pocket of his jeans. Beside him, tiny Iris drums impatient fingers against the butt of her own rifle. "Us. He's trying to keep *us* safe."

Us. As if we're in the same boat. I don't need to be kept safe. If something happens to Nicolás, I have no reason to live. Death is something I came to terms with years ago.

I stare at the sizable vice president. I know about his plight with Jonathan Laurent and the extent he went to to protect Isabelle. Clubhouse stories paint him as a savage, a warrior, an unstoppable force, but here he stands, the big bad James Creed, sidelined on the same hill as me, staying out of harm's way while his brothers fight without him.

And he didn't even put up a fight.

"The way they speak about you around the clubhouse, the way Isabelle speaks about you, you're like a god," I say, seething, earning a frown from him. "You're supposed to be uncontrollable. Indestructible. You're such a disappointment."

"First of all." Iris scowls, her soft, pretty features turning sharp. She steps forward, planting a slender leg in front of her. Dressed head to toe in black, save for her brown cut, she's ready to defend her vice president. "He doesn't give a shit what you think of him."

I turn my attention from her to Creed as he sets his jaw tight. *If I can provoke him, or her, enough to let me go...* "It's what they're all going to think when they get back."

"Be grateful we're even here," Iris snaps. "This isn't our fight."

"It's our fight," Creed cuts in, not taking his gaze from me for a second. "It became our fight the moment Judge fell in love with her and her son."

I pull a face even though my heart races at the thought of it being true. "Judge doesn't love me."

Creed saunters closer. Dry leaves and twigs are crushed under his heavy boots and crickets grow quiet the closer he comes to me. I swallow as he towers over me.

Tilting his head, Creed asks, "How does a detective miss all the clues?"

Clues? What clues? Judge and I shared a mutual adoration for each other's paternal and maternal qualities. We shared a mutual physical attraction too, but I don't think it can go any deeper than that. The fact I'm an ex-law enforcement officer makes him uncomfortable, and the fact he's a criminal doesn't sit well with me. And *love?* The word sends a chill down my spine and a sickness through my stomach. In another life, I'd let myself fall head over heels for Damon Judge, but in this life, the only boy I love is my son. He needs so much love I can't possibly spare any for anyone else, and I won't. Not even a drop.

I inch closer, straining Judge's bike. If I pull hard enough, it will topple over. I'm so close to Creed I can smell his cologne, hints of asphalt and burning rubber. He smells like Judge…and it makes me lightheaded in the most delightful way.

"He doesn't love me," I repeat, my voice firmer this time.

"If he didn't, we wouldn't be here fighting for you and your kid. He wouldn't risk the entire chapter for anything less than—"

"They're here fighting," I cut in, dropping my attention to the narrow rectangular patch on the breast of his cut. *Vice President.*

"What?"

"The rest of the members. They're here fighting. You're just here as a look out."

His dark, whiskey eyes flare as he bares his teeth. He hates it. He looks like he wants to slap me. I need to hit Creed where it hurts—his pride and loyalty—and pray he takes me down the hill with him. I open my mouth and it's loud—the gunfire, drowning out my insult. I'm glad it did. I don't think I would've come back from calling Creed afraid and weak. Lava zips through my veins as panicked heat pools in my face.

"You're his best friend, his right-hand man," I say, and it takes everything I have to keep fear from manifesting in my expression, to keep my tone calm. "I pray he doesn't need you down there."

Creed whirls away from me and storms to the edge of the hill. He pauses at the lip of the decline and stares into the dark abyss, the moonlight offering little refuge from the blackness. He turns from the hill and paces, only growing more agitated the longer the gunfire continues. It softens over time, as the battle moves from outside to inside. I close my eyes and pray Nicolás is somewhere safe, tucked away from the danger and the noise.

The gunfire goes on and on, an unbearable racket in the distance, rivaled only by the approaching thunderstorm. The moonlight is swallowed up, and dry lightning flickers, the flashes spiking my anxiety. On the tail end of a not so distant rumble, the apparently dense clouds begin to spit.

Creed tilts his head back and stares up at the foliage, then tosses his rifle to the floor. "Screw this."

He rushes the decline, leaving me behind.

"Creed, wait!" I shoot forward, nearly yanking Judge's bike from its stand. "Please, please!"

He slams to a halt and whips to face me. Pointing an angry finger at a motorcycle six feet from Judge's, he bares his teeth. "Key is in Armi's bag. You want it so bad, get it yourself."

He turns away, ignoring me as I shout after him. Iris follows, not paying me any attention as I demand for her to help me. When she leaves, my chest tightens as if I'm being crushed in a metal corset. I open my mouth, desperate to drag more air into my lungs, but it only makes me dizzy. I still and drop my head, resting my chin against my chest.

I breathe, short inhales in and even shorter exhales out. Then, I drag longer ones in through my nose and hold it for a few seconds, then breathe it out more controlled than before.

You want it so bad, get it yourself.

I set my sights on Armi's motorcycle and I pull hard on Judge's bike, toppling it over, getting me closer to Armi's bag where he's hiding the key. I reach, stretching so far my shoulders ache, and brush my fingertips along the sewn edge. I curse, then try again, coming up shorter this time. A strangled shriek squeezes out my throat and my feet slip out from underneath me, sending me plummeting into the mess of leaves below.

You want it so bad, get it yourself.

I clench my teeth until their surfaces ache and my jaw throbs, and I stretch more. I dig my boots into the ground and push off. The metal of my cuffs cut into my skin and it feels like fire at my wrists, but I keep pushing, uncaring if I sever my wrist. I groan, and that groan transforms into a gravelly shout as I straighten my legs and feel the ground give away beneath my boots. I gain an inch, then another, as I drag Judge's heavy motorcycle behind me. By luck, I snag Armi's bag in my hand and pull it, using it as leverage. I contort my body using as much force as I can to get it off balance, but it's not enough and I can't get Judge's bike to move any further.

A sob chokes me.

Then another.

But I keep pulling…

...until my muscles burn, and I...and I can't physically do it anymore.

I cry as I release Armi's bag and I roll onto my back. More thunder growls, more lightning flashes, and there's more water on my face from crying than there is from the rain. I scrunch my face, pinching it tight to hold back the onslaught of emotion and tears, but like a full cloud, it rips open and the waterworks surge. My dampening hair sticks to my face and I stare up at the canopy, deaf and blind to everything going on around me. In the leaves, I see Nicolás's face. I see his big eyes and gentle, lopsided smirk, and I cry harder. It seems no matter how hard I try for him, I come up short. It's never enough.

Lightning lights up the sky and a loud crash next to my head startles me. I jerk my head toward Armi's fallen bike and peer up at the shadow standing above me, watching from over the top of the motorcycle. I blink, clearing away the blur of tears and see Creed as clear as ever.

I glance at the bike, then back at Creed, who demands my silence with his intense stare. How much of it did he see? Warmth blooms in my cheeks at the thought of him witnessing my emotional meltdown. I don't know what it is but being in the presence of him—of any of the Devil's Cartel men—makes me want to be brave. I don't want them to see me as weak.

When he leaves, I let out the air I didn't realize I was holding and I waste no time digging through Armi's saddlebag, uncaring that my hand brushes against grenades and bullets. At the very bottom, I feel the thin, jagged edge of a key and I pinch it between my fingers. My pulse skyrockets as I take the key from the bag and use it to free my goddamn self.

EIGHTEEN

JUDGE

My first mistake was underestimating Elias and thinking we had the upper hand.

Bullets chipped away at the thick stone wall I leaned against and I blinked repeatedly as the residue burned my eyes. *Shit.* My chest heaved and I pulled my arms tighter against me, squeezing my shotgun in my grip, desperate to keep out of the line of fire.

My second mistake was leaving Creed on the hill. I needed him. I needed all the men I could get, and he was a fucking overpowering force to be reckoned with. I turned my head and looked at Armi as we rested against the stone wall of an indoor courtyard. Elias's men were relentless in their fire, but they weren't accurate. I imagined Elias Vergara was rarely attacked. His men were out of practice—mostly. Outside, we took down thirteen men

315

without issue. Inside, they had time to man their guns and get into position.

Armi lifted his arm and checked his watch. I peered at it and watched the minute hand tick, then I held my breath. That same moment came a deafening boom that shook the colossal stone lodge and the firing squad of twenty paused in their assault.

They shouted in Spanish and the sounds of boots against hard stone was prominent over the buzzing in my ears.

"Go!" Armi demanded, pushing off the wall.

He gripped the well-oiled steel of Creed's weapon, pressed the stock into his shoulder, and rounded the corner. Bullets sprayed with every squeeze of his trigger and they snapped and cracked through the air. One after another, my men stormed past me, moving further into the lodge. Guns went off and each roar carved its way into my ears, and as Kace pulled up his skull neck gaiter, covering his mouth, I was ready to go. I followed close behind Kace and kept my eyes on the prize—the massive stone staircase at the center of it all. At the sight of it, my thoughts swayed from the fight at hand to the intricate details carved into the stone.

Was this how Minnie lived? In such grandeur? Insecurity I wasn't used to feeling wormed through my stomach. I bet she thought the clubhouse looked like shit. I put a lot of money into the design, decoration, and the upkeep of our place, but its chromium accents and leather trimmings were nothing compared to the gold fixings and marble sculptures, carved with such precision they looked soft. Images of Minnie dripping in diamonds on superyachts and in magnificent mansions assaulted my mind. It must've been hard to leave it all behind…another testament to the unconditional love she had for Nicolás.

"Judge!" Creed's voice hit me like a train, then came his body, colliding with mine.

Bullets ripped apart the hard floor, sending clouds of dust into the air. I was yanked by the back of my cut and dragged behind a chunk of glossy marble. I shook my head as Creed pressed against the base of a crumbled statue on bended knee, and emptied his clip. Cursing, he dropped low and dug into the pocket of his cut.

"What the hell are you doing here?" I demanded, sitting upright.

"Saving your ass." He freed a clip from his pocket and dropped the empty one from his gun. Clicking the new one in place, he cut his eyes at me. "What the fuck were you thinking?"

"I was thinking how rich this bastard is. Is Minnie still—"

He threw himself back into the gunfight, shooting his handgun like a mad man. Creed flew out from behind the marble and disappeared into the fray. To my right, a smoke grenade burst, and I rolled into it. I held my breath until it was tight in my chest, and headed for the stairs. From somewhere, Armi shouted for the men to keep driving Elias's goons out the back. I buried the stock of my shotgun into my shoulder and approached the stairs. Creed flanked me from the left, sporting a long, sleek rifle now. Blood splattered his face and seeped from his lower lip.

"I should've known you'd never stay put."

"If you *ever* strand me as a look out again, I will shoot you." He cut his eyes at me, his white-dusted eyebrows narrowing. "We fight together or not at all."

Clenching my jaw, I nodded my head. It didn't feel right, breaching the premises without him. He was my righthand man, and now he was here, I had the confidence to get in and do what needed to be done.

Creed and I bounded up the long staircase and swept the upper level. We stepped over large chunks of expensive debris and countless dead bodies. Room after room was barren of life until we hit the upper right side of the building. Breathless, I turned the handle, but it didn't open. I shook it. Nothing.

"Locked," I said to Creed, and I stepped aside and braced against the frame.

Creed stood in front of the door and pulled back,

cocking his leg back, bringing his knee closer to his chest. A mighty growl ripped from his chest as he slammed his leg forward, crashing his boot into the finely polished wood. The door splintered as if it were made of thin plywood and he rolled his body to the other side of the frame, adjacent to me.

He blew air out of his cheeks, then flicked his chin. I flexed my fingers against my shotgun and turned my body into the broken door. I entered the room, my shotgun up and my finger eager against the trigger. Elias sat behind his big oak desk, relaxed in his leather chair. The jacket of his black suit was haphazardly thrown open, exposing a neatly tucked white button up shirt.

Other than him, there was no one else in the spacious room. He pinned me with his black eyes and dragged his index finger thoughtfully across his lower lip as he gently swayed side to side. He had no fear on his features, nor a weapon in either hand, and the sounds of gun fire weren't so muted in the distance. That put me on edge.

"Whatever she's offered you, I can double it," Elias said, his smooth tenors not betraying any fear he might be feeling inside. "Triple it."

"Well." Creed laughed under his breath as he entered the room and stopped three feet to my left, his rifle pointed at Elia's ugly face. "Three pussies *are* better than one."

I smirked. That was one way of letting him know

Yasmine never offered me any money, I suppose. Elias clenched his jaw and his eyes thinned, sharp and accusing, underneath his deep frown.

"You slept with the enemy."

I flexed my fingers against my gun. "She's not my enemy."

"She's a pig."

"Was."

Elias sat forward and Creed jolted, stepping toward him. "Always will be."

"Where's the boy?" I demanded, sparing a glance to my right.

Nicolás wasn't in here—unless Elias had him stashed behind a fake bookcase.

"Boy? You mean my son."

"No." I lowered my gun and barreled forward. "He's not your son. You lost the right to call him that."

"Is that what she told you?" Elias looked me up and down, his lips quirking with smug disgust. "I'm not surprised. You see, my darling wife is..." he tapped his temple. "Unwell."

"*Ex*-wife."

His smug lips pulled into a wide, wolfish grin. "Funny. I don't remember signing any divorce papers."

His words triggered a jealousy unlike anything I'd ever felt. It was hot in my blood, mixing dangerously with emerging anger. My nose twitched. It fucking bothered me he felt he still had claim to her. She was mine—she said she was mine—but if he was telling the truth, she was still legally *his*. *His* wife.

"I told you, she's unwell," he said, as if it was all he needed to say for me to lower my gun and retreat. "Give her back to me and I'll make sure she gets the help she needs."

I aimed my shotgun at the surface of his desk and squeezed the trigger. It fired, vibrating my arms, and kicked into my shoulder. I blew a massive hole in his desk and shrapnel scattered from the blast, cutting exposed parts of Elias's wrists as he shielded his face.

"Mierda!" he shouted, his face flushing an angry red.

"Give me Nicolás!"

"Sobre mi cadaver," he seethed, shooting forward and slamming his fists against his destroyed desk. *Over my dead body.* "What kind of father would I be handing my only son over to murderers and rapists?"

Creed's rifle went off—a quick burst of noise and fire from the tip of his weapon. Murderers we were happy to admit, but rapists? None of the men in my chapter had ever been involved in a rape. Any that were I dealt with personally. Elias howled, his body jolted, and he fell deeper into his seat. Creed marched forward and I followed, approaching the desk. Elias squeezed his eyes shut and clamped his palm over his shoulder. Blood flowed freely over the back of his hand and spattered his crisp, white shirt. I felt my pupils dilate at the sight and saliva flooded my mouth.

Elias gasped and dragged deep inhales through his nose. "I-I can give you N-Nevada."

Creed peered sideways at me and I tightened my jaw. Nevada was the only state the Devil's Cartel didn't have a chapter in. It was quite an offer. It was an offer I had no business turning down without a meeting with my men…but they'd forgive me. Scoring a new territory or not, I had no intention discussing business with the likes of Elias Vergara and I trusted Creed not to mention it to the others.

"The Ventillis own Nevada," Creed said.

Elias shrugged his good shoulder. "For now."

I had no doubt he could take this state from Marco Ventilli, but so could I, if I really wanted to. The old president would've struck the deal with Elias and thrown Nicolás and Yasmine under the bus, but I was a man of honor. Yeah, I was a criminal, but I was loyal, and my loyalty couldn't be bought.

"Fuck Nevada," I said, and I meant every word of it.

Sighing, Elias closed his eyes and focused on his breathing. I glanced at Creed and he shrugged, then

Elias pushed his seat back and lifted himself off it. He swiped at his nose, smearing blood against his nostril. Groaning, he made his way around the desk and Creed let him go. I lowered my shotgun, then held it out for Creed to take.

Blowing air from his lips, he stopped gripping his shoulder and straightened his spine. "I thought you'd be a smarter man, Damon Judge."

The corner of my lips quirked. "And I thought you'd be taller."

For an injured man, he moved quick. He shoved his hand underneath his jacket and whipped out a small handgun. My heart leaped into my throat and I reacted. I grabbed his wrist in one hand and the barrel of the gun in the other. Growling, I snapped the gun back on him and, in the fumble, he squeezed the trigger. The bullets that exploded out the end kissed the tousled, charcoal colored hair by his temples. We froze and his volcanic glass eyes widened at the near miss.

"You kill me and you'll never find Nicolás's body."

Body? My heart sank, then burst with homicidal rage. If he touched a single hair on that boy's head, I'd break him into little pieces, and I'd keep him alive as I did it.

I knocked the gun out of Elias's hand. If we were gonna go head to head, I'd do it with my bare hands. Minnie was afraid of him and I'd show her he was nothing, that I crushed him without breaking a sweat. I bent my knees, dropped my shoulder, and slammed my fist into his ribs. I clenched my teeth as I threw my bodyweight into it—into him—twice! Air was forced from his lungs and blood spat from his lips and sprayed my face. I thought I had him. I thought I'd hit him so hard he'd never recover, but he deflected my third punch and shoved me onto my back foot. He swung his fist and hit me in my jaw, tossing my head to the side. Pain erupted and blood pooled, the metallic flavor overbearing. I pushed my tongue against the roof of my mouth, gathering blood, and I spat it on the floor.

"You're going to kill me? For *her*?" I gripped him by the collar, pulling him in close. Behind him, Creed exhaled and sat on the corner of the desk. "She's—"

"Mine." I drew my head back and slammed it into his nose. His body slackened in my grip. Pain crepitated across my forehead, but Elias was worse off. Crimson blood sprayed from his nose as his eyes rolled in his head. "Yasmine and Nicolás are mine."

I released him with a shove and he dove at me. He drew his fist back and ploughed it into my torso. I hunched as my organs smashed together and my ribs touched each other under the force. It was a good punch, I'd give him that, but he wouldn't beat me. I launched forward, unrelenting in my assault as

I slammed my fists into him. He couldn't stop me. He could barely defend himself. I continued battering him until he collapsed to the floor and closed his eyes. His chest rose and sank with each shallow breath he drew in.

"Take my whore wife and the retarded boy. What do I care?" he gasped, his hands moving over his body like he didn't know which injury hurt more. Finally, he settled on the gunshot wounds in his shoulder. "I was using him as revenge on her. Not to start a war with you."

I kicked his arm away from his shoulders and planted my boot on his chest. "Revenge on her means war on me."

Elias laughed, then choked on his own blood. I put pressure on his chest so he couldn't clear the blood from his throat easily. I held out my hand and Creed placed my shotgun in it. I extended my arm, pointing my gun at Elias's face. I placed my finger over the trigger and applied pressure.

"Minnie!" A distant shout pulled my attention and I removed my finger from the trigger.

I looked over my shoulder at Creed for confirmation and he shrugged his shoulders.

"Hold him," I ordered, not wanting the slimy bastard to get away.

Creed sauntered forward. I took my foot off Elias and Creed planted his own boot in my place. Elias groaned, choking again, and I slung my shotgun over my shoulder and left the room.

I walked along the upper level, peering down at the destruction below. A handful of my men were shooting it out with a handful of Elias's. My men defended the stairs that led to Creed and me, while Elias' men tried to breach it. A flash out of the corner of my eye drew my attention. By the main entrance to the room, Minnie drove her knife into a man's chest. I turned to watch as the wild woman bared her teeth and shoved the man forward, using him as a shield to catch the bullets whirring in her direction. Taking the handgun from his side, she extended her arm over his shoulder and shot, killing three guys in front of her, clearing the lower level of Elias's remaining men.

I looked at Modo, who stood at the bottom of the stairs, an axe in one hand and a sawn-off shotgun in the other. His blue eyes were wide, his skin spattered in blood. *What the fuck?* He mouthed at me.

Yeah. *What the fuck?*

I turned my attention to Minnie, and she was already storming in my direction, her eyes narrowed, her lips held in a tight pout. She was covered in blood, her hair no longer in a tidy ponytail. She looked fucking wild. I loved wild.

I headed toward her. On the stairs, my men parted, letting me through, and I came to a stop in front of her at the bottom. She craned her neck to look up at me. Pride swirled in my chest. This whole time I treated her like I needed to protect her when she was more than capable of protecting herself.

"Where's Elias?"

I flicked my head up the stairs and stepped aside. This was her fight and she wanted to finish it. Who was I to take that away from her?

"Find Nicolás," she ordered and stepped closer. She spoke in a tone meant only for me. "And don't ever cuff me against my will again."

I smiled at her and she hated it. Turning from me, she marched up the stairs, ignoring the surprised looks from my men, and entered the room where Creed kept Elias trapped by his boot.

YASMINE

My spine wavers at the sight of Elias pinned underneath Creed's shoe. He's beaten and bloodied, already the pulp I wanted to turn him into. Disappointment licks at me, but the fact he's already so weak and injured is for the best. Physically, I've never been a match for him and, it seems, he isn't a match for Judge.

Creed offers me a small wave as I enter the room, but I keep my attention on my ex-husband. My heart races in my chest as I flick my gaze around the room, searching for Nicolás. The state of this house is horrific now the Devil's Cartel has barreled through it. If he's here, *I hope*...a lump forms in my throat and I clear it, then swallow hard. *I hope he's okay.*

I close the distance between us, and Creed lifts his boot when I stop beside him. We stare down at Elias and I barely recognize him. His face is swollen, his own blood painting his flesh. It's strange to see him like this—fallen so far from the pedestal he put himself on. He made me believe he was untouchable, that he was a god. Damon broke him in minutes, his palatial lodge barely standing, and I finally see him for who he really is. *No one. He's nothing.*

I crouch as Elias splutters, spitting blood between his lips, the red liquid bubbling, like a volcano about to blow its lid.

"Look at you," I whisper, tears welling in my eyes. "Not so mighty now, are you?"

His bloodshot gaze fell on me and a chill moved down my spine. I know the look all too well. It holds the same level of disgust as it did the day Nicolás was born. The same level of hate it's had since he discovered I was working for the Feds. I can't believe I loved him, that I thought he was the most beautiful man I'd ever seen, that I risked it all for him.

Elias's chest caves as his frame trembles with rage and pain. "I didn't hurt him." He licked his lips. "Not a hair on his head."

"You took him from me. That *is* hurting him."

"I'm s-sure it hurt you m-more than it hurt him." He gritted his teeth. "I s-should've h-hurt him. You k-killed Antonio."

"And I'd do it again." A flash of Antonio standing in front of me, sneering, and calling Nicolás that disgusting word flickers through my mind. I lean close, smelling the metallic scent of his blood as it mixes with his rich cologne. "I *wish* I could do it again."

"So, that's it?" He coughs. "You're gonna be some biker's whore? S-such a role model for your son."

If he were standing, I'd hit him with my gun, but he wasn't. He didn't stand a chance, not even against me, so I let him run his mouth because there's nothing he can say that will bury under my skin anymore.

"When Nic a-asks about his f-father...what're you going to tell him?"

I haven't thought about that yet. Exhaling, I stand up and pull my handgun from the waistband of my jeans.

"What makes you think he'll ever ask about you?" I ask, stepping over Elias to plant a foot either side of his waist.

Elias releases his shoulder and grips my calf—if I can call it a grip. It's weak and pathetic, more of a gentle caress than a hold. I straighten my arm, pointing my handgun in the middle of his ugly face.

"H-he'll ask about me. He'll want to k-know what happened a-and he's not going to underst-stand a word you say. H-he'll force you to relive th-this memory. It will h-haunt you for the r-rest of your life." He smirks at me—a wicked, evil smirk I never thought I'd see again. "K-killing a disabled boy's father. You're a bigger monster than me, Yasmine."

Anger flares. It swells in my chest and shoots down my arms to my fingertips. Baring my teeth, I pull the trigger and blow a hole in Elias's face. His hand falls away from my leg as smoke seeps from the tip of my gun. I drop it and it makes a small thud as it hits Elias's lifeless body. I stare down at the gaping hole, watching blood as it fills the cavity in his head.

This is it.

The end of a chapter I thought would go on for the rest of my life.

I inhale, and my chest caves painfully. I can't breathe.

Creed lowers his rifle and flashes me his palm, as if trying to steady me. "Minnie?"

I stumble backward, tripping on Elias's long legs, and hit the wooden floor. Debris stabs into my hands, but I don't care. I inhale again, deeper this time, and exhale even quicker. *I can't breathe.* Bile burns like acid in my gut and gushes up my throat. I twist my body and crawl on my hands and knees to the silver wastebasket next to the desk and I puke. Barely anything comes out, but I keep going, hoping the full feeling in my stomach will leave with whatever I expel. Acid burns my throat, leaving a bitter taste on my tongue as I force it out.

"Ah, shit, Minnie." Creed brushes his fingers up the back of my arm, up my bicep, and bunches my hair in his fist.

With his free hand, he rubs his giant palm over my back. I keep dry retching and it's awful. My eyes water as pressure builds behind them. I try to think about other things—nicer things—but the smell. *God.* The smell. I sob and it jams a retch in my throat. The sob squeezes itself out, bringing with it a surge of tears I don't want to shed.

"Hey, cut that shit out," Creed demands, pulling my face out of the wastebasket. He swipes at my face, at my mouth and my eyes. "Suck it up, baby. Don't let them see you like this."

I sniffle, forcing the tears back. I don't want *him* to see me like this. I don't want any of them to see me like this. I close my eyes and inhale, finally filling my lungs. Weight is lifted off my shoulders, a weight I thought I would live with for the rest of my life. And while a new weight settles, it's not half as heavy as it was when the day started. At this point in my life, it's all I can ask for.

"There you go." He pulls me to my feet and dusts me off. "You did good. Now, let's find our boy."

I frown. "*Our* boy?"

Creed smiles and it's warm and genuine— something I rarely see on any of the Devil's Cartel men. "He's part of the family now."

NINETEEN

JUDGE

I stood at the base of the stairs as my men filtered in from other areas of the lodge, from out the front and down the back. By headcount, I lost seven men. Add that to the eight I lost during the clubhouse attack this morning and I was down a significant number of members for a chapter who wasn't actively at war. The mother chapter would ask questions when I paid our chapter's dues in a couple weeks, but I guess that was future Judge's problem.

I sent uninjured men in different directions, instructing them to pull this place apart in search of Nicolás. I demanded they pull on candelabras and rip down bookshelves. Who knew where Elias was stashing the kid in this big ol' house? There were wine cellars to be explored and panic rooms to discover. Nicolás was here somewhere...and I squashed down the possibility of finding a lifeless body.

"Judge," Amani called from behind me.

I turned to face the direction of her voice—a wide hall opposite the damaged statue of The Rape of Persephone, a depiction of her kidnapping by Hades. I leaned to the left, peering around the statue, and my eyes widened at the sight of Amani carrying a pale boy in her arms.

My heart leaped into my chest and my beaming smile stretched wide on my face as she carried him in her arms. I started forward and Amani's pretty face twisted with…pain? My smile faded, my happy heart wrenching painfully as Nicolás's head hung over her elbow, his lips parted and void of color. Then I saw it, the dark reddish-brown stains on his orange shirt.

No.

I stopped and stared, hating the way oxygen was siphoned from my lungs—from the building. I remembered the last time I felt something so…sickening. I remembered my blood draining the same way it did when Creed carried my baby girl to me. I swallow hard, meeting Amani's scared dark eyes. She was looking for me to take the boy, and the burden. I didn't want to. I didn't want to be the one who delivered Nicolás to Minnie like this…but I was president, and this was my run.

My chest tightened, my lungs suddenly unable to

move against my heavy ribs, as I lifted Nicolás's shirt, peeling it from his bloodied body. I stared at the first hole in the lower right quadrant of his abdomen. A gunshot wound. Cursing, I lowered his shirt. He'd been hit by bullets, and they could've been anyone's—ours, or theirs.

And that killed me.

I blew air from my lips and pulled Nicolás out of Amani's grip. I held him close to my chest and stared down at him. He looked so much like Minnie—even had the same freckle on his cheek. My eyes burned and I blinked repeatedly, desperate for it to go away. I hadn't cried since I lost Nila.

"I tried…" Amani sniffled and pursed her lips to hold back the emotion. "I tried so hard, but he's bleeding too much."

"Nicolás?" Yasmine's voice stabbed into me, sharper than any blade to ever cut my skin.

Amani turned her back and swiped at her face, then walked from the building, not wanting to witness the ripping of Yasmine's heart from her chest. I didn't blame her.

I held my breath and slowly turned around. Yasmine's eyes were glowing, holding all the happiness in the world, only to fade when her gaze fell from me to Nicolás. I watched the blood drain from her face, her heart sinking with it. A strangled noise left her throat and her knees wobbled. She dropped and Creed caught her by the wrist, forcing her up straight.

"Oh, no," she whispered.

She gripped the bannister and descended the last few steps with Creed right by her side, stopping her from collapsing. I walked closer, carrying her whole world—her whole reason for living—in my arms.

She rushed forward. Touching Nicolás's face, she sobbed, her voice broken and strained, as she begged for him to open his eyes. *For Mommy,* she kept saying. *Mommy's here. Do it for Mommy.* Each plea for him to wake up and be okay wrenched my heart as her hands touched him all over. Nicolás s eyelids flickered and light lit up Minnie's face. She pulled him from my arms, and they fell to the floor. She cradled him in her slender arms, groaning when she grazed her palm over his injuries, over the heavily soaked fabric that stuck to his wounds.

"Call an ambulance," she demanded, not taking her eyes off Nicolás for a second.

I lifted my stare to Creed and clenched my jaw. *I can't tell her.* He nodded and stepped forward, debris crunching under his boots.

"There's...there's no service road out here, Minnie."

She shook her head, raking her fingers through her son's dark tuft of hair. "Th-they'll come. Call an ambulance, please!"

No one moved. No one would call, and not because Nicolás would be dead in minutes, but because it was the rule of the run—no police, no emergency health services. To die on a run was an honor and, for the first time ever, I hated that rule.

She looked directly at me, wanting *something,* but I did nothing except watch her heart shatter in her irises. She lowered her eyes to Nicolás, and I flinched, my face screwing up with the guilt that carved through my bones. Members began to leave, exiting the building at a slow and somber pace, until only Creed, Armi, and I remained.

"Bring the truck closer," I asked Armi, and he left to do the job.

Nicolás moved his hand and touched Yasmine's face, barely a graze against her cheek. She smiled at him, continuing to caress him all over, and it was a smile full of pain. She knew he wasn't going to make it.

"It's okay," she whispered, crunching her body to kiss him on the cheek. "You're going to be okay."

She kept kissing him, closing her eyes, and pressing her face into his touch…before his hand fell away from her and dropped against his body. Her face screwed up and spears of her loss impaled me. I clenched my jaw as my muscles flexed and I breathed rapidly through my nose. Mist fogged my vision. Whose bullets were they? Mine? Did I do this?

She cried hard as she clenched her son to her

body, so hard her wails were silent, and grief swept me into the same river she drowned in. All I could do was stand there and watch, my limbs frozen.

"I didn't want this," she cried, talking to me even though she never looked at me. "This wasn't what I wanted."

A honk sounded outside, and I moved forward. I took Nicolás from her arms as Creed helped her to her feet. I held the boy close, clenching him in my embrace as if he were my own. I wished it were different. I wished we could take him home and get to know him. Most of all, I wished I could show him what a real father's love felt like.

I gently placed Nicolás on the backseat and closed the door. I turned to tell Creed to find someone to ride my bike home when another door slammed shut. The red parking brakes on Armi's SUV stopped glowing and the car rolled forward. I swore and ran to the driver's side. I banged on the window as Yasmine rolled the vehicle across the front lawn. She didn't open it, she kept her stare ahead, her knuckles white on the wheel. I grabbed the door handle and yanked on it, but it was locked.

"Yasmine!" I shouted and she didn't react. "What the fuck—"

She sped off, leaving me staring at her taillights as she disappeared into the forest.

YASMINE

I drove for hours.

The sun was up.

The light on the dash begged for gas.

I didn't know where I was going or which direction I was headed. I just drove.

And drove.

I spoke to Nicolás. I told him about the day he was born, how his existence completed me, and how his birth saved my life. Before him I had nothing to live for. After him, I feared dying and leaving him behind. I told him about Exeter, my time with Judge, and how I got him to help. Mostly, I apologized for every day of his life that led to this moment. My ultimate failure.

His untimely death.

I swerve on the road as I blink through a never-ending stream of tears, then correct myself, only for the engine to stall and the car roll to a stop. *Out of gas.* I swipe at my nose and sniffle.

It's quiet, so quiet my ears ring. I look out the window for the first time since leaving Elias's lodge. Endless mountains and tall trees as far as the eye can see.

What the hell am I going to do?

I glanced in my side mirror and catch the sight of three black SUVs as they roll to a stop behind me. None of them belonged to the Devil's Cartel. If my heart still worked, it would've sunk into my feet. I keep my gaze on the first car. The door opens and out steps a familiar face. The last time I saw it, it was dark and obscured by shadow, but I remember his height and his width. The tall and imposing Ben Campbell kicks his door shut behind him and lifts his handgun.

Sighing, I open my door.

"You're out of time," he shouts.

I know. I swing my legs off the seat and step out of the car. My shoes touch the earth and my legs fall out from under me, exhausted. I fall to my knees on the rocky asphalt and drop my face into my hands. Tears flow. They're unrelenting. Painful, even.

Ben approaches on his own, his gun still outstretched, and I lift my head as he peers into the backseat. He curses when he sees Nicolás, and his face falls.

"What happened?"

A gentle breeze blows, drying the tears wetting my upper lip. *What happened? I lost everything.* I hang my head.

"Get me water," he demands of his men, and they bring him a small plastic water bottle.

Ben tucks his handgun into his waistband and unscrews the lid. Crouching, he shuffles forward, and the breeze blows his cologne past my nose. I breathe it in. It's like Judge's and it threads comfort through my bruised soul. I gently lift my chin and

Ben places the mouth of the bottle against my lip. He gently tips it, letting water trickle over my dry lips. I part them, allowing the cold water to swirl around my tongue before I gulp it down.

"What hap—"

I choke as the water repeats on me, flying up my throat quicker than I swallow it. I keel over and puke the water onto the road. Nicolás's tiny palm felt like heaven on my cheek. He didn't open his eyes, but I felt the pure love in his touch. Then he left. And that moment of loss impacted my world with the force of an atomic bomb. I built my future on making it up to him, on making new memories— *happy* memories. Instead, I'm left with mistakes I can never fix, a hole I can never fill, and kisses I can never give.

I cough, spitting up the last of the water. Ben touches my arm and I shrug him off. "Don't touch me!"

"You'll die if you stay in Nevada," he utters, his brows furrowing. "Let me take you closer to Exeter—"

I laugh and it's ugly and bitter.

"I don't care if I die." I point at Armi's car. "My son is dead. I want to die." I glance at this hip, at the gun tucked into his waistband. "Give me your gun. I'll do it myself."

He swallows hard. "Do you need a hospital?"

I chuckle, my chest moving sporadically, and it

341

swiftly turns into sobbing. *It's too late for a hospital.* I cover my face with my hands and Ben stands up with an exhale and kicks a rock across the road.

"Boss said to kill anyone still on our soil," another male says, and I don't bother lifting my head to see who.

"She's not a Cartel member," Ben argues.

"Maybe she's a clubwhore. Can clubwhores be members?"

"I don't think she's that either."

I feel soft fingers under my chin and my head is lifted. I blink through the tears and look into Ben Campbell's dark eyes. "Are you with them? Or not?"

With them? Yes, I'm with them. Or was. I was with them.

"She's with us," Judge shouts, and I hear boots on the road. "If you want to keep your hand, I'd take it off her."

How'd they find me? I didn't hear their bikes. Ben drums his fingers underneath my chin, then stands up. His demeanor changes in the presence of the Devil's Cartel. He's taller, straighter, and his movements more calculated. He flicks his fingers toward Ventilli's SUVs and men spill from the black vehicles. I peer over my shoulder at Creed and Judge. They're outnumbered, but you can't tell it bothered them. They stand side by side, their rifles up, their faces pinched into angry scowls. My gaze meets Judge's and his tough façade softens.

"We're gonna bring you home, Minnie," he calls out. "Nicolás too."

"You missed your deadline," Ben shouts. "I can escort her out safely, but there's nothing I can do for you two."

"We can give Ventilli more money in exchange for more time to get home."

Ben laughs. "Unless you're hiding half a million dollars in your pockets, I doubt it."

Ben's men shuffle nervously as Creed reaches into his pocket and pulls out his phone. "I have a contact in my phone. That's pretty much the same thing."

He taps the screen and lifts the phone to his ear.

"We found her," he says. "But they're not gonna let us take her without—" He listens to what the person on the other end is saying, then he lowers it from his ear and holds it out to Ben. "If you've got a minute?"

Ben saunters forward, but not too far, and Creed meets him. Ben takes the phone and lifts it to his ear.

He listens intently, then his lips quirk. "Isabelle Laurent. I should've known you were funding their little excursion. He doesn't want any more of your money and I can't agree to anything without discussing it with him."

343

Ben's jaw tightens. What's she saying to him? Eventually, he hangs up the phone and returns it to Creed. Pulling out his own phone, Ben dials a number and strolls away. The low hum of his voice is all I can hear over the sounds of nature.

"Minnie," Creed grumbles, placing his rifle on the ground beside me. He touches my hair, smoothing it over with his palms, and grabs my face. "What the fuck are you doing?"

My chest shudders with the remnants of my sobbing. "I ran out of gas."

Creed looks exhausted. Why wouldn't he be? He's been up all night. "We're taking you home."

Home? Where the hell is my home? With them? "I don't have a home."

Creed pulls his head back a little, offended. "You've got one."

I do. I know that. I felt at home at the clubhouse. I felt wanted and appreciated. I never felt alone, not for a second. But right now? I'm depleted. I don't want to go back. I don't want to go anywhere. I blink. None of this even feels real. It's like I'm here, but I'm not here. What I wouldn't give to wake up, for this to be a nightmare.

I pinch the collar of my shirt and wipe my nose with it. "Is he mad at me?"

"Uh," Creed glances at Judge and swallows. "Yeah…but he'll be happier once we get back to Exeter and you're safe."

344

Exeter is ages away. "I have to take Nicolás to a hospital—"

"We'll stop at the first one we pass as soon as we're in California, I promise."

A lump wedges in my throat and I feel my face pinch as I hold back another surge of tears. Suppressing the grief sends sharp slices of pain through my chest. "I can't do that drive, Creed, not with my dead son in my lap. Not for that long."

"Then I'll hold him."

I shake my head as tears spill over the rims of my eyes. *Oh God.* I'm going to have to plan a funeral and purchase a plot. I have to do it all for a child no one knows exists.

"A hospital here can take care of him, clean him, and transport him to Exeter," Ben chimes in as he approaches. "You're free to go," he tells Creed, then points at me. "But she's staying."

"Get fucked," Creed bites out, standing up. "She's coming with us."

The sound of hammers being clicked bombards my ears. I don't want anyone else to die—especially Judge and Creed, who went out of their way to help me.

"Her car is out of gas. Are you going to transport the boy on your motorcycles?"

"If we have to."

"I want to stay," I say. I twist my torso and look at Judge. "I want to go to the hospital with Ben."

A hospital will take care of my boy, and I need time to process, to grieve. I can't be with the Cartel right now. They'll want to recap, they'll want to talk, and I don't have it in me. I need to be somewhere no one knows me and no one cares. Judge lowers his rifle and the look on his face is gut-wrenching. He's disappointed—heartbroken— but I need to put my boy first for the first and last time. I look away from Judge as Ben holds out his hand. I take it and he eases me to my feet, all while telling someone else to grab Nicolás out of the car. He escorts me toward the SUVs and eases me into the backseat. Ben slides in behind the wheel and the back-passenger door is opened. A brutish man avoids my eyes as he places Nicolás on the seat like a sack of potatoes and closes the door. If it weren't for the blood soaking his shirt, I'd have thought him peacefully asleep.

My heart stutters and I shuffle closer, crying as I lift Nicolás's head and slip my legs underneath. The SUV rolls forward and I look out the window as we pass Creed, then Judge. Judge is furious, his eyebrows furrowed, his jaw tight. I offer him a small wave and he gives nothing back. I don't expect him to...I just hope he knows I'm not blaming him, and it isn't anyone's fault but my own. I hope he knows I need to grieve on my own—just me and Nicolás, like it's always been.

TWENTY

YASMINE

○

EXETER, CALIFORNIA
SIX DAYS LATER

I tilt my head, lifting my chin to the sky. The sun shines brilliantly, basking me in all its glory as I stand beside my son's unfilled grave. It's convenient that the worst day of my life is the most beautiful I've seen. The grass is as green as ever, and the flowers are blossoming earlier than the year past. I should be thankful for such a stunning day, but it feels like betrayal for the day to be anything but overcast and miserable, like my soul.

"Anyone else?" the Father asks, and I bring my attention to the white wood of Nicolás's casket as I stuff my hands into the pockets of my flowing, black dress.

Squinting behind my big sunglasses, I shake my

head. Nicolás has no one else. Not even my parents know about him. Even if they did, they wouldn't make the trip from Washington since we haven't spoken since I was seventeen.

I've been in Exeter for five days and avoided the Devil's Cartel like the plague. I'm sure they know I'm here, but I haven't heard from them since I deserted them in Nevada. I left Creed and Judge on a road somewhere, and Isabelle half a million dollars poorer. I don't doubt they hate me for wasting their time and resources—for the loss of many of their members. I can't just send them a letter asking them to join me at a funeral when I shunned them from the night of his death. I owe them more than I can ever repay, and I'm terrified they'll never accept my thanks, or my apologies. I want to talk to Judge, to tell him it isn't his fault, but how can I go back there? How can I slip into his life like I didn't lose my heart and soul? I stare at the giant photograph of my boy. What I wouldn't give to kiss his round, pink cheeks, and ruffle his dark curls, and listen to him giggle as I did it.

The minister speaks and I'm unable to hold back my grief. Behind my black sunglasses, silent tears flow steadily down my face and it hurts. I've cried so much my insides feel battered and bruised. I will never see his face again or feel his embrace. The warmth in his eyes has been extinguished for good, the playful curve in his lips forever straight.

I hunch forward with a sob and the minister pauses in his speech. I gesture for him to keep going, to ignore me as realization of Nicolás's death settles in my soul. He continues his service, but the words he's saying takes the backseat to a constant buzz, much louder than a swarm of bees can make. It grows louder the closer it comes, the buzz turning to a hum, the hum morphing to a roar. Then they crest over the distant hill, spilling into the cemetery like ants on their shining, metal machines.

The Devil's Cartel.

My stomach rolls. How'd they find out I was burying Nicolás today? I kept it out of the papers for that reason alone. Worry pricks at me. Are they here to ruin it? To cause a scene?

The minister hesitates and casts an uneasy glance as the men draw closer. "Friends of yours?"

I swipe at my cheeks, clearing away the tears. "I'm not sure anymore."

My response makes him uneasy. The hoard of bikers stop not far out, a foreboding sea of leather and faded black denim. At the forefront, Judge swings his leg over his bike and stands beside it. Next to him, Creed and Isabelle do the same. He looks in my direction through his mirrored Ray-Bans and I can't tell if he's a friendly or an enemy. My heart tries to punch its way out of my chest as I stand and stare back. *Please don't be here to break me anymore than I already am.* Anxiety is a crushing pressure in my chest, but I won't let him see it. Swallowing hard, I lift my chin, holding my head high. I'm not going to let them ruin this.

"Please continue," I tell the minister, and he carries on with the service, his voice quiet, his face wary.

The Devil's Cartel lift off their bikes and every muscle in my body tenses, holding so tight a headache brews at the base of my skull. My vision blurs as the bikers move forward, an army of memories thrust to the forefront of my mind on a day I'd rather forget them. In a single file line, they approach Nicolás's grave and stroll past, lowering objects onto the grass beside it. Frowning, I blink to clear the blur and push my glasses off my eyes to the top of my head.

Flowers.

And teddy bears.

And toy planes.

They brought…gifts? One by one, and more than I can count, they place their gifts around Nicolás's final resting place and stand silently, listening to the minister. I feel Judge's presence at my side, tall and looming, but I keep my attention on Nicolás's casket, which is the only thing giving me strength right now. If I look at Judge or focus on the beauty of what the Devil's Cartel is doing for me, I'll lose it. I know I will.

Judge takes my hand in his. My heart stutters and

I part my lips to let out a gentle gasp. He's so strong and warm. His touch sends zips of electricity up my arms, reminding me that even though I've been feeling disassociated with myself lately, I'm still very much alive. The feeling overwhelms me. After abandoning him in Nevada? After costing Isabelle a ridiculous amount of money? I thought he'd hate me. But he doesn't. He stands beside me, holding my hand and caressing my soft skin with the rough pad of his thumb. He doesn't need to speak because his actions are loud. He cares about me, despite my mistakes, and he cares about my son even though he never got the chance to meet him.

As the minister finishes his service and Nicolás is being lowered into the ground, the minister turns to me. "Nicolás would be happy to know there's so many people to see him go."

I nod and thank him for his time. He plants a gentle kiss on my cheek and gives Judge a small smile of farewell. I thread my fingers together and inhale the fresh morning air deep into my lungs before turning to face Judge. He lifts his sunglasses onto the top of his head and our gazes meet. My ribs clench around my organs at the sight of his dark, ocean eyes as he flicks them over my face. The longer he watches me, the more uncontrollable my emotions become until they're bubbling right under the surface and my skin is alight with tingles. I blow air out of my lips and cast my attention across the

351

SKYLA MADI

cemetery to tall, decaying tress down the back, irritated that I can't keep it together in his presence.

"Come here," he says, and he pinches the front of my dress and tugs me forward.

He pulls me into his embrace and holds me tight, his big arms a strong rope that replaces the frail twine I've tried keeping myself together with. I press my cheek into the warm leather of his cut and breathe him in. Peace slithers through the chaos inside me and my muscles release from their tight clench as I lift my arms and wrap them around his waist.

"He would've loved you," I tell Judge, not bothering to fight the quiver in my lower lip.

"And I would've loved him back."

I close my eyes, turn my face into his body, and cry. I cry because I've lost my son, because I wasn't enough, because the strangers standing around his grave cared for him more than his own father did, and because every word out Judge's mouth is true. He would've loved Nicolás with everything he had.

Judge holds me for what feels like hours. When I finally pull away from him, Creed and Isabelle approach and offer their condolences with a side of more warm hugs. A part of me is wary, worried they're manipulating me for payback, but I'm sure that's the automatic negative thoughts talking. What will they gain from it? I have nothing left to lose.

"There's a barbeque for Nicolás back home, if

you're feeling up to it," Isabelle says, brushing her long blonde hair out of her face. "We miss you."

I miss them too, more than I thought I would, but I don't belong there. Do I? I start to shake my head, then stop. I could use a distraction. Besides, what better things do I have to do? It's a barbeque for Nicolás. It'd be rude not to go.

"We're gonna go for a ride first," Judge tells them before I get the chance. He takes my hand in his. "Then we'll come home."

Home. There's that word again. Judge escorts me away from Creed and Isabelle and I wave to the rest of them as he leads me to his bike. He gets on and holds out his hand. I reach out to take it but pause when I notice the ink of a beat-up teddy-bear on the inner side of his wrist. I move my palm over his to graze his wrist. Pursing my lips, I touch the cursive writing as it wraps around the bear and seemingly blows away in the wind.

"The longest walk home…" I whisper as I read it.

I think about his experience with his daughter and what I know from third party information. They say he carried her lifeless body for miles…

"You have me." He gifts me a sad smile. "You don't have to walk the whole way."

He grabs my hand and I climb onto his motorcycle, carefully tucking my dress around my legs and against his back so it doesn't fly away on me. He's slow to leave the cemetery and I watch the green grass as we roll over it.

We ride for hours, it feels like, and every minute of it I remind myself it's not a dream. By the time we stop, the sun is higher and hotter in the sky, and dewdrops have long since dried on the grass and on the crisp leaves of the tall, lean trees that tower above us. Straightening my spine, I peer over Judge's shoulder and spot the fireworks shack not far ahead. My tummy flips at the thought of revisiting our first meeting place. I followed him that night because something in my gut told me he was the one who could help me. He scared me, but not in the ways Elias did. I knew there was a gentle heart hidden deep within the MC president's chest. I just had to find a way in.

I clench Judge tighter in my arms. He slows his motorcycle and rolls us into the thicket. Once we stop, he grabs my hand and we leave the bike behind as we push through the shrubbery and exit onto the riverbank on the other side. The lake is different during the day, more impressive, but less magical...or maybe that's the way I'll see things from now on. *Less magical.*

I release Judge's hand and bend to take off my kitten heels so I can feel the warm grass on my feet. He leans against a nearby tree, watching me as I sigh and wiggle my toes in the rocky, grassy soil below, grounding myself.

"I was worried about you," he admits, and I turn my head. "You should've been at the clubhouse with us."

"I know. I just needed..." I rub my face. "I don't know what I needed. I don't know what I need."

Judge tilts his head and gestures for me to come closer. I saunter toward him and lean my torso against his.

"I know what you need." He brushes hair out of my face and touches my cheek. "You need someone to be there for you. You need someone who understands, who knows that empty feeling better than anyone else. You need me."

I lower my gaze to his firm lips. "I left you."

"You did."

"You could've been killed."

"I could have."

"And you still want me?"

His lips quirk. "More than anything."

I lift myself onto the tips of my toes to reach his lips. He gently touches my chin, guiding my mouth to his. Our kiss is gentle, barely a touch, but it washes away all my anguish.

Judge breaks the kiss as he pushes his fingers through my hair and toys with the ends. "Do you want to come home?"

A heavy fog settles on my shoulders. If I go back with him, that's it for me. There's nothing else in my life besides him. What if it doesn't work out?

What if…there's a million what ifs I can drop on him, but what if he wants more from me down the track? I clear my throat.

"You should know I can't have any more children," I say, the last secret I have from my time with my ex-husband. I spare him the gory details of being drugged in my sleep and having my reproductive organs ripped out of me. "Elias made sure of that."

Judge shifts uncomfortably. I know something as heavy as children aren't on his radar right now, but it's best he knows for the future. I expect him to retreat or to shrug it off because he doesn't see us going that far. What I don't expect is for him to plant a gentle kiss on my forehead and smile.

"We have children," he says, kissing me again. "A perfect daughter and a perfect son. We don't need more."

We have children. That's all I need to hear to fall head over heels in love with him—and the realization is terrifying. Emotion bubbles up my throat and I hide my face against his chest as my face pinches tight. I try to fight back the tears, but I haven't been any good at that these last few months, so I let them flow. And Judge doesn't rush me. He rocks side to side and rests his head against mine and peers out over the lake. Eventually, I turn my head to look too.

It's quiet. Peaceful.

In the distance, a dark flock of birds release from a cluster of trees and move through the bright blue sky, like a thunder cloud. I can't help the smile on my lips or the warmth spreading through my limbs. Nicolás loves birds and I choose to take it as a sign of his approval. *He would've loved Judge...he loved anyone who took the time to get to know him.*

"I could leave," Judge whispers as he tucks his head into my neck, afraid if he speaks too loud the universe will hear. "We could leave and never look back."

If we were to leave, where would we go? I don't want to be more than ten feet from Nicolas's grave—ever—and Damon will go mad having no one besides me to boss around. I pull away to look him in the face. His expression tells me he's dead serious in the way he holds his lips in a straight line and in the slight downturn of his brows. It's his eyes that give his heart away. He doesn't want to leave. He needs his chapter. He needs Creed and Armi, Amani and Modo—he needs them all in order to be happy.

"We don't need to leave," I tell him, and my palms grow clammy at the words bubbling up my throat. Here goes nothing. "I love you as you are."

Judge doesn't skip a beat. As if that's all he was waiting for me to say, he kisses me with a bruising passion, gripping my head in his hands, and the world falls away. I hold him closer, running my

357

hands down his back, pulling him closer until there's no space left between us.

I hope he knows every word out of my mouth is the truth.

I love him.

I love him as president.

As a criminal.

As a father.

I love him as he is, and as he always has been, the man who burned up all my daylight and consumed all my nights.

<u>**NEXT IN THE SERIES:**</u>

Burning Revenge

A Devil's Cartel MC novel

Book Three

Acknowledgements

A big thank you to everyone still following me on this writing journey! As always, I am forever grateful for my husband, three children, my publisher, my editor, and my readers for your endless patience and encouragement over the last few years. Thank you for tolerating my slow writing output, missed deadlines, and unanswered messages, comments, and emails. The last few years have been hard, and long—and God knows 2020 hasn't been any easier—but I am working on getting back into the groove! Here's to a healthy and happy 2021!

About the Author

SKYLA MADI is an Australian writer from Brisbane, Queensland.

Skyla started her writing career fresh out of high school and at 21 she is a giver of both real and fictional life.

She is an aquarian, lover of the written word and author of the #1 BESTSELLING Consumed trilogy.

Skyla LOVES to hear from readers! Here are some of ways to get into contact with her:

FACEBOOK:
https://www.facebook.com/SkylaMadi

TWITTER:
https://twitter.com/Skyla_Madi

GOODREADS
http://www.goodreads.com/author/show/6554179.Skyla_Madi

Join our Reader Group on Facebook and don't miss out on meeting our authors and entering epic giveaways!

Limitless Reading

Where reading a book
is your first step to becoming
limitless...

LIMITLESS PUBLISHING *Reader Group*

Join today! *"Where reading a book is your first step to becoming limitless..."*

https://www.facebook.com/groups/LimitlessReading/